FOR JUS her ow about h just exp love and *pain*.

His teeth were in her neck, drinking from her, showering her in goose bumps and spearing through all her defenses. She cried out, tumbling headfirst into another oblivion as he drove into her, taking her with a force that hurt in a beautiful way, one that touched her very soul.

This was her life.

Her purpose.

Her meaning.

She loved this man. This Sethios. This male who had shattered all her beliefs and had broken through the harshest of her resolves.

Caro clung to him, weeping, her time with him too short. The sacrifice they would make would change the future of the world. But what if they couldn't come back from it?

She would never voice that fear, the knowledge of what was to come. Because her mother would find her when she failed to locate Astasiya. Caro would endure rehabilitation. And she would survive.

That was her purpose, her one secret, that she never gave up. With Sethios forever etched into her very soul, the council couldn't separate them. They would try, and they would fail. She would return to him. Always.

"I love you," he whispered to her, his lips a caress against her ear. "I will forever love you."

"I love you, too," she breathed. And this time it was her. Her voice. Her heart. Her body. Her soul. She'd fallen into the memory, enraptured and ensnared and never letting go.

His eyes burned into hers. "Come back to me, Caro."

"I'm right here."

"Come back to me, angel."

She frowned. "I'm here."

"I miss you."

It didn't make any sense. How could he miss her? He was inside her. Making love to her. Only, everything began to blur, the memory slipping from her fingers and surrounding her in a cage of literal glass.

She frowned. *Where am I?*

Immortal Curse Series Order

.

BLOOD SEEKER

AN
IMMORTAL
CURSE NOVEL

USA TODAY BESTSELLING AUTHOR
LEXI C. FOSS

Editing by: Outthink Editing, LLC

Proofreading by: Katie Schmahl, Jean Bachen, Joy Di Biase-Giachino, Diane Dykes, & Julie Robertson

Cover Design: Julie Nicholls with Covers by Julie

Cover Photography: JW Photography

Models: Aidan Stewart & Kristen Lazarus-Wood

Published by: Ninja Newt Publishing, LLC

Digital Edition

eBook ISBN: 978-1-950694-21-1

Paperback ISBN: 978-1-950694-90-7

To Casey, for convincing me to ponder and play with a certain blond-haired Ichorian. ;)

To Jean, Katie, and Bethany, for making this book possible. I'd be lost without you!

To Heather, for your love and support of this series and for always making me smile. Kylan sends his love <3

BLOOD SEEKER

BOOK SIX

BLOOD SEEKER

Seraphim do not feel.
Seraphim do not love.
Seraphim do not react.

Those are the rules every higher being lives by.
And Caro broke them all for *him*.

Now she's lost in a vacant sea, punished for the ultimate sin
of choosing an abomination—*a vampire*—over her duty.

Sethios promised to come for her, to find her, to save her,
but with each passing breath, her hope melts into despair.

Will he find her in time? Or will her mind shatter from the
madness?

Welcome to the Immortal Curse world.
The High Council of Seraph will see you now…

GLOSSARY

PRETERNATURAL BEINGS

Fledgling (noun): The child of a male Ichorian and a human female, who has not yet been reborn as a Hydraian; they do not typically possess supernatural or psychic gifts until their immortal rebirth.

Hydraian (noun): An immortal offspring of a male Ichorian and a human female, who possesses two supernatural or psychic gifts and does not require human blood to survive.

Ichorian (noun): An immortal being of unknown descent who possesses one supernatural or psychic gift and requires human blood to survive.

Immortal (noun): A general noun designating a being who does not age and is immune to natural human death.

Progeny (noun): The term Ichorians use to refer to those they created through the Ichorian turning process.

Seraphim (noun): A being who belongs to the highest order of angelic hierarchy.

GLOSSARY

KEY TERMS

Arcadia: Notorious Ichorian club in New York City that also serves as the primary meeting location for the Ichorian government.

Blood Laws: A series of ordinances created by the Ichorian governing board in response to the Treaty of 1747.

Catastrophic Relief Foundation (CRF): A global humanitarian aid organization headquartered in New York City with a secret paramilitary unit designed to destroy rogue supernaturals.

Conclave: The Ichorian governing board.

Edict: A law or rule issued by the High Council of Seraph.

Elders: The original Hydraians who also serve as the Hydraian governing board.

Fated Line: Seraphim who can foresee the future.

High Council of Seraph: Seraphim governing board.

Nizari: Ancient Ichorian assassins who hunt and kill fledglings.

Nizari Poison: A green substance notorious for killing fledglings and preventing their rebirth.

Sentinel: A soldier in the CRF unit designed to slaughter rogue immortal beings.

Treaty of 1747: An armistice between Hydraians and Ichorians to cease fire and live in their designated areas. Those who opt to cross these boundaries do so at their own risk.

INTRODUCTION

STAS

A LOT HAS HAPPENED over the last year of my existence. So I'm going to try to break it down for those of you who might need a refresher…

There's an immortal war coming that's probably going to destroy humanity as we know it. And somehow, I'm at the center of it all.

My grandfather, Osiris, is the Seraphim of Resurrection, which means he controls life and rebirth. He's used this gift to his own benefit over the last several millennia, creating an army of Ichorians and Hydraians all meant to serve him.

Some of you may be asking, *What the fuck are Seraphim, Ichorians, and Hydraians?*

Ha. Yeah. I know how you feel. I had no idea what they were until recently. Seraphim are easy—they're essentially angels. The others are harder. So I'll try to explain it for you: in a nutshell, they're immortal beings.

The longer explanation is Ichorians are like vampires, only they don't have any of the weaknesses. They can even eat normal food. But they do require human blood to survive. They also have a power of some kind that was amplified to supernatural levels during their rebirth.

1

For example, Issac, my bonded mate, can control vision. His progeny, Tristan, can control sound, and his other progeny, Mateo, is a technical wizard.

Scientifically speaking, the ability comes from an affinity that already existed in their bloodline when they were human. During the resurrection process, that gene is triggered, and a supernatural talent is born.

Hydraians are a little different. They are created when an Ichorian male breeds with a mortal female. The child is actually human, which the Ichorians call a *fledgling*, and remains mortal until death. Once killed, they are then reborn as a Hydraian and possess not one but two gifts— one from each bloodline. They also don't require human blood to survive.

You're probably wondering about this immortal war I mentioned and how it pertains to all this scientific bullshit. I promise I'm getting there.

See, the Ichorians hate Hydraians.

Why?

Jealousy. Or that's my take on it, anyway. Hydraians are not only immune to the imbibing-human-essence requirement, but they also have two gifts *and* their blood is actually toxic to Ichorians.

So yeah, they don't get along.

They went to war a long time ago, only to reach an accord between the races when the Ichorians realized they couldn't exterminate all the Hydraians. Everything was quiet for a few hundred years, but animosity brewed in the background.

The kicker? This was all Osiris's plan. He's the master creator. But he hasn't spent all this time creating pawns to go to war with each other. No. He wants them to go to war as a unit against the Seraphim.

I'll be honest, I don't know a lot about the Seraphim

yet. I mean, I just found out recently that I am one. My best friend, Lizzie, is pregnant with one, or that's the speculation, anyway.

Because the CRF created Lizzie in a lab.

What's the CRF? The Catastrophic Relief Foundation. They're a humanitarian agency that isn't so humanitarian. It used to be run by an Ichorian who wanted to dominate the world. Instead, we killed him, and the rest of his Sentinel division went down in flames with him. Well, a few survived—we have them in custody—but the sinister aspect of the organization is dead in the water.

Except they left a lasting imprint, one of those items being my very pregnant best friend. Her genetics indicate that she's a Seraphim, which is how Jayson and Lizzie were able to procreate and also why everyone believes their child is going to be an angel.

According to Leela, a Seraphim of the fertility line, immortal genetics don't work like they do for humans. I believe her because I sprouted wings just after my twenty-fifth birthday. My mother is a pure-blood Seraphim, and now, so am I.

Anyway, in summary, Osiris has created an army, and he intends to go to war with the Seraphim with all of us as his pawns on the battlefield. A lot of the immortals don't know this yet; it's something we've only recently begun to understand. Until I learn more about the Seraphim, I'm not doing shit.

The prophecy that says I'll destroy the immortal race can go fuck itself.

I make my own decisions.

And I invite you to make your own choices, too.

Pick a side. Protect yourself. And for the love of God, do not go anywhere near Osiris. He's a monster. Hell, the dick put my mother at the bottom of an ocean to drown over and over again for the last eighteen years. He also erased my father's memories of everything that had ever happened to him.

That's where we are right now—I just saved my dad, and now we need to find my mom. But as I said, she's drowning somewhere, and this globe is pretty much all water.

So finding her is going to be quite a task. Fortunately, we have a lot of support for the mission.

Read on to continue the journey.

Remember, trust no one. Pay attention to the details. Don't believe everything you hear. And watch your back.

A war is coming.

Which side will you choose?

PROLOGUE

CARO

EVERYTHING IS SO DARK HERE. Cold. Painful. Agony personified.

I used to count the seconds. They later turned into days and weeks. It's hard to know what's true down here. I die. I live. I die again.

My mind wanders once more, and I swear I hear Sethios's voice. So smooth. Warm. Concerned.

I miss you, I want to say to him. *Why haven't you come for me?* I want to demand. *Why hasn't anyone come for me?*

We did this for a reason.

I left my daughter behind to protect her. Has she grown up? How old is she now? Is she safe? Did Osiris find her in the end? Is Gabriel alive? Is Sethios?

My lungs fill with ice once more. I'm used to it now. I can only hold my breath for so long.

I allow it to consume me, to pull me under for those brief moments of blissful reprieve found only in the afterlife.

Sometimes my daughter visits me. It's all a dream, an unrealistic expectation, but I indulge in it anyway.

Just as I allow myself to fall into a vision now of black

wings and a cruel grin. Not Sethios, yet so much like him. I sigh. *Where are you?* I wonder. *Does your heart break like mine?*

I feel light. Reborn. The chains a shackled reminder of my fate.

This isn't a happy story. I sacrificed everything for those I love, only to reside in perpetual anguish.

But as long as my little angel lives, there's hope.

The prophecy says she'll be the one to destroy us all. Does that include me? Her father? All our friends and family? Has the High Council of Seraph found her?

I shiver.

This world is so bleak and dark. So absolute in its obscurity.

Another inhale.

More burning.

Death.

On and on I go.

Drowning in circles, longing for escape. Longing for *him.* My love. My existence. The one I can no longer feel. The one who makes my heart break even in the afterlife.

Free me, Sethios… I beg him. *Free. Me.*

But it's a lost cause. No one can find me now.

It hurts. It burns. It slays me once again.

Death. Sweet death. I can breathe here, if just for a moment. But those black feathers tickle my vision once more. What are they? Why are they here?

I wake again to something new.

The water has disappeared.

The world is filled with stones. A chair. More chains. *Where am I? Another vision?*

But this one is so different, driven by the source of madness standing before me.

A bolt of panic strikes my heart. I jolt alive in the chair, my eyes widening.

This can't be real.

After all this time, why now?

"Welcome back, Caro," he says, his voice flat and emotionless. "You and I need to have a chat."

That cold voice is how I know I'm truly gone. Dead. Never to resurface again.

Oh, Sethios. I love you. Please know that I'll never regret our choice. She lived. I died. I'll always love you both. For eternity, my darlings… for eternity.

CHAPTER ONE

SETHIOS

WHERE ARE YOU, angel? Sethios wondered for the thousandth time, his gaze on the stars above. *Why won't you talk to me?*

No answer.

He sighed, his hands in the pockets of his jeans, his heart in his throat. A week had passed since Astasiya had freed his mind. Not entirely, but enough for Sethios to think beyond his father's control.

There were still holes inside his mind.

Pockets of missing memories.

But he remembered his angel, his Caro, his love.

"Fuck," he muttered, his eyes closing as he pictured her at the bottom of the ocean, dying over and over again. He'd left her in that state for eighteen goddamn years, completely oblivious to her fate. All because his father had wiped her clean from his mind, suffocating him in a world of nonexistence.

Sethios hadn't known his mate.

They were bonded in a way his mind couldn't comprehend because of the fog inflicted upon him by his father's persuasion.

And now, he couldn't find her. Because she'd given up

on him, on the world, on anyone ever rescuing her from the chains binding her beneath the sea.

His knees threatened to give, his chest an empty cavern drowning beneath a wave of anguish. In a way, Osiris's torment had been a blessing. He'd provided Sethios over a decade of nothingness. No pain. No understanding. No care in the world.

Now it all crashed over him with the heat of a million suns, burning every molecule inside him.

He had to pull it together. Not just for Caro, but for Astasiya.

Ah, his little angel. She'd grown into a woman in the blink of an eye. She was seven yesterday. At least to him.

Sethios blew out a breath and ran a hand over his face, shaking his head. This self-pity bullshit wasn't going to fix a damn thing. He needed to find Caro. Then he needed to find a way to take his father down. Killing the old man wasn't an option—Seraphim couldn't die—but he could immobilize him. Perhaps by pouring a vat of concrete over his head.

Sethios shuddered at the thought of his last "punishment" orchestrated by his asshole of a father. Osiris had forced Sethios to bury himself alive by dousing himself in liquid concrete. It had hurt like a son of a bitch. And yet, oddly, it still didn't compare to the agony inside him now.

He felt as though his soul was ripped in half. Shredded. *Destroyed*.

Caro remained unattainable, her last whisper in his mind reminiscent of a dream. Had that been her or his own mind playing tricks on him?

Fuck, the pain she must feel…

He swallowed, his eyes briefly closing once more. He needed to get over this pity party and start the search.

There was just one problem.

He had no idea where to begin

Gabriel had shown him on a map all the places he'd looked so far—of which there were thousands—and none of them revealed even a hint of her location. This planet was mostly composed of water, leaving the possibilities endless. And without her talking to him, he stood little to no chance of discovering her whereabouts.

Not that she could help much from below the surface.

Sethios began to pace, something he'd done quite a bit of out on this beach. Gabriel owned the entire island, his house only taking up a small speck of space. Some of the underbrush could use a little trimming, but it was otherwise an ideal piece of real estate out in the middle of the Pacific Ocean. The waves were rough, crashing against the shore with a fury that rivaled Sethios's mood.

He walked alone, indulging in the night, seeking out the solitude offered among the stars. Nearly two decades flashed behind his eyes, there and gone in an instant. It was such a minuscule scrap of time. And yet, it was profoundly life-altering.

Three thousand years of existence had not prepared him to feel this way. So alone. So devastated. So *wronged*.

His hands curled into fists, his mind wandering to his angel once more. *Where are you, Caro? Talk to me.*

"Dad?" a voice called instead, his daughter appearing in a flurry of translucent feathers a few feet away. Her wings fluttered around her as she found her footing, the plumes a brilliant opal shade beneath the moon. Then they disappeared as she took her corporeal state, her expression one of astute concentration.

She was still learning how to control her angelic talents, including the one that allowed her to compel others.

"Hi, little angel," Sethios murmured, doing his best to

tamp down the anger he felt inside. He didn't want to scare her, not after they'd been so recently reacquainted.

It was a bit strange having a fully grown daughter whom he hadn't seen in years, one who had already found her other half. Sethios almost felt replaced in a way, her loyalty split between the family she once knew and the one she'd created on her own.

He hadn't decided how he wanted to react to that yet.

A darker part of Sethios wanted to slaughter the immortal who thought he was good enough to date—no, not just date, but *mate*—his daughter.

Meanwhile, a wiser part of him respected Issac Wakefield's confidence. The Ichorian hadn't once bowed to Sethios, his main priority very clearly Astasiya and only Astasiya.

Time would tell whether the darker side would win out against the wiser side.

Right now, he embraced the latter. For his daughter's sake.

He opened his arms for her, offering a hug that felt right yet foreign at the same time. If she noticed, she didn't mention it, just returned the gesture before following his gaze upward into the stars.

"Your mother and I used to enjoy nights like this," he explained softly. "There was very little light around Seeley Lake. It provided us a sense of peace and security."

A false security, of course.

They'd never been truly safe, just as they weren't safe here either. Not with the Seraphim residing so close by and his father trying to hunt them down.

The two of them stood in silence for a long moment, his arm around her shoulders, their gazes on the sky.

Serenity surrounded him for an instant, his heart

reveling in the choices he and Caro had made. Their separation hurt, but in the end, they'd done the right thing.

After a few more minutes, he released Astasiya and took a step away to face her fully. She hadn't come here to stargaze. He could see the resolve in her green eyes, so similar to his own. However, the rest of her was all Caro—athletic with feminine curves, long blonde hair, soft yet elegant features, ethereal and beautiful.

It almost hurt to look at her.

And yet, he found himself grinning.

"What?" Astasiya asked.

"You just remind me so much of your mother," he admitted softly. Something he'd mentioned before yet felt the need to say again. Because it was so very true. "Although, your emotions are a bit more impressive than hers. I suspect you get that from me."

"If you're talking about earlier, well, Stark deserved it."

Sethios's lips twitched. "Can't deny that," he agreed, amused.

Astasiya was nowhere near ready to forgive her brother for his choices over the last two decades. While Sethios understood many of the Seraphim's decisions, he had to admit that Gabriel Stark had royally fucked up a few details. One of those decisions had even led to Astasiya being buried alive, which was unacceptable to all parties involved.

"You know he meant well," Sethios offered as a consolatory statement. "But I agree he could have handled it a little better."

"A little better?" she repeated, incredulous. "He let me think I was *toxic* to Issac. Not to mention the whole death incident. Oh, and letting us all think he was working with John." She scrunched her nose, reminding him of her favorite stubborn expression from childhood. "The memory manipulation thing sucked, too."

He chuckled under his breath, saying, "Yeah. As I said, he could have handled it better."

"You said 'a little better,'" she replied. "He could have handled it *a lot* better."

"He's young and learning." Not necessarily an excuse so much as a fact. "And his experience with non-Seraphim beings is sorely lacking."

She grunted. "No shit." She considered that for a moment. "Is Mom…?" She trailed off.

"Similar to Gabriel?" Sethios asked.

Astasiya nodded.

"At one time, yes," he murmured, recalling how he first met Caro at the Arcadia in New York City.

His lips twitched fondly with the memory. She'd shown up in her regal Seraphim form, wanting to deliver an edict to his father. Only, Sethios hadn't allowed her to utter that message to the intended source. Instead, he'd persuaded her to remain silent, then he'd taken her home for some fun.

"She learned how to feel," he summarized, not wanting to provide his daughter with the details of how she was created. Something told him she wouldn't be interested in hearing the story about how he'd used her mother's favorite knives in the bedroom.

Do you remember that night, angel? he thought at Caro. *How I fucked you up against the glass? Then taunted you with your blades the next morning? You came all over the steel edge before I fucked you to oblivion and back.*

A spike of heat caressed his heart, there and gone in a second, causing him to frown.

Is that what you need, angel? Visuals of our past? He would send her thousands if that was what it took. His mind contained an arsenal to last a lifetime. Even with a child running around, they found time to indulge in his dark depravities. Mostly because there was just so much he'd needed to teach Caro.

Which drew him back to Astasiya and her questions regarding her mother's emotions. "She's much more in tune than your brother," he said.

"I think everyone is more 'in tune' than Stark," she muttered.

Sethios couldn't argue with that. Even Leela and Vera appeared to be more emotionally inclined than the warrior Seraphim.

He studied his daughter for a long moment, curious as to why she'd sought him out. "What do you want to ask me?" He pitched his voice low, letting her know with his tone that she could demand anything and everything from him, and he would ensure it happened. She meant the world to him. Just like his Caro.

But does she really mean enough? he wondered idly, some of his guilt peeking through. *You forgot her for eighteen years. All because of Osiris's compulsion.*

Sethios's jaw ached from clenching his teeth, annoyed with that pesky line of reasoning. Yet it continued to haunt him, the very realization that he'd let his entire family down for eighteen fucking years.

Astasiya must have read the change in him, because she took a step back, her throat working over a swallow. "I… I wanted to talk to you about Mom. I had another dream."

His focus sharpened. "In the water?"

She nodded, then frowned. "Sort of."

That didn't sound good. "Sort of?"

"It was strange. We were in the water, but she could breathe."

"Did she say anything?"

Astasiya shook her head. "No. She was too terrified to speak." His daughter paused, her brow furrowing. "It was just really weird because we didn't drown. Yet everything was dark and heavy, like we were in the water, but the atmosphere didn't feel right. I don't know; maybe it was just a standard nightmare." Her lips twisted to the side. "Except, it felt like Mom."

Sethios considered the description, his own mind seeking out Caro for an explanation and coming back with nothing once more.

It frustrated him to no end.

Yes, all right. He'd fucked up. His father had broken him via a method he never could have anticipated.

The issue was he *should* have expected it.

Osiris was creative and always one step ahead. Sethios knew better than to think he could possibly best him.

And yet… he had bested his father in a way. By keeping Astasiya a secret.

Maybe having his mind completely wiped had actually been a gift, granting Sethios a way to guard everyone he held dear.

He'd have to ponder that train of thought later. There would inevitably be a hole he could crawl into, one that allowed him to return to his state of self-loathing. But, for now, he allowed that benefit to empower him into action. Because wallowing wasn't doing a damn thing for him.

"Did Issac see your nightmare?" Sethios asked.

"Yes." Astasiya grimaced. "He woke me up when it turned too dark."

"Too dark?"

"Consuming," she whispered. "I couldn't seem to swim out of the hole."

He frowned. The imagery unnerved him. However, he

wanted to see it for himself. "Where's Issac now?"

"At the house. He would have come with me, but I wanted to mist."

And he currently couldn't travel via mist with her, or his control over Skye's mind would lapse, sending her into a fit of insanity. Osiris had broken her mind entirely, compelling her to kill herself should someone take her away from him without approval. Which was exactly what Ezekiel and the others had done during Sethios's rescue—they'd kidnapped Osiris's prized asset—his pet seer.

"When was the last time Issac slept?" Sethios wondered out loud.

"He hasn't," she replied. "Not since Skye arrived."

Because if he slept, the seer would awaken and try to take her own life. "We need to find a better solution to that problem."

"I know. I've been trying to find a way to warp Osiris's compulsion or break it, but nothing I've done works. He's just too strong."

"You'll get there," Sethios said, fully confident in his daughter's abilities. "He just has a few years of experience on you, is all."

"A few years?" She snorted. "Try ten thousand years."

"More, actually," Sethios murmured. "But you have something he's never mastered, little angel."

"Oh yeah? What's that?"

"Heart," Sethios replied, smiling. "You care. That's a powerful weapon, one he will never understand." He reached out to squeeze her shoulder, giving her his best indulgent look. "Let's go talk to your *boyfriend*." Sethios really hated that fucking word, especially when in reference to his daughter's life. "I want to see this dream. Then perhaps you and I can give Skye's compulsion a go together."

17

CHAPTER TWO

SETHIOS

THE DREAM WAS as dark as Astasiya had described, the webs around her thick and complicated. He searched the visual Issac provided, finding nothing that gave away Caro's position.

But he sensed her fear.

What's changed? he asked her. *Why are you suddenly terrified, sweet angel?*

Again, nothing.

How strange. He used to adore silence. He'd even compelled her to be quiet the first time they'd met. Now he would give anything to make her speak. Even a scream would do.

He sighed, shaking his head. "I can't hear her." If he said those four words out loud one more time, he might lose his ever-loving shit.

How the fuck was he supposed to find her when he couldn't even sense her?

Oh, he felt the cord tied to his heart, the frayed edges stabbing his insides like angry little thorns.

But apart from that pesky sensation, he felt nothing. And he *hated* feeling nothing.

"I can try to sleep again," his daughter offered softly. "Maybe the dream will be clearer?"

"Or it could consume you again," Issac said, sounding far too tired. Sethios could see the concern in his gaze, not for himself but for the female he clearly loved.

How will Caro feel about their relationship? Sethios wondered idly. It would shock her, just as it had him. However, he suspected she would approve, if nothing more than because of the way Issac looked at their daughter.

Sethios shook his head. *Enough of that.* "Let's see what we can do about Skye," he said, needing a distraction.

He also wasn't keen on the idea of returning his daughter to the black hole of her dream state. There hadn't been anything useful in that reverie, making it more dangerous to her psyche than useful to their search. And Caro would never approve of putting Astasiya at risk for her own benefit.

"Okay," his daughter agreed, her relief palpable.

Issac flashed Sethios a grateful look, then followed Astasiya as she walked toward the stairs.

Poor Gabriel had each of his guest rooms occupied. Most were sharing space with a few sleeping on couches. But Skye had been provided her own bed.

Ezekiel stood as they entered, his hair tangled and unkempt, his clothes at least four days old. "You need to take a fucking shower," Sethios told him. "Right now."

His oldest friend snorted. "I'm fine."

"Oh, it's not for your benefit but for mine. You look like shit."

"Says the man who resembled a Neanderthal last week."

Sethios rolled his eyes. One of Osiris's favorite torments was to compel hair growth. It hurt like hell. So did the razor he used to remove it. Just to begin the agony again. That had been Sethios's punishment for removing the stitches from his mouth a few weeks, or months, or maybe years, prior.

Time was a funny thing. While Sethios could remember almost every detail of his time in captivity, he had no concept of when things occurred, thanks to his bruised mental state.

Regardless, he needed his friend to take a damn shower.

"Skye's nose will thank you," he said, arching a brow. "Unless you're trying to torment her by forcing her to remain in close quarters with you in this state?"

The question was carefully phrased, the word "torment" one of Ezekiel's hot buttons when in reference to Skye.

It provoked the male into action, his lithe form moving with lightning speed as he attempted to send a fist into Sethios's jaw. The two of them rarely sparred, but when they did, it was an even match. At least when they were both at full health.

Today, Ezekiel was not at full health.

Sethios dodged him by stepping to the side, causing his best friend to lose his balance. It sent Ezekiel right into the wall, but the bastard traced to behind Sethios and tried again.

They danced in a circle, Sethios ducking while Ezekiel swung.

"I can do this all night," Sethios taunted. He had a lot of fury to burn off, as did Ezekiel. Osiris had taken Skye from him a century ago and had been abusing the pair ever since.

She'd predicted Ezekiel would be her downfall, had tried to escape him on numerous occasions, but he'd been infatuated with the dark-haired beauty, chasing her all over the earth.

He tracked her with ease, his assassin roots assisting in his pursuit. However, a day after her capture, Osiris had arrived and demanded Ezekiel hand her over.

Which was why Sethios's best friend had opted to work with Osiris.

Not because he approved of the old man's inane plans, but because he held Ezekiel's heart—Skye.

Saving her had been a clear course, except it was driving the poor woman mad inside. Ezekiel bore the brunt of the guilt, his infatuation with her the reason she'd been imprisoned in the first place.

That all led to Ezekiel's current state and the pent-up rage riding his spirit.

Sethios allowed a fist to graze his cheekbone, hoping it would be enough to pacify the ancient assassin.

It did.

The darkness overriding Ezekiel's wary features receded, the gold flecks in his black gaze blazing with knowledge. A curse passed through his lips, followed by a shake of his head, sending his unwashed dark hair sprawling across his lean shoulders.

If hell had a "look," it was Ezekiel.

"Go shower," Sethios said again. "We're going to analyze Osiris's compulsion and see what can be done."

"Nothing can be done." Ezekiel's haggard tone revealed a part of him others rarely glimpsed—the part of him that cared for someone other than himself.

"We're going to try anyway." Sethios owed it to his best friend after everything he'd sacrificed for him and Astasiya and Caro. "Let us try."

Ezekiel appeared ready to tell them all to fuck off, and if he did, Sethios would listen. But he suspected his old friend needed this break. And if Ezekiel was going to trust anyone to guard Skye, it was Sethios.

"Your daughter already tried."

"Then let me try," Sethios rephrased.

"You've tried before, too," Ezekiel muttered.

Yeah, and it hadn't gone well. "Do you have a better idea?" Sethios countered, knowing full well his best friend had no alternatives other than to allow her to remain in this magically induced coma.

The assassin's jaw ticked, then he took a step back. "Fine." He started toward the door.

"Steal some clothes from Gabriel," Sethios called after him. He'd already raided the Seraphim's closet himself, which was where his current outfit of jeans and a T-shirt had come from.

Ezekiel didn't reply, disappearing from the room with a trace.

Issac lifted a dark brow. It was the only reaction he provided before shifting his sapphire gaze to Skye. He grimaced at whatever vision he found lurking inside her mind.

His ability to control mental imagery proved useful in this instance, as he could not only force the prophetess into a dream state but was also able to warp her nightmares into something less violent.

However, the strain of having kept her in that state for over seven days showed on his features. It required him to remain awake and alert at all times, something he could do as an immortal, but even one as powerful as Issac required some rest eventually.

Sethios also suspected the male was using a great deal of energy to monitor Astasiya's mind, which was how he'd managed to pull her out of her latest dream of Caro.

Astasiya cleared her throat, her brow furrowing. "So

I've tried compelling her on my own, just with verbal commands for her to dream a certain way. But each one always returns to a suicide attempt."

Issac nodded. "Yes, the persuasion is harsh and wrapped around her mind in every feasible way."

Not her mind, but her spirit. However, Astasiya spoke before Sethios could clarify.

"I can see it. Well, not see it physically, but I can sense it. Like a dark strand of barbwire wrapping around her psyche. I don't know how to explain it."

"I understand what you're feeling," Sethios murmured, his own senses picking up on the compulsion woven around Skye's spirit. "We need to pull it apart. I just don't know how." If he did, he would have applied that knowledge years ago. "How did you break Osiris's control over me?"

If she thought it weird that he referred to his father by name, she didn't react. Probably because she called him Osiris, too. Not "Grandfather."

"I… I don't know. I was out of it. You didn't recognize me, which hurt, and then I started thinking about you and Mom. My memories. How you made me run that day." She swallowed, then cleared her throat. "And then I thought about where Mom is now. That's when your compulsion seemed to fracture."

Sethios considered that for a moment, his heart skipping a beat in his chest. He'd been enraged by the cement encasing him, suffocating him, *killing* him over and over, and then he'd been freed. It'd taken too long for him to understand why because his mind had refused to recognize the female standing before him.

When it'd finally registered, he'd thought it was his Caro, only the eyes were all wrong. They were *his* eyes.

He sighed.

That method wasn't going to work on Skye. Neither Sethios nor Astasiya had that kind of history with the prophetess, making it impossible to unweave this compulsion through a familial bond—which was what he suspected Astasiya had done. She'd used his paternal tie to her to infiltrate his soul, thereby snapping Osiris's hold.

Skye needed something else. She required them to unravel the mental strings, not cut through them.

He twisted his mouth to the side as he considered the energy signature surrounding her. It was one he understood far too well. But he had no idea how to sever it. If he had, he would have used that knowledge long ago to destroy every single one of his father's mental mindfucks.

"Compelling her isn't going to work," he said slowly. "It'll only worsen her state." Sethios had tried it once at Ezekiel's request. "Osiris built in safeguards long ago to prevent me from tampering with the compulsion. I imagine they're still in place."

"That would explain why her mind reacted so brutally to Astasiya's attempts," Issac replied. "It seemed to be a defense mechanism."

Sethios dipped his chin, recalling a similar reaction from decades ago. "We're going to need to—"

He cut off on a curse, a mental spike ramming through his mind as Caro's voice roared to life inside his head. *Where are you?!* she shrieked at him. *Find me! Find me now! No! Don't! It's not—*

The words cut off abruptly, his breath leaving him on a gasp as an array of images assaulted his mind.

"It's okay," he heard Issac saying from somewhere within the room.

"Shh," Sethios hushed him, focusing on the message his angel appeared to be trying to send him.

A street.

A building.

What is that? he thought at her, trying to decipher the darkened blur phasing in and out of her visual. *Feathers? Wings?*

A sign obliterated the previous vision. Not a theoretical sign, but a physical one. With a street name. English. Green. American, from the looks of it. But where?

Another visual slammed into his mind, this one of a shoreline and a windmill spinning wildly in a storm.

Slow down, he told her, that sable swirl consuming the visual. *I can't see, angel.*

Letters scrawled across a building, some old manufacturing plant with brick siding. Then the shore and windmill again. Followed by the street sign. All of it whirled through his mind like a tornado, her scream echoing in his ears until all of a sudden everything went silent.

He blinked, finding himself on his knees, his head in his hands.

"Show me," a deep voice demanded. Not Issac, but Gabriel.

Several others had joined them, including Ezekiel in a towel, a pair of guns in his hands. Issac's progeny—the Irish one—stood beside him. A Hydraian with dark skin behind them.

Names escaped Sethios, his ears ringing from the assault.

Skye remained blissfully unaware, still fast asleep beneath Issac's spell.

It all happened so quickly, or it felt that way to him. He'd been in the middle of trying to help her. Then Caro's screech had brought everything to a halt. She'd sounded frantic, her visuals scattered in a chaotic manner that made no sense to him.

"Slow it down," Gabriel said.

"Slow what down?" Sethios asked, his palm against his forehead. *Fuck!* It felt like he'd been assaulted by a damn freight train.

"Issac's showing us the scenes Mom shared with you," Astasiya explained. "It reminds me of the East Coast."

"We need to search that name, including the plant. I think she's trying to show us her memories from when Osiris had her drowned." Gabriel's emotionless voice made Sethios frown.

"What was the blur?"

"Perhaps Osiris in ethereal form," Gabriel suggested.

Sethios shook his head. "It felt… intrusive." Like Caro had been trying to tell him something while sharing the visuals. He couldn't say why or how he sensed that. His instincts just insisted there was something more to that scene. Something she'd been attempting to convey behind a mask of urgency.

What are you trying to tell me, angel? he asked.

But, of course, he received no response. Perhaps she'd drowned again and would reach out when she surfaced.

However, five minutes later, she still remained mute and Gabriel had already pulled up a location on his phone. Sethios recalled a time when mobiles weren't powerful enough to hold such vast information.

"We need to scout," Gabriel said, his light green eyes landing on Sethios. "You and me."

"What?" While Sethios agreed that he should be the one to accompany the red-feathered Seraphim, he really wanted his head to stop spinning first.

"You need to confirm it's the right location. You're also bonded to her. If we get close enough, you might be able to sense her." He looked at Astasiya. "You need to stay here."

"Excuse me?" Her tone indicated just how she felt about that edict.

"This property needs a Seraphim on it on the off chance the council sends an emissary. Until Leela or Vera returns, you're the only one who can speak on behalf of the island."

"What does that even mean?"

"If the council sends a messenger, you'll understand. Otherwise, I'll explain it later." Light green eyes focused on Sethios once more. "Let's go."

CHAPTER THREE

SETHIOS

"YOU REALLY NEED to reconsider your approach with Astasiya," Sethios advised as he and Gabriel materialized on the shores of Maine. The actual city name had escaped Sethios on the way, his head clouded and aching from Caro's visual attack.

He felt the wrongness in this approach even as they arrived, his stomach twisting with dread. Caro had been trying to tell him something.

Yet, as he glanced around, he recognized all the images from the ones in his head. They'd definitely found the right location.

"Recognize anything?" Gabriel asked, ignoring Sethios's commentary on Astasiya.

Typical. The Seraphim preferred logic and practicality over emotions.

"It's definitely the place she showed me," Sethios replied. "But otherwise, no. I don't recognize it. Nor do I sense her."

The only indication Gabriel gave that he'd heard Sethios was a slight twist of his lips that served as the Seraphim's equivalent of a frown. He walked along the shoreline, his hands loose at his sides. He had at least three guns strapped to his person, all concealed by his brown leather jacket. Sethios suspected he had a knife in his boot as well, tucked securely beneath his jeans.

Unlike Gabriel, Sethios hadn't bothered with a single weapon. His hypnosis and manipulation abilities made such items irrelevant. He also refused to touch a knife until he had Caro back. Those were her preferred items in a fight. He wouldn't hold one again until she stood before him. Then he'd either hand it to her as a gift or use it in another manner. Preferably the sexual kind.

"I left Astasiya behind as a protective measure," Gabriel said without looking at him. His light blond hair practically glowed, the sun high in the sky in this area of the world. "It's only a matter of time before the council sends someone to check in on my estate. They'll have sensed all the immortal traffic in and out of my home."

He turned then, his expression far more tired than Sethios had ever seen it. That appeared to be the common thing among them all at the moment.

"I don't know how they're going to react, Sethios. But it won't be good."

Sethios frowned. "Why do I feel like you brought me here for a reason, Gabriel?"

"I merely took advantage of an opportunity to have a moment alone with you," the Seraphim admitted. "You are the only one other than Leela and Vera who understands our politics. The council isn't going to sit by and allow me to harbor abominations."

"So your response to that threat was to leave my daughter in charge and steal me away for a moment?"

He ran his fingers through his hair, the unruly ends touching his ears. "The council won't touch Stas. She's too valuable to them. But they may try to take Skye. Not to mention Elizabeth. If they find out she's pregnant..." He trailed off, flinching at wherever his mind went. "We're in trouble, Sethios. Hiding Owen was one thing—he kept to himself and never left. But now the Hydraians are teleporting in and out of my house like it's a damn airport."

"Why haven't you said anything?"

"I have. No one listens to me."

"So you're hoping I can make them see reason," Sethios translated. "And you brought me to Maine for that conversation?"

"As I said, I took advantage of an opportunity. Caro provided the location."

"Yes, by showing you an eighteen-year-old memory," a deep voice murmured. "I expected it to be sooner now that you've regained your senses. Which makes me wonder about your Seraphim's current mental condition."

Ice drizzled through Sethios's veins as his father fully materialized beside them, the olive-toned skin of his bald head gleaming in the afternoon sun. His black wings disappeared, leaving him clad in a smart tailored suit, his white dress shirt unbuttoned at the top and lacking a tie.

"Don't fight me. Don't mist. Don't run." The commands left Osiris's mouth in rapid succession, each statement underlined in persuasion. "Actually, don't move your legs at all. I have things to say and would prefer to make this quick, given the circumstances of our meeting."

"Hello, Father," Sethios greeted on instinct, his millennia of existence aiding his bored tone. He refused to show fear around this man. Anger, maybe. But nothing else.

This is what you were trying to tell me, wasn't it, angel? The black blur had been Osiris. But this was an interesting development. His father had referred to this "vision" as an eighteen-year-old memory, thus implying Caro had been here before. And if he was the black blur, then she'd visited this location *with him*.

His heart skipped a beat.

There was only one reason they would have been here together.

This is where he took you…

"Son," Osiris returned. "You look healthier than the last time we saw each other."

It took physical restraint not to show any outward reaction to the inner chaos rioting inside Sethios's mind. All he wanted to do was kill the bastard before him and find Caro. But he couldn't move his legs or fight, thanks to his father's fucking compulsion.

So he feigned nonchalance, a skill set he'd spent a lifetime perfecting. "Well, my hair is growing more naturally now," he drawled. "My skin also appreciates the fresh air rather than being burned by molten cement." The calmly spoken words were at odds to the utter agony those experiences had caused him.

"Hmm. And your mind is enjoying its freedom, too?"

"Is it free?" Sethios countered, aware that his father enjoyed deploying delayed persuasive tricks.

He didn't acknowledge the inquiry, instead asking, "Tell me, how's Skye? Has she died yet?"

"Is that why you're here? For an update on those you enjoy tormenting?" Sethios wasn't interested in playing this game and allowed that sentiment to reflect in his tone. "What do you want, Father?"

It would be wise to keep the old man talking and think through an escape plan, but Sethios found he was fresh out of patience.

Gabriel said nothing, merely folded his arms and watched Osiris with a complete lack of concern. The Seraphim feared nothing. Not even his own death. He was probably working on a plan and just giving nothing away. Meanwhile, Sethios's only idea was to endure whatever his father had in mind, then break free later.

That hadn't worked out so well last time.

Except Sethios and Caro had been captured with the notion of not trying to escape. They'd wanted to protect Astasiya. Now that her presence was known, Sethios could fight back.

"Always direct," his father mused. "Also a wise decision, given that I'm not the only one monitoring this area, and as it's not tourist season, we'll absolutely be noticed."

Sethios remained silent but internally wondered what his father meant by that. *Who else is monitoring this location? And why?*

"Has the High Council of Seraph demanded an audience with Stas yet?" his father asked. "I imagine they'll be most interested in her talents. She'll be a prime candidate to replace me at the table. Of course, if you ever find your wings, so would you."

Sethios didn't miss the jab. His father had always faulted him for not being a pureblood. It was Osiris who'd chosen to procreate with a mortal rather than another Seraphim, yet he lay the blame at his son's feet.

The insult usually rolled off Sethios's shoulders without leaving an imprint, but today he felt the slice of pain across his heart. Because he should have wings now, thanks to his bond with Caro. Yet he didn't, and he suspected it had something to do with their time apart.

She'd claimed nothing could break a blood bond.

An insecure part of him worried she might have been wrong.

However, he couldn't ponder that right now. Not in front of Osiris.

His father fed off fear and pain. Sethios possessed both

in spades. But he'd suffer in silence and flay himself alive inside before he ever allowed an ounce of it to grace the air in the presence of his creator.

Osiris studied him for a long moment, his lips curling just enough to hint at his growing amusement. Or maybe it was pride. The old man was hard to read, his mind too psychotic for anyone to truly comprehend.

"Maybe you're ready after all," he said, his voice softer than usual, almost as though the words were meant for himself and not his audience. "That's good, son. You'll need that strength for what's coming. Especially now that you've left my circle."

It took all matter of control not to ask him to elaborate. Sethios couldn't afford to appear intrigued, even though the ominous threat about "what's coming" had certainly piqued his interest.

"If the High Council hasn't called upon you yet, they soon will. They're going to want to talk to your daughter. I suggest you don't allow that to happen if you value her life."

"And let me guess your next suggestion," Sethios drawled. "You want me to hand her over to you for safekeeping."

"It would be a wise move."

"Sure." Sethios infused a healthy dose of sarcasm into that single word. "I'll get right on that."

His father made a noise of annoyance. "I retract my comment regarding your preparedness."

"Astasiya is her own person," Gabriel interjected before Sethios could lay another sarcastic comment at his father's feet. "She would need a very good reason just to speak to you right now. The notion of going to you willingly?" Gabriel snorted. "That's entirely impractical. It'll never happen."

"Are you saying I need to win my granddaughter's trust?"

"I'm saying that from what I've observed of her power, she will not be easily compelled by her father, or you for that matter." Gabriel twisted his wrist, his watch catching in the sun. A quick move, one that Sethios registered while the rest of him remained utterly composed, his legs stiff, thanks to Osiris's compulsion. "The only way she'll even consider such an absurd notion is if you give her a reason to. And so far, I haven't seen any."

Sethios's mouth threatened to curl down, the young Seraphim's proclamation strange. Astasiya would never agree to go anywhere near Osiris, even with a decent "reason."

What are you doing, Gabriel? Sethios wondered, trying to follow the strategic path the male had set in motion. Because he was clearly after something. He'd also done something with his watch. Had Osiris noticed?

"Perhaps I should take both of you prisoner," Osiris proposed. "That ought to provide the motivation she requires for a visit."

Gabriel lifted a shoulder, unbothered by the looming danger. "You could, but that will only infuriate her more."

"I can work with fury."

"Can you?" Gabriel countered. "Your granddaughter was raised by humans, Osiris. She thinks with her heart, not with the logic of her birthright. Hurting her will only drive her further away from you."

"You should probably listen to him, Father. He's currently on the receiving end of her wrath. She broke his nose just this morning. Which was what? The third time this week?" Sethios pretended to consider. "Or was it the fourth time?"

"Second," he corrected, his tone emotionless despite

Sethios's attempt to ruffle his feathers. He also never once looked his way, his focus entirely on Osiris.

"You're right," Sethios conceded, matching his flat tone while internally grinning. "The first one just gave you a black eye."

Gabriel ignored him. "The point remains, Stas won't go to you willingly, Osiris. Not even if you kidnap everyone she loves. She'll just fight you, and while you may be able to best her, she won't stop until she's utterly broken. If that's your goal, then so be it. But I think we both know that a broken weapon isn't in your best interest."

Ah, so that's the angle you're playing at, Sethios realized. He was indeed suggesting Osiris try to win over Astasiya's trust, something that would be impossible to do. However, his father would be just arrogant enough to try. Because Gabriel was right—Osiris needed Astasiya intact and functional for his plans.

He wanted to go to war with the Seraphim. Sethios had known that was his goal for centuries. And they'd finally reached the point in their existence where the chess master could place the influential queen on the board.

"You've not done yourself any favors," Sethios added, playing off Gabriel's commentary. "And Gabriel's observations are correct. I'm not strong enough to compel her, so even if you provided me with the motivation to try, it wouldn't do much."

Sethios ensured his voice and expression gave nothing away. He infused each word with certainty, sounding apathetic by even the prospect of being forced to persuade his own daughter.

Oh, it might work.

But his father didn't need to know that. And the gleam in his green irises—the same shade as Astasiya's and

Sethios's eyes—said he was taking their statements seriously.

Good.

That meant they might just make it out of this alive. Not that Osiris could kill either of them. Sethios also suspected Gabriel had set off some sort of alert with that watch on his wrist. His father hadn't seemed to notice. Or perhaps, more accurately, he'd actually allowed it, simply because he wanted his granddaughter to arrive.

Hmm. Too bad, old man. The call had likely gone to Vera and Leela, who weren't with Astasiya at the moment but with the Hydraians.

"All right," Osiris said, sending a wave of shock through Sethios's system.

Those were two words he never expected to hear from his father's mouth, and they immediately put him on full alert.

He waited for the Seraphim of Resurrection to say more, but he didn't. He merely clasped his hands before him, his expression giving nothing away.

What are you playing at? Sethios wanted to ask him, his defensive instincts firing as power rippled over his skin. It caused every hair on his arms to rise. He recognized the compulsion yet couldn't determine the purpose.

A ringing sound broke the suffocating silence.

None of them moved.

It continued until Osiris sighed, "Answer it." Persuasion underlined that statement, forcing Gabriel into action.

He pulled the mobile from his pocket and pressed it to his ear. "Yes?" His eyes widened a fraction at whatever was said, his light eyes landing on Sethios. A hint of alarm met his features, confirming an unexpected change. One that couldn't be good.

"What have you done?" Sethios demanded, the

invisible strands of power seeming to slink backward into Osiris. Each cord brushed Sethios's body on another plane of existence, reminding him of just who had provided him life.

Your power is my power, it whispered across his senses. *I own you.*

"I've offered my version of a gift," Osiris explained, the electricity fizzling out around them as he absorbed it all into his system. "It also happens to serve as a practical course, considering you need the guidance more than I do right now."

A practical course? Sethios repeated to himself, the air cooling around him. He slowly began to relax, the electricity humming over his skin subsiding.

His father gently rolled his neck, a slight shudder passing over him from harnessing all that energy.

Gabriel still hadn't spoken a word, but surprise radiated off of him.

"I had hoped we would have more time, but I can feel the tide shifting." Osiris looked up at the sky, releasing a sigh. "That's the problem with being as old as I am. I miscalculate in terms of centuries, not minutes. Alas, here we are. I've provided all the tools. It's up to you to use them."

Sethios nearly snorted. The only "tools" his father had provided were via lessons on physical and mental torment.

"You released Skye of your compulsion," Gabriel said, causing Sethios's eyebrows to hit his hairline. "While a worthwhile gift, I believe Astasiya would look more favorably on having her mother back."

Holy shit, Sethios thought, stunned by Gabriel's announcement. *Gabriel's suggestion actually worked.*

The prophecies surrounding Astasiya all depicted her as powerful and a force that would destroy all in her path.

Sethios wasn't naive; he knew why his father wanted her. But he had no idea that Osiris would go to such lengths to secure her allegiance.

Clearly, Gabriel had guessed just how far his father would go to ally with her. And he'd used that notion brilliantly to his advantage.

Sethios's respect for the man intensified greatly in that moment.

Osiris slowly lowered his face to meet the young Seraphim's gaze. "That's not within my control."

"You could tell us where you left her," Gabriel suggested.

"I could." He looked out at the ocean. "But it won't help you." He canted his head. "She's no longer there."

Gabriel and Sethios shared a glance, both of them trying to decipher the evil man's words.

"My offer for Astasiya's protection remains," his father said softly. "She's going to need it." His feathers appeared around him half a beat later. "I'll be awaiting your call."

Osiris vanished.

Sethios said nothing for a long moment, his gaze on Gabriel. The Seraphim studied him right back. "Caro's not underwater."

"What?" How had he gleaned that information?

"Osiris said the vision was an eighteen-year-old memory. Then he commented on her mental state, which I thought was a reflection of her dying over and over again. However, he just said she's no longer here. He also implied that he doesn't know where she is, which means someone found her before we could."

Sethios considered the evidence, recalling every word his father had said. Osiris thrived on strategy, his decisions and words always uttered with his own best interest in mind.

It was possible that he'd meant to send them on a fool's errand while he crafted a trap to take them all. Yet he hadn't provided enough information to truly give them anything.

"Who else would have been looking for her?" Sethios wondered out loud, thinking through Gabriel's comment suggesting someone had already saved her from the ocean floor.

"That's not what worries me," the Seraphim replied. "It's who had the ability to find her that is a greater concern."

Sethios stared at him as a conversation from the past filtered through his mind. One that had occurred shortly after Astasiya's birth. Caro's bloodline made her untraceable. He frowned. "She said you could track her."

"Yes," he agreed. "I should be able to. Yet, I've not been able to feel her since shortly after Osiris disposed of her in the ocean. I thought it was because she's underground. Now I'm wondering if something else has been interfering with my ability to track her this entire time."

"Are you suggesting that she hasn't been drowning these last eighteen years? That she's been somewhere else entirely?" Even as the questions left his lips, the possibility of them being correct filtered through his thoughts. "Is that why I can't feel her?"

Osiris's compulsion not to move his legs was all that kept Sethios standing.

Fuck. Me.

"But you and Astasiya dream of her," he said, speaking his thoughts out loud. "She's sending you visions."

"Is she?" Gabriel asked, his expression showing the first signs of emotion. "Or is it a loop meant to distract us?"

"A loop?"

"A memory feed," he elaborated. "We need to evaluate the visions. We need to evaluate everything." He looked at his watch, then back at Sethios. "There's only one other being who has the ability to find my mother."

"Caro's mother," Sethios said, recalling the other individual from that discussion twenty-five years ago. "But I thought Leela was monitoring the council." That'd been her job and the reason she'd refused to pledge fealty to Astasiya. "She was supposed to tell us if they decided to wake Caro's mother from her angelic coma."

"Correct, she's our eyes and ears inside," Gabriel said softly, frowning down at his watch again. "Just as she's supposed to be monitoring my alerts."

Sethios's legs twitched, the persuasion holding him in place snapping with a jolt of residual energy. His father had completely released him and Gabriel, allowing them to move their legs again.

Gabriel misted as though to test his wings, then he reappeared in his corporeal state. "We should check on Skye. Then we need to have a discussion with Leela. And after that, we'll evaluate all the dreams. Because if Osiris is right about today's vision being a memory, then I suspect the others are as well."

Sethios swallowed, his heart in his throat.

All week, he'd sensed that something was seriously wrong. He should be able to at least feel Caro, yet the only tangible thread between them was the barbed wire shredding holes in his heart.

He'd worried it was because she'd blocked him out because of the pain.

But what if that wasn't it at all? What if someone, or something, had severed their bond?

Oh, angel… His heart broke all over again. *Where the fuck are you?*

CHAPTER FOUR

CARO

CARO FELT NOTHING. Not the cold metal chair beneath her. Not the stale air of the room. Not the heat of the sun warming the window.

She merely existed in a fog.

Forgotten.

No, that wasn't right. She hadn't been forgotten at all. But she needed her mind to remain clear. Open. Vacant. It was the only way to operate here.

They were all inside her, their powers rehabilitating her Seraphim soul, trying to re-create the being she should be. She allowed it. Accepted it. Encouraged it.

Because deep within, she'd found a small fracture in the programming, and she didn't want them to locate her current whereabouts.

Deep within her psyche.

Exploring.

Tugging.

Gently prodding the memory loop that'd been inserted into the link. It took all of her mental strength not to flinch at her own agony, the visual one that left her breathless and terrified.

Seraphim do not feel.

Seraphim do not love.
Seraphim do not react.

She whispered the words through her mind, feigning a pretense of giving in to the reprogramming of her soul while reminding herself of the battle existing within her.

So much power. So much authority. So much *weight.*

Caro strove for focus, finding the thread she desired, the one that would connect her to the forbidden place.

Quiet.

Slow.

Easy.

She couldn't afford to give anything away, and there were so many of them around her, all reprimanding in nature. They wanted her to conform. To change. To be the Seraphim of her past.

Caro was no one.

She ceased to be.

A vessel of magic. A being to be owned.

Those thoughts rolled through the front of her mind, an intoxicating presence of reformation. She didn't fight. Not obviously, anyway. Instead, she quietly retreated to that place she craved, the one she shouldn't touch. Every time she altered a contrived memory, the message changed. She couldn't risk it being too much, or one of them would notice. But the feed was on a loop.

Caro drowning.

Caro crying.

Caro screaming in agony.

It all felt centuries old to her. She couldn't even feel the water now or remember how it'd suffocated her. Yet the pain remained as a visceral scar against her heart.

She crept forward, wishing to leave another footprint, hoping to be able to alter a sentence or a phrase.

How many times had she died and regenerated?

The loop only showed a handful of memories, causing her to wonder how long she'd actually been at the bottom of the ocean. Minutes? Hours? Days? Months?

Did it truly matter?

No. Not really. She had a mission in mind, a memory to tweak, a way to—

A spike of presence had Caro blanking her mind once more.

One of *them* was checking on her increased mental activity.

Seraphim do not feel.

Seraphim do not love.

Seraphim do not react.

She took a shallow breath, falling back into line, far away from that precious place. There would be no altering today. Not with *him* in her mind, poking around to search for any faults in her rehabilitation.

Silence overcame her.

Calmness.

Nothingness.

Caro no longer existed.

No bonds.

No family.

No love.

Just a Seraphim soul, floating… floating away.

TIME NO LONGER HELD MEANING.

Caro was reborn. Died. Reborn again.

Drowning without water.

Flushed from her body and reattached once more.

Did it hurt? Maybe. She couldn't sense anything, her mind existing in a stratosphere removed from her spirit.

Not true. They were connected in a way. Blinking. Swaying. Dying again.

A strand of light caught her focus, so subtle and slight, a sliver of insanity brightening her shadows. She carefully, quietly, clandestinely swam toward it, seeking the outlet her soul desired.

No one was watching today. Not closely, anyway. Her restoration was almost complete. Soon she would wake with a renewed purpose. She felt nothing in regard to that development, just acceptance.

They would provide her with a task.

She would fulfill it.

To disobey was impractical.

Just like following this tarnished, barbed thread. Visions of the past swirled around her. She hid her intentions, choosing to watch them through a passive mind's eye.

No one stopped her.

Not even a prick in her conscious.

She was fully reformed now and no longer a concern.

Which allowed her to play, to subtly alter the message once more. They'd established this memory loop to play over the strands, to pass on to those she couldn't name—not without risking discovery.

Subtly, subtly, subtly, she touched and stroked, adding her own words, blinks, and sounds.

She remained alone, unbothered, her mind still deep beneath the spells of Seraphim power, but not openly monitored.

Caro added another blur. Tweaked another detail. Removed the water from one loop. Waited.

Nothing.

Were her visions even working? Was this all just a trick of the mind established by those meant to guide her through the reformation? What if this was a test? Was she failing even now?

She mentally touched the loop once more, seeking the memory from the day of her drowning. The blurs were too fast, imperceptible.

It was a risk.

But she needed them to see.

Rightness settled over her, a subtle shift that almost bled warmth into her forever frozen state. A trick of the mind? Another experiment?

If she didn't pass, they would just start over.

If she didn't try, she might never escape.

Sacrifice wasn't new to her. She could withstand more pain if it provided her with a chance.

She slipped deeper into the memory loop, careful to avoid detection by the one who had created it, and entered the mental maze deep inside.

This cycle fed into a link somewhere. And that connection was her key to survival.

She had to warn them.

Before it was too late.

CHAPTER FIVE

SETHIOS

"Osiris released Skye from his compulsion as a gift?" Astasiya looked as incredulous as she sounded. "For me?"

Sethios dipped his chin in confirmation. "Gabriel convinced him that you required a sign of good faith in order to consider working with him."

"I will never work with him," she replied immediately.

"Obviously," Gabriel said from the recliner chair in his great room. He had his eyes closed and one ankle crossed over his opposite knee, the picture of ease. The rising sun outside indicated the very early hour, confirming yet another sleepless night for all of them.

"Osiris doesn't know you or your resolve," Sethios added when the Seraphim in the chair remained stoic and silent. "Your brother played on that because, I believe, he wanted Osiris to provide us with your mother's current location. But he gave us Skye instead."

"So he thinks by undoing one evil thing, I'll forgive him?"

"My father is a master strategist. Therefore, I suspect he also removed his compulsion for a self-serving reason." Something that his comment regarding it being a practical course had indicated. "He stated we needed her more than he did, suggesting he intends for her to deliver some sort of prophecy that will likely put us right in his path."

Astasiya visibly shivered. "No, thank you."

Issac wrapped his arm around her, pulling her closer to him on the couch. It was such a natural move, one she accepted with trust and an open heart. While the thought of her having a mate irked Sethios to no end, every moment in their presence indicated the strength of their connection.

Rather than comment on it—or break Issac's arm—Sethios took the chair across from Gabriel, leaving the lovebirds on the couch. "Have you heard from Leela yet?"

"No."

"That's troubling."

Gabriel lifted a shoulder, his version of disagreeing, apparently. "According to Owen, she's with Jayson, Balthazar, and Elizabeth."

"And where's Vera?" Sethios pressed.

"That one is more troubling," Gabriel murmured, finally opening his eyes. "My alert goes to her as well, and she's neither here nor in Hydria."

Sethios considered that. While they'd charged Leela with monitoring the council, Vera possessed the same insight.

"You mentioned when you returned that it's possible Caro's mother—Astasiya's grandmother—might have found her." Issac glanced first at Sethios, then at Gabriel. "How are Leela and Vera related?"

"Leela was supposed to monitor the council's decisions," Sethios replied. "It was her job to warn Gabriel of any sign that they'd chosen to awaken Caro's mother."

"Awaken?" Astasiya repeated.

Right. She was probably not aware of the Seraphim penchant for taking century-long naps. Sethios hadn't known about it either until Caro had explained it all to him. "How much do you know about the Seraphim?" he asked, curious as to where they needed to start this discussion. "Are you aware of their political structure?"

"We haven't reached that part of her education yet," Gabriel put in.

"Yes, because someone spent the last eighteen years of my life fucking with my head," she shot right back.

Gabriel rolled his eyes, an action that would have entertained Sethios on a normal day.

Alas, today was not a normal day.

So he ignored the show of annoyance and focused on his daughter instead. "The High Council of Seraph is the governing body of the Seraphim. They issue edicts and rely heavily on the Fates to guide them in those decisions. That's actually how your mother and I met—she was sent to deliver an edict to Osiris."

His lips threatened to curl at the memory of that night. He'd seen her pretty blue wings glowing from across the Arcadia nightclub and sauntered over for a chat. She'd been the opposite of amused by his interest. Then he'd persuaded her to remain silent and still when his father had approached—an act that had saved her life—and she'd threatened to kill him soon after.

It'd been lust at first sight for Sethios.

The feisty little angel and her penchant for blades.

Fuck, how he missed that night. How he missed *her*.

But that wasn't the topic at hand. He needed their daughter to understand the history to be able to work through the present.

So he told her everything he knew, including how the council members were all the oldest and most powerful of Seraphim kind. How each councilman or councilwoman was the head of their proverbial bloodline, and each line possessed a power or trait.

For Caro, she came from the messenger line, her natural gifts allowing her to conceal her whereabouts. She also inherited a healing ability from her mother, but it remained dormant inside of Caro. At least for now. The Fates had said she would need it one day; however, that day had not yet come to fruition.

Gabriel's father, Adriel, was the leader of the warrior line, which had Astasiya snorting, "Of course he is," in the middle of Sethios's lecture.

After he detailed the structure of the family lines, he went into the society operations and how Seraphim governed themselves. "The council is in charge of every decision," he told her. "So if your grandmother was pulled out of her sleep, it was under their authority. And it would have been with the purpose of finding your mother."

"She was the only one who could do it, other than you, me, and Sethios," Gabriel added then. "I thought I couldn't locate her because she was underground—sort of like when Issac buried you. I couldn't sense your location at all when I should have been able to."

"So it's entirely possible that she's still drowning," Issac replied.

"Yes," Gabriel agreed. "Except there are other signs we need to consider, such as Sethios not being able to sense her. When you bonded with Astasiya, I warned you that if anything like that ever happened to her, you'd be in constant agony as a result." He gestured at Sethios. "He's decidedly not."

"I used to be," Sethios said, thinking back on his captivity. "There were several times that I felt Caro die, never understanding who she was or why I experienced the death with her. But it subsided shortly after Osiris's compulsion took over." He frowned. "There were moments here and there where I experienced her pain, but it wasn't consistent. Now it's like she's not even here."

He recalled the first time Caro had died, how excruciating it had been to not understand why he felt as though he were drowning on land. The ache in his chest had nearly undone him, the anguish crippling his soul. Only it all disappeared a breath later, then repeated several more times that day until his father had arrived and silenced him with a command.

How long had that gone on? The hours or days of dying on repeat and being unable to scream or move?

He blinked. When had it all stopped? Had Osiris compelled it out of him due to boredom? Or had it been something else entirely?

"I thought you heard from Caro daily?" Issac asked, his focus on Gabriel. "Isn't that what you said when you arrived in Hydria? Something about your headache?"

"Her visions haunt me, yes," Gabriel replied. "But that's more metaphorical. I don't actually hear or see her, but I dream of her drowning every time I sleep. It's vivid, yet always the same. Which is why I want to fully evaluate them now, to see if it's a looping memory or not. I want to evaluate Stas's dreams, too."

"Mine are always different," she replied, frowning. "They usually tie into something else. Like after the Conclave I attended, the drowning vision morphed into him torturing me like Sierra."

"Who's Sierra?" Sethios asked. He didn't recognize the name.

"An Ichorian who found me in New York City and didn't give me up to Osiris," Owen explained as he entered the room and collapsed onto the couch beside Astasiya and Issac. "It's my understanding that he made a show of her disobedience." The words were flat, yet regret touched his dark features.

Sethios imagined the female had suffered greatly, especially if she was the star of the Conclave that night. "And you witnessed this show?" he asked his daughter.

"Yeah." She visibly swallowed. "That was my introduction to Ichorian life."

Right. Grand introduction, indeed. He narrowed his gaze at the *Ichorian* beside her. "You took her to a fucking Conclave?"

The male snorted. "Not by bloody choice."

"One doesn't just accidentally attend a Conclave, Issac."

"I never claimed it was an accident. I stated it wasn't by choice."

"Elaborate," Sethios demanded, ready to wring the male's neck for endangering his daughter in such a way.

"Tom told her about the Arcadia," Gabriel replied before Issac had a chance. "He thought it would be a good way to show her Issac's true nature. He didn't realize it was the night of a Conclave."

"If you'd like to kill him for it, I'll happily watch," Issac said, his own fury over the experience palpable and somewhat cooling Sethios's mounting ire.

"Look, I'm fine. I didn't die. Can we focus on Mom now?"

"No, I have another question," Sethios interjected. "Who the fuck is Tom?"

"Jonathan Fitzgerald's son." Gabriel shifted, lowering one foot to the ground and lifting his other ankle to rest against the opposite knee. "He's a Hydraian, and valuable. You can't kill him." He looked pointedly at Issac. "It would greatly upset Amelia."

"Bollocks," the male muttered in reply.

"Seriously, none of this matters. You said Mom might be in a memory loop. I want to know what that means, how it works, and what to do if it's true." Astasiya's tone resembled Caro's no-nonsense voice, the kind she used when reprimanding without much emotion. It caused Sethios's heart to pang softly, his concern regarding the Conclave vanishing in an instant.

His daughter was right—they had more important matters to discuss.

"Show Issac your dreams, Gabriel. Then he can play them for all of us, and we can search for loops. Astasiya can do the same. Then I'll offer what little I can. We'll see if your theory checks out."

Gabriel nodded, the practical course one he would obviously favor.

Issac visibly flinched, the Seraphim already unloading his thoughts without another word.

Sethios glanced at his daughter, catching the worry in her expression. He decided to distract her by answering one of her comments.

"As you know, Vera can manipulate and change memories. But she's not the only one with that gift. If your mother has in fact been taken by the Seraphim, it's possible they've been trying to rehabilitate her, and during that process, they may have put her memories on a loop."

"But why would they do that?"

"To ensure those connected to her didn't sense the change in her location," Sethios replied. "Unfortunately, if this is true, it implies Gabriel is no longer within their circle of trust."

"It also implies they know about my fealty pledge to Astasiya, something they've not indicated in any disciplinary hearings yet." The Seraphim spoke without taking his gaze away from Issac. "However, if we're right about this, then we're being monitored. Which means we're not safe here."

"Jesus, slow down," Issac said, sounding breathless. "You're quite literally drowning me in details."

"Work faster."

Issac's eyes narrowed, and the Seraphim suddenly choked. "Fast enough for you, mate?"

Gabriel coughed and sputtered as though he were drowning himself while power poured off of Issac, his expression one of astute concentration.

"That's a very useful ability," Sethios mused.

"Indeed," he returned. "And I can already tell this is a manipulated loop. Her movements are restricted."

"She's tied to a chair," Gabriel pointed out, his voice hoarse.

"That's not what I mean. Look. Watch her eyes and mouth. They move in the same sequence on repeat."

Caro populated Sethios's mind, so real and tangible and not two feet away from him. He reached for her on instinct, his fingers brushing air. *A vision.* And a horrid one at that.

Agony etched a scar into her pretty face, her screams muted yet present in the way her mouth formed wordless sounds. She began to choke, causing his heart to beat faster, his own anguish pouring out of him in waves.

"No!" He dove toward her, going through her and landing on the floor.

"Stop!" Astasiya demanded.

The vision vanished, Caro's pain disappearing into mist and revealing Gabriel's great room. Sethios wheezed on the ground, his chest vacant, his heart no longer beating.

His angel... *Oh, fuck...*

He curled into himself, the pain threatening to shred him inside.

All of Osiris's tortures combined hadn't compared to this. Oh, how she'd suffered. He searched for her, his soul in tatters, his blood refusing to flow. *Goddammit, Caro. Talk to me!* He shouted the command through their bond, his fury a whiplash to his senses. *Talk to me now!*

Shh, her voice hushed him in reply. *They'll hear you.*

Sethios froze. *Caro?* he breathed, worried his mind might be playing a cruel trick on him.

When she didn't reply, he growled both through the bond and out loud. *If you don't start talking—*

Stop, she whispered urgently, then he felt her tug on his soul, yanking him closer. An odd sensation, considering he remained in Gabriel's house. *They know you're here. Oh, Fates! They're coming. You need to run. Run!*

But it was already too late.

A Seraphim with translucent gold feathers misted into the room before Sethios could even speak.

Fuck.

CHAPTER SIX

STAS

THE WORLD SWAM AROUND STAS, her vision whirling in a cacophony of colors. One minute, she'd been kneeling on the floor trying to talk to her father, and in the next second, she was flying.

Not of her own volition. Not with her own wings, either. But a black blur she couldn't decipher.

When her feet touched sand, she shoved herself away from a body much larger than her own and froze upon meeting a pair of tired black eyes. The gold flecks of his irises swirled with a touch of insanity, his long, dark hair pulled back into an uncharacteristic ponytail. He was also missing his trademark leather coat.

"Ezekiel?" It came out as a question. Of course she knew the assassin's name. She just didn't understand why he'd—she frowned, taking in her surroundings—yeah, she didn't understand why he'd taken her to Hydria. "What the hell?"

"Skye," he rasped. "She had a vision and I reacted."

"A vision? What kind of vision?"

"One involving golden feathers and your capture," he explained as Jacque appeared beside them with Luc and Alik on either side. "I need to trace back, but stay here."

"What about Issac?"

"He can handle himself."

"And I can't?" she demanded.

Silence.

Because the damn Ichorian was already gone.

She had half a mind to follow him back to Stark's house and teach him a lesson, but her intelligent side held her in place.

If he'd traced her here, it'd been for a reason. One Issac confirmed less than a second later as he murmured, *I assume Ezekiel kidnapped you because of the golden-winged Seraphim in Gabriel's great room?*

He said Skye had a vision of golden feathers and my capture.

I see, he replied, his English accent thicker inside her thoughts than when he spoke out loud. She rather liked the sexy inflection. Not that now was an optimal time for her to think about it in that manner.

If Gabriel's surprised by the intrusion, he's not showing it, Issac continued. *Sethios appears equally unfazed by it. Where did Ezekiel…? Actually, no, never mind. Don't tell me in case they can locate you through me.*

"Stas?" Luc prompted, his muscular arms folded over his chest. "What's going on?"

Jacque had already disappeared, perhaps to Stark's place to check in on the situation there. Or maybe he'd been called to another part of Hydria. The poor teleporter was constantly working.

"A Seraphim just arrived at Stark's place," Stas said. "Ezekiel traced me here before I could be seen. Or I assume that was the purpose, anyway."

"Which Seraphim?" a feminine voice asked as a swirl of purple graced the air. Leela materialized, her blonde hair glowing in the moonlight. It'd just been morning on her side of the world. It seemed to be closer to eight or nine at night here.

This whole teleporting thing was intense.

Stas narrowed her eyes at the stunning Seraphim, recalling her father's commentary with Gabriel regarding Leela's job to monitor the council. She'd either failed in her task or was playing a dangerous game of double agent.

The female blinked. "What the hell is that look for?"

"Is my grandmother awake?" Stas countered.

Another blink. "I… Your grandmother? Why would she…?" She cocked her head in a decidedly inhuman manner. "Why would you ask me that? What has Sethios found?" Then her eyebrows lifted. "Wait, does he think…? Oh… Oh, no…" She flickered out before she could elaborate, disappearing from view.

Stas scowled after her. "That's helpful."

"What has Sethios found?" Luc asked, his emerald irises blazing with unworldly knowledge. Sometimes his omniscience frightened her. Yet she couldn't doubt the useful nature of his strategic abilities.

Her heart gave a slight pang for the loss of his father, his death having occurred on this very beach.

If it bothered Luc, he didn't show it. However, the bags beneath his eyes indicated he hadn't slept in quite some time. While Hydraians didn't require sleep, she suspected it hurt to go without it.

She cleared her throat to focus on his question, telling him about the conversation she'd just had with her father and Gabriel and how they were speculating that her mother might not be at the bottom of the ocean at all.

"They ran into Osiris?" Alik asked, his dark brow winging upward. "And I wasn't invited to the party?"

"He ambushed them in Maine," Stas explained. "I guess he knew they'd show up there eventually because it was near my mother's drowning site. But he told them she's no longer there."

"And they believed him?" Alik didn't bother to hide his irritation at the concept.

"He released Skye from her compulsion," Stas added. "He claimed it was a gift for me."

Luc stared at her. "A gift?"

"Yeah, Gabriel convinced him that I needed a show of good faith to consider talking to him." She snorted. "Not that it will ever happen."

Alik scoffed, just as Stas had when she first heard the asinine idea. Luc, however, nodded, mostly to himself.

"That's a decent strategy. I imagine he also suggested your mother as an offering, which Osiris claimed he couldn't do because she's not where he left her." He dipped his chin again. "Yes, I see why they believe him. Caro would be the best card for Osiris to play, and he hasn't. That indicates it's not his card to play. Interesting."

Alik considered it and shrugged. "Maybe he plans to play that card later."

Aya, the Seraphim just issued Gabriel an edict to rid his premises of the abominations—preferably by death—and then report to the council. With you. Issac's warm tones belied the ice of his words.

Stas froze. *What did he say to that?*

He vaguely agreed.

Has Ezekiel returned? she wondered.

Not to this room, no. The Seraphim has only seen me, Sethios, your brother, and Owen. My guess is he's tending to Skye.

What about Tristan? He was the only other Ichorian at Stark's right now. Everyone else had returned to Hydria for the time being.

He's staying silent upstairs.

Stas didn't particularly like the sound-controlling

Ichorian, but he was Issac's progeny and therefore important. So she felt a small measure of satisfaction at learning he was all right.

Do you need me to find Jacque and send him to you? She phrased it in a way that didn't give her location away since he didn't want her to tell him where Ezekiel had taken her.

No, the Seraphim seems to feel the edict is enough to force Gabriel's compliance.

Is it? She'd meant that as a musing more than a real question, but Issac replied anyway.

Was it enough for your mum? he countered, a smile in his voice.

No.

Then I doubt it's enough for your brother.

"The Seraphim delivered an edict to Gabriel. They want the abominations removed from his property, preferably by death. And they want him to appear before the council. With me." Stas looked at Luc. "That's not going to happen."

"You're right. It's not," Leela agreed, reappearing again. "If they have your mother, then she's being rehabilitated. Which is exactly where they'll take you and Gabriel after you arrive. That's where I'll end up as well if the theory about Chanara—your grandmother—is accurate." She visibly shuddered at the words.

"How does one rehabilitate a Seraphim?" Luc asked.

"Rehabilitation is used to correct the broken ones of our kind," she replied softly. "It's a program that helps us relearn our status in life and reminds us why emotions have no place in our society."

"By doing what?" he pressed.

"Whatever is necessary." She swallowed. "If Caro is there, well, they would do everything they can to break her blood bond with Sethios. Or, at the very least, degrade it to a point where she no longer considers it relevant."

"Which would explain why my father can't sense her."

"Yes," Leela whispered. "Because there would be nothing to sense. She would consider herself nonexistent and therefore be nonexistent. No heartbeat. No thoughts. Just a being waiting to be reborn into whatever purpose the council chooses."

That sounded… *awful.* "Gabriel thinks her memories are playing on a loop."

Leela's bright blue-green eyes flickered with understanding. "They're using her pain in a practical manner to manipulate the emotions of those bonded to her. If it hurts too much to pay attention to her mind and soul, then you ignore the obvious."

Stas didn't know how to reply to that. Mostly because she couldn't wrap her head around such cold cruelty. But with every piece of information falling into place, it seemed more and more likely that her mother was no longer drowning. She'd been transferred to an even worse prison—Seraphim rehabilitation.

Issac, Stas whispered before relaying to him everything Leela had just said. *I think Stark and my dad are right,* she concluded. *The Seraphim have my mom.*

No, Aya, he replied, already knowing what she was going to suggest. *You are not going there with Gabriel.*

But it makes sense, doesn't it? They've just presented us with a perfect opportunity to find and save her.

Or trap you in the same damn state, he snapped. *Absolutely not.* However, even as he said it, she sensed his mind working through the same calculations that she'd already done.

I'm not saying I'll go right now, she confirmed softly. *I just… I think we need to explore the opportunity.*

He didn't reply, his hesitation and fear vivid in their bond.

Tell Gabriel, she said, the two words more of a suggestion than a command. *See what he says.*

I already know what he'll say, Issac muttered back at her. *I'm going to tell your father instead. He'll see reason.*

She snorted. *Ganging up on me with my dad now?*

If that's what it takes to keep you safe, then yes. Just consider it.

No.

Liar, she accused softly. *I know you see the opportunity here.*

She could admit it was a rash decision, one she intended to think through entirely before agreeing. But she wanted her lover to at least consider it with her.

Instead, he fell silent once more, causing her to sigh.

"Your brother is being stubborn," she told Luc. They technically weren't brothers by blood, but they shared a father figure in Aidan. He was Luc's dad by blood, and Issac's maker.

Jacque teleported in with a plate in his hand and a fork at his lips. He appeared to be eating some sort of cake. "B needs you, Feathers. He says to meet him at Jay's place." He was already teleporting again as the last word left his mouth.

"Feathers?" Stas repeated.

"Leela," Alik explained, rolling his eyes. "It's Jacque's pet name for her."

The Seraphim smiled. "Have you come up with one for me yet, handsome?"

"Trouble," he drawled.

Her sea-colored eyes sparkled. "I like it."

"I'm sure you do," he returned. "Go play with B. He's more your style."

"And how would you know?" she asked him.

61

"Because you saved his life on the beach?" Stas suggested, arching a brow. "Not that I'm complaining, but why did you do that, exactly?"

"She saved Balthazar's life?" Luc asked, his eyebrows shooting upward.

Leela put on an expression of contrived innocence. "I'm sure I have no idea what any of you are talking about." She shot a look at Stas, then disappeared into a flurry of purple once more.

"What did you see?" Luc demanded. "Are you talking about the night of the wedding reception?"

Uh, oops. She hadn't meant to step into a situation she knew little about.

"Um, yeah, she was there that night and took a few bullets that were meant for B. At least, I think that's what I saw. But everything happened in a blur, so I could be wrong." She wasn't wrong. She knew what she'd seen that night. It had distracted her so entirely that it'd caused her own death in the process. Which had led to being buried alive, and yeah, that had sucked.

She cleared her throat. "So, how's Lizzie?" Her best friend was very pregnant, despite having conceived in October. And it was only January, or was it February now? Stas had lost track of the time, what with dying and coming back to life and then saving her father from an insane, millennia-old immortal, and everything else that had happened in between those events.

Her head spun from the events that had occurred since Christmas. Learning her best friend wasn't exactly human and likely about to give birth to a Seraphim was just the icing on the cake.

"Can I see her?" she asked when no one responded.

"That depends. How do you feel about hormonal women?" Alik considered her while he spoke. "Never mind. You'll be fine." He turned on the beach, walking away from the homes and toward a more remote area. "If anyone needs me, I'll be patrolling."

"I'll take you to see Lizzie," Luc offered, his voice soft. "If you tell me exactly what you saw that night."

Yeah, he wasn't going to drop that anytime soon. Primarily because he was all-knowing and the Hydraian King. He needed to understand what had happened to better process the situation. "Can I detail it along the way?"

"Yes," he agreed, gesturing toward the path behind them rather than to the trail Alik had created with his sneakers. "Then you can tell me the plan my brother disapproves of. Perhaps I can be of assistance."

Stas hadn't mentioned that Issac disapproved of her idea, but she wasn't surprised that Luc had inferred as much from her "your brother is being stubborn" comment. It also didn't shock her that Luc might want to help. He tended to be the voice of reason. Which was why she obliged him with the details he craved as they walked, leaving nothing out, including her seeing Aidan fall.

It hurt to discuss that night. Yet it also provided her with a therapy of sorts. Jonathan had taken so much from them. He was dead now, yet his legacy hung over their heads in an ominous cloud, one she very much wanted to dismantle. And with every word, she could feel that presence weakening.

It was fascinatingly cathartic.

She only hoped Luc felt the same because if anyone needed to release some of his anger over the events, it was him.

Unfortunately, something told her it wouldn't be that easy for him. He'd lost so much that night. Rather than grieve, he bore the brunt of those events and carried all of it on his shoulders. Because he had to be strong for his people, which didn't allow him to break.

How lonely he must feel, she realized, her heart aching for him. Alas, she knew better than to breathe a word of it. He couldn't afford for anyone to see through his show of strength. So, instead, she confided in his wisdom, providing him with the power he needed to thrive.

We're on our way there, Aya, Issac informed her just as she reached Jayson's house. *See you in a few seconds, love.*

CHAPTER SEVEN

SETHIOS

ASTASIYA's best friend was very pregnant. Sethios had met the woman once before under less-than-comfortable circumstances. He'd helped her escape his father's captivity by compelling her to run.

While his actions probably appeared gallant to her, they weren't meant for her. Sethios had merely wanted to infuriate his father.

The bastard had persuaded Sethios to sew his mouth shut as a punishment for his lack of obedience—something he hadn't understood at that time but realized now was a residual for his dalliance with Caro. To get the old man back, Sethios had encouraged the curvy redhead to flee.

Then his father had paid him back by forcing his hair to grow.

That'd been excruciating, yet worth it. Especially now that he knew the girl's importance to his daughter.

The two of them were sitting on the couch with bowls of ice cream. Elizabeth, or Lizzie, as she preferred to be called, was talking animatedly about the nursery Jayson had built for the baby. Sethios had never heard of a Hydraian being able to procreate, which he said now to Issac.

"Elizabeth was created in Jonathan's lab," the male replied softly, his voice pitched low so as not to be overheard by the females in Jayson's living area. The reason for his softness was evident as a result of the sensitive nature of his comment.

"Jonathan, as in the Ichorian who forced truths from others?" Sethios asked, clarifying whom he meant.

"Yes. He and your father were working together on experiments through the Catastrophic Relief Foundation."

"I'm familiar with the CRF and my father's pet projects," Sethios confirmed. "But I wasn't privy to the details." Nor had he honestly tried to learn more about it. He just assumed it was another one of his schemes to craft and mold a stronger army against the Seraphim.

"One of those pet projects is Elizabeth. She has Seraphim genetics but was carried to term by a mortal female," Issac murmured. "From what Ezekiel has said, your father had her created for mating. To replace you."

Sethios snorted. "Sounds like something he would do. But the baby isn't his, right?"

"Jayson's the father."

"Interesting. I'm surprised Osiris allowed her to keep the child." Another thought occurred to him immediately following that statement. "Ah, I see. He considers this a test run."

It would be just like his father to fully trial the experiment before bothering to use the product. Unfortunately, that meant Elizabeth was a ticking time bomb. The moment she proved viable, Osiris would come for her again.

"What security measures are in place to protect her?" Sethios wondered out loud. "Aside from the usual Guardians."

"Should I take that as an insult?" Jayson asked as he

entered the kitchen area that overlooked his living room. "You don't think I can protect my wife?"

"Wife?" Sethios's eyebrows hit his hairline. "Is that your pet name, or did you actually buy into that human bullshit?"

Issac grinned, explaining, "Elizabeth was raised in a mortal society. She very much values the sanctity of marriage. I'm waiting for her to plan Astasiya's wedding."

Sethios gaped at the man. "You're going to marry my daughter now?"

He lifted a shoulder. "It's a frivolous ceremony meant to appease family and friends."

Yeah, fuck that. "It would not please me in the slightest."

"Does that mean I don't have your blessing?"

"Considering she's still seven in my eyes, no. You absolutely do not."

"Then I suppose it's fortuitous that Astasiya doesn't require your approval to marry," Issac replied without missing a beat.

"I'm doing what now?" Astasiya asked as she joined them, her green eyes wide as she gaped at the suit-clad male. "We're already married."

Issac's lips twitched. "Indeed we are," he agreed.

Sethios's blood ran cold. "You *married* my daughter?"

"I'm sensing a hint of animosity surrounding the whole wedding thing," Jayson interjected, waving his hand in the air. "I had no idea you bought into this '*human bullshit.*'"

There was a time when others feared Sethios and what he could do. He wondered when the fuck that had changed. Less than two decades of imprisonment did not compare to several millennia of life.

"Did you just call our wedding *bullshit*?" The feminine

voice drew everyone's gaze to the pregnant female in the doorway.

And the pigment in Jayson's skin went from tan to stark white in a second.

Sethios smirked, delighted by the change.

Until the female began to cry.

That put an immediate end to his amusement and struck a chord of terror inside him instead. Dealing with upset women was not in Sethios's repertoire.

"No, Red. I swear, that's not what I meant at all." Jayson tried to console the female with his outstretched arms, but she stepped back, her lower lip wobbling in a way that had Astasiya jumping in to wrap the female in a hug.

"They were talking about me and Issac," she quickly explained. "You know Jay loves you. He planned the whole wedding, Liz. He did it for you."

"But considers it bullshit," the girl said, her shoulders hunching.

Oh, for fuck's sake. "I said it was bullshit," Sethios interjected. "He was throwing my words back at me. Weddings are a human invention, one I clearly don't understand."

How the hell had they gone from discussing Caro's whereabouts in the Seraphim world to bantering about weddings?

Sethios shook his head and left the room, not having time for this asinine discussion. He'd explained the situation with a few words. If the girl chose to give in to her pregnancy hormones, that was on her.

He stepped through the threshold to breathe in the island air, his heart thudding painfully in his chest.

A part of him couldn't stand being around the pregnant female inside because she reminded him too much of Caro and her pregnancy with Astasiya. What he wouldn't give to go back to that time and hold them once more, to safeguard them within the protection of his arms.

Caro hadn't spoken to him again since the Seraphim's arrival. It almost made him wonder if he'd imagined the entire thing. Yet he'd *felt* her. Just for that brief moment, she'd been inside him, much different from the visual he'd been sent a few hours prior.

He suspected that image from the coast of Maine had served as a test of sorts, one he and Gabriel had failed. It wasn't a coincidence that hours after they'd visited the area, a Seraphim had arrived with an edict. They'd planted that memory into his mind with the purpose of drawing him out, to find them. And they'd likely tracked him and Gabriel right back to the South Pacific.

Which suggested it hadn't been Osiris at all, a thought that left Sethios decidedly uneasy.

"…viable, yes." The deep baritone came from a male Sethios hadn't seen in a very long time.

"Lucian," he said as the blond, godlike man stepped into view. He had a charisma and power about him that made his role as leader of his people a natural expectation. Sethios had always maintained a level of respect for the man, despite their clear differences.

"Hello, Sethios," Lucian replied.

Gabriel stood beside him, his expression as vacant as always. "I was bringing him up to speed."

"Good. Meanwhile, I've been causing problems inside," Sethios admitted. "I'm rather certain Jayson wants to kill me now." He'd welcome the challenge, if only to amuse himself for a minute. The Hydraian Elder could control metal, which was a fascinating gift to battle.

Of course, Sethios could just use that ability to his own advantage with a few carefully worded commands.

"Stas says she wants to go with Stark to the council. While I agree that it's an ideal opportunity for reconnaissance, we've discussed an alternative plan that may work better," Lucian said, getting straight to the point.

This was why Sethios liked him—he never wasted time. "Does it still involve her going to the council?" he asked. "Because if it does, I'm going to veto it."

Issac had told him Astasiya's thoughts on going with Gabriel to see the council. He commended her bravery; however, it was exactly what Osiris had predicted would happen and had advised against. And while Sethios typically ignored his father's instructions, on this, they were in agreement.

"The council wants her, just like Osiris does," Gabriel said, stating the obvious. "I think we should apply a similar strategy. Which means I need to go alone."

Sethios listened as Gabriel detailed the plan, his admiration for the Seraphim growing with each passing second. Caro had once mentioned that Gabriel came from an old line of warriors. He'd assumed that meant the young Seraphim could handle himself well in battle in a physical sense, but by the end of the discussion, he realized it applied to strategy as well.

"I had no idea you were so manipulative," Sethios drawled.

Gabriel merely blinked at him, then continued his plotting. "I need someone to test my current level of mortal influence. Is there an empath on the island?"

"You want to make sure the Seraphim can't detect any emotions in you," Lucian translated.

"Exactly."

The Hydraian King studied him. "I thought you were immune to our abilities."

"I am," Gabriel confirmed. "But there are ways around it."

He arched a blond brow. "Enlighten me."

"Do you have an empath?" Gabriel countered.

"I do. But she might not be a willing participant."

Gabriel stared at him. "I don't need her to necessarily cooperate. I just need some of her blood."

Well, that's interesting. "You need to imbibe her essence?" Sethios guessed.

"Yes." Gabriel's tone was flat. "But not much."

"That's not why she'll be unwilling," Lucian informed them. "The only empath on the island is currently in custody."

"Clara," Gabriel said.

"Who's Clara?" Sethios asked, hating all these new names and associations. This would be so much easier with just a handful of acquaintances, but the Hydraians operated as a family unit. Hence, their hierarchal structure resembled more of a brotherhood than a dictatorship.

"An Ichorian. Aidan made her. And she betrayed us all to Jonathan." The anger in Lucian's voice rivaled the green flames flaring in his vibrant irises. "She's locked up in the utility hut off the beach. I suppose we could have B read the reaction from her mind, if you think that'll be sufficient enough. But she's not being all that forthcoming with information."

Sethios considered him. "Is she the reason my daughter was shot and subsequently buried alive?" Technically, Gabriel possessed some of the fault in that sequence of events. But the burial wouldn't have been needed without the initial attack.

"Yes," Lucian replied. "She told Jonathan about the wedding."

"Then perhaps I should tag along," he suggested. "If

there's one thing my maker taught me, it's how to intimidate someone into cooperating." Sethios's reputation for cruelty spanned millennia, something they could use to their advantage now.

Unless she failed to fear him like the immortals inside Jayson's home.

His lips curled down at the thought. He'd only been out of the game for twenty-five years. That was a few blinks in their overall life spans. Did they all assume he'd reformed himself while under his father's version of house arrest?

"Actually, that might help us," Lucian said, his expression thoughtful. "She's old enough to know who you are. That she placed your daughter in harm's way should also sway her to cooperate at least a little. And you bring the added benefit of having no history with her. Which means she'll know you won't go easy on her."

"Yes, and as an empath, she'll be able to feel my rage." Of which he had plenty to go around. Particularly as Caro had shut him out again and he was getting really tired of not being able to feel her.

"When do you need to report to the council?" Lucian asked.

"Edicts are expected to be followed. They'll anticipate my swift compliance, but I have a few hours, or perhaps days, before another messenger arrives. They may allow me more time due to the request to handle the abomination problem on my property."

Sethios snorted. "What happens when Issac and I grow wings? Will we still be considered abominations?" The blood bond would eventually turn both of them into Seraphim.

Eventually, Sethios repeated to himself, annoyed. He

should already have his wings, at least according to what Caro had told him twenty-five years ago.

"It's not a precedented situation, so I imagine the council will need to meet to declare your fates."

"And they haven't already decided mine?" Sethios asked, surprised.

"Not that I'm aware of. But as my grandmother may have been awakened without my knowledge or consultation, my expertise on the matter is likely null."

Always so practical and stoic.

Sethios really thought Ezekiel would have loosened him up over the years, but the Gabriel before him was just as bland as ever.

"Right. Shall we go chat with the empath?" Sethios suggested, needing a distraction.

Balthazar appeared on the path in a T-shirt and shorts. "Let's go" was all he said, leading the way without another word.

Lucian must have communicated the plan to the mind reader. As his fellow Elder, it made sense. There were five of them who essentially led the Hydraian race. Or there were five the last time Sethios had checked.

Lucian, Balthazar, Alik, Jedrick—who now went by Jayson—and Eli.

Sethios considered the last one with a frown. He hadn't seen the giant immortal anywhere. Alik had been playing sentry on the beach. Jayson was inside dealing with his pregnant wife. So where was Eli? Off with Amelia, perhaps?

Only, hadn't Gabriel mentioned Jonathan's son being important to her? Sethios hadn't bothered to ask why, his concern with the prick revolving around an entirely different matter—telling his daughter about the Arcadia.

Rather than ponder it all damn day, Sethios asked,

"Where's Eli? I haven't seen him yet." And he rather liked the big brute. He could kill with a single touch. A very useful trait.

Lucian and Balthazar stopped walking, both of them turning to study him closely.

Sethios's eyebrows lifted. "That's a pair of ominous looks."

"Eli's dead," Lucian replied flatly. "Jonathan killed him."

The world fell silent with that announcement, Sethios's heart skipping a beat in his chest. "Jonathan killed Eli? How the fuck did that imbecile take down a Hydraian Elder?"

"By taking advantage of our trust."

"Why would you trust him?" Then it dawned on him, the reason it'd been so simple for him to infiltrate their world and cause all this havoc. "Right. Aidan took him in as a stray immortal." And as Issac's maker, and Luc's father, anyone else who affiliated with him would be perceived with some level of familial trust. "Fuck. I'm sorry to hear that."

Eli had been a formidable adversary, and Sethios respected that.

Balthazar dipped his chin in gratitude, while Lucian just turned to continue walking.

"What else have I missed?" Sethios wondered out loud.

"No other deaths, if that's what you mean," Balthazar replied. "None that you would know, anyway."

"Jonathan took Amelia and experimented on her for several years," Lucian said. "Another of his experiments is being kept in the utility hut. She and Tom are determined to rehabilitate him."

"And Tom is Jonathan's son," Sethios said, not a

question but a statement. "You trust him after everything his father has done?"

"We do," Balthazar confirmed as they turned off the cobblestone path onto a narrow concrete walkway that would take them down to the beach. "He and Amelia killed Jonathan together."

"He was also instrumental in taking down the CRF," Lucian murmured.

"And he's Amelia's chosen lover," Gabriel interjected. "She's the reason they trust him."

Amelia's dating the son of Eli's killer? Sethios thought, whistling to himself. *That's sort of fucked up.* Although, he wasn't all that fit to judge. His relationship with Caro hadn't exactly started with sunshine and roses. He'd negotiated her into his bed, then reneged on the deal and tried to keep her. She hadn't been thrilled with him.

Do you miss your knives, Caro? he asked her, amused by the memory. *If you talk to me, maybe I'll let you play with them after I find you.*

The resounding silence only made him sigh.

I'm going to find you, angel, he promised. *Then I'm going to fuck you for months, just to hear you scream. Because I can't stand not hearing you.*

Was this how she felt when he didn't know her? Had she tried to reach out to him, only to be ignored?

He considered what he remembered, his lips curling downward with each revisited memory. Sethios couldn't recall a time she'd tried to reach out. Only mental visions of her drowning and the searing pain of experiencing it with her. But even those felt less and less painful over the years, like he'd somehow numbed himself to it.

Or perhaps it was because the visual cycle's effects on him had declined with each repeated experience.

If it'd all been a sequence, as Gabriel suggested, then it

was falsely contrived, and the bond would more or less overpower it. Was that why he couldn't sense her? Because she'd been truly cut off from him, and the feed the Seraphim had created to keep him temporarily occupied no longer applied?

"We need to finish comparing the dreams," he said, interrupting whatever Balthazar and Lucian were discussing. "We only reviewed yours."

"Yes, but if my theory about the council having my mother is accurate, then reviewing the dreams is null and void."

"Not if she's been trying to communicate through the visions," Sethios said. "I heard her briefly before that messenger arrived. She warned me."

"You're sure it was her and not a forced vision?"

"I could sense her, Gabriel. It was her voice in my head, not a fuzzy image." And now she'd gone silent again. *Stubborn angel.*

Gabriel considered him, then nodded. "We'll see what level my empathy is operating at, then we'll talk to Stas about her dreams. After that, we'll evaluate a plan and proceed accordingly."

CHAPTER EIGHT

GABRIEL

GABRIEL CHECKED his phone as he entered the bunker. Ezekiel had messaged to say that he'd arrived at an undisclosed location with Skye and Owen. Since the latter was considered an exiled Hydraian, he wasn't exactly welcome back in Hydria yet.

Okay, Gabriel replied.

Then he scanned his phone for any notes from Vera. Nothing. His lips threatened to twitch, something they rarely did. She should have called by now.

He hadn't mentioned his suspicions yet to the others, but they grew with each passing minute. They were just too coincidental.

Vera could manipulate memories, which made her qualified to create a mental loop of Caro's memories. Further, Vera had access to Stas and Gabriel to influence their interpretations of those visions through dreams. She could essentially insert the images into their minds while they slept without either of them sensing the disturbance.

However, she wouldn't have been able to access Sethios's mind. The fact that he hadn't dreamt of Caro for years suggested that either the circular enchantment didn't work on him, or the Seraphim initiating the visions hadn't been able to infiltrate his dream state.

The remembrance from earlier of Maine could have been sent to him from nearby, and Gabriel wouldn't have sensed any intrusion because Vera was a welcome member on his property. His wards wouldn't alert him to her presence.

That she wasn't answering his texts or showing up to present her innocence only further confirmed Gabriel's concerns.

He would mention them after he finished this test with the imprisoned Ichorian. He wanted Leela there for the discussion. It would exonerate her and also confirm the council's awareness of her involvement—because Vera had likely told them.

Loyalty among the Seraphim varied. He wouldn't necessarily fault her if she'd betrayed them. She would have seen it as a practical course.

Just as he would see killing her as a practical response. Or perhaps that was emotional. She'd eventually regenerate, so it wasn't like his punishment would be final or anything.

He slid his phone back into his pocket and followed the others along a short corridor. The Hydraians only had a handful of holding cells, all protected by solid doors. Prisoners were clearly rare on this island.

Two females stood in the hallway, one with ash-blonde hair, the other with a mane of silky dark strands. Both Hydraians. However, the darker-haired female was newer. He recognized her as a recent fledgling, but her name escaped him.

"Luc," the older Hydraian said, giving him a nod. A seductive gleam entered her azure-colored eyes as she looked at Balthazar. "B."

The mind-reading Hydraian merely dipped his chin, his expression uncharacteristically void of emotion. He typically oozed sensuality yet seemed a bit withdrawn today. Perhaps he was dreading the task at hand. That left Gabriel wondering just what they were walking into.

"What are you doing down here, Eliza?" Lucian demanded, his focus on the brunette.

She visible cringed at his hostile tone. "I… I was just…"

"You were just what?" The dark quality of his voice had the hairs along her exposed arms standing on end, yet her expression morphed from contrite to annoyed in an instant.

"Ash was teaching me about Guardian responsibilities," she snapped. "I'm a Hydraian now, so I need a job. I thought that might be a useful area for me."

Lucian snorted. "Like you have what it takes to be a Guardian."

Gabriel evaluated the female, curious. She had on a pair of jean shorts and a pale tank top, revealing her toned arms and athletic legs. That probably made her light on her feet. Perhaps even fast.

"Are her powers not of a defensive or offensive nature?" he wondered out loud. Because her overall physique suggested strength, confirming her warrior potential.

"Her power isn't the problem," Lucian said between his teeth. "It's her discipline."

"What he means is, I won't put up with his shit, so he thinks I'm disobedient," she translated.

"I see." Gabriel wasn't sure what else to say. Lucian's assessment was valid—an insubordinate soldier was an unfit soldier. "Which room is Clara in?"

He wanted to get this next part over with as soon as

possible. To counteract his defensive rune, he needed to imbibe the Ichorian's blood. It was a magical marker he'd altered on his lower back for a slightly different purpose, but it would benefit him now.

If he imbibed from the Ichorian, she would be able to use her gift on him. And in return, he also temporarily inherited her ability. That had been the primary purpose of his rune—to be able to steal powers as required when in the field. It just came with the negative consequence of lowering his defenses momentarily as well.

Power lurked in the blood. Everything was give-and-take. And fortunately for the Hydraians and Ichorians, this rune wasn't one many could replicate. It was Gabriel's bloodline on his father's side, in addition to the marking, that facilitated the exchange.

Sethios possessed a similar ability as the son of an original Seraphim. Unfortunately, that gift diluted with each generation, which meant Stas likely didn't possess that ability. Gabriel would have to teach her more about the enchanted drawings later to test the theory.

"This way," Balthazar said, taking over. Lucian didn't follow, his darkening gaze on Eliza. She didn't back down, confirming the warrior spirit inside her. The female would likely prove useful once she understood the purpose of hierarchy.

Gabriel turned away from her to follow Balthazar. Sethios joined him, his gait casual as they approached the final door at the end of the hallway.

Balthazar sighed, shaking his head. "She's still repeating the same words in her mind. No apologies. Just excuses. She won't let me hear anything beyond them."

"Let's see if that thought process changes upon seeing me," Sethios suggested, stepping forward.

Balthazar intercepted him, standing in front of the

door. "Don't hurt her. That's not how we do things around here."

"A topic we are still evaluating," Lucian called over to them. "Some infractions require pain as punishment."

The mind reader's jaw clenched. "Not today."

Sethios shrugged. "Fine. I can intimidate her without true physical harm. Just open the door."

"Or perhaps I should enter first. I have no quarrels with the Ichorian. I just need to borrow her ability."

Balthazar's irises flashed with instant suspicion. "Borrow?"

"Yes." Gabriel didn't see the need to elaborate. He'd purposely used that term.

Balthazar narrowed his brown eyes. "Explain how you intend to 'borrow' it."

"It would be more prudent to show you instead." He didn't necessarily care if they learned about Gabriel's rune. It wasn't like they could remove or replicate the charm.

Gabriel took a step forward, only to have Balthazar block him like he'd done Sethios seconds before. "Will it hurt her?"

"Minor scrapes cause pain in some beings, so potentially, yes." He planned to use a blade against her palm or wrist, whichever proved easier.

Rather than wait for a reply, Gabriel misted through Balthazar and the door to reach the prisoner inside. Lucian had already provided his permission for this experiment. He didn't need the mind reader's acceptance as well, just his willingness to convey the captive's thoughts. Which he would do once he realized the girl was mostly unharmed.

Only, the sight of her had Gabriel pausing upon his entry.

She sat in a corner with her slender arms wrapped around her exposed legs, the long shirt she wore barely covering her thighs. Her crystal blue eyes held a manic gleam to them that enhanced her odd rocking.

Back and forth.

Back and forth.

Sideways.

Repeat.

He frowned at her quick repetition, his surprise at her condition costing him precious seconds and allowing Balthazar the chance to unlock the door and enter.

Gabriel materialized but didn't try to approach the female. Instead, he studied her, noting the bizarre aura around her. Her blonde ringlets were tangled, indicating it'd been a few days since her last brushing. But that wasn't what confused him—it was the bathroom attached to her cell with the shower she'd clearly not used for some time. If ever.

Was she rebelling? That would explain the uneaten food as well. But what practical recourse did that serve? She was hurting herself more than others, as evidenced by the dark bags beneath her eyes.

Ichorians needed blood, and this woman had clearly not imbibed much lately. Balthazar had worried needlessly about Gabriel harming her. She was doing that just fine on her own.

Fortunately, Gabriel didn't need her coherent to borrow her abilities.

He misted to her side, a blade already in his hand, and knelt. "I need a sample of your blood," he informed her softly.

The words just sort of came out of him without permission or purpose. She didn't need to know what he wanted or why he intended to touch her. Prisoners had no rights. She'd also more than earned this fate. Yet some part of him felt the need to explain himself.

Rather than evaluate the oddity, he quickly sliced the knife across her forearm. She didn't move or react, just continued that inane twisting, her eyes focused on some point ahead of her.

His lips nearly curled down at the sight, but he busied himself by tasting the essence coating his blade.

Blood never really appealed to him, despite it being a primary source of power for his kind. However, Clara's essence contained a tangy flavor that briefly caught his attention as he swallowed. Then the tingling began at the base of his spine as his rune engaged, distracting him from the female's taste.

He sheathed his blade, waiting for the power to ignite. The last time he did this—about two decades ago—it'd taken only a few seconds for him to feel the effects of the new talent.

This one appeared to be coming to him gradually, likely because he'd imbibed less blood than the other experience. He could take more if—

His knees nearly buckled as the full force of her ability stole his breath.

Fuck!

The pain.

It hurt his heart, squeezing the organ so tightly he couldn't breathe. It overwhelmed him, bringing tears to his eyes. He'd never felt anything like it, as though someone had taken a dagger to his chest and shoved deep.

Wind blew through his ears, roaring with rage, inundating his senses and handicapping him entirely. Where was it coming from? How was this possible?

More tears streamed down his face, his cheeks aching from the assault. Fuck, he was wheezing, and at some point, he'd ended up on the floor beside the female. She stared down at him with sharp blue eyes filled with the agony he felt inside.

How was she doing this to him? Crippling him beneath this wave of unknown *pain*?

Deep voices boomed overhead, their presence flaying the skin right off of Gabriel's prone form. He'd never experienced such brutality, nor did he comprehend the source.

What was this power? It reminded him of Alik's ability to mentally torture his victims. But Gabriel was immune to those gifts. Unless Clara's blood was somehow connected, but he doubted it.

Her blood, he thought to himself, trying to regain his focus. *This is her blood*.

No, not her blood.

Her *power*.

He was feeling the results of her empathy. *Emotions*.

His eyes widened at the realization that he was experiencing *her* emotions through empathy. And all the emotions surrounding them. At once. Something he'd never been exposed to in his entire existence.

He'd only meant to test his own levels of humanistic sensibilities. He hadn't considered what turning on this ability would mean for him in regard to others.

All their emotions became his own.

And Gabriel had no training in how to handle this forced sensation. He never had a practical reason to learn it.

Yet it was the anguish emanating from Clara that startled him more, and the fact that he wanted to help her. Because no one should ever endure that kind of agony.

Except, no, she'd earned that pain.

But did she? he wondered, conflicted by what he sensed in her emotional aura.

He shook his head, attempting to clear it. The words of the others started to infiltrate his mind, Balthazar commenting that it seemed Gabriel had more than just borrowed Clara's ability—he'd consumed it.

Which was an obvious statement.

What they should be paying attention to was Clara's pain. Did they not sense it? Couldn't Balthazar hear it? Could no one else *feel* it? The emotions burned against Gabriel's conscience, forcing him to act. He needed it to stop so he could concentrate! To find himself again and wait out these negative consequences of her ability.

One thing was astutely obvious to him—he was not at emotional risk levels.

However, he might be after this. Because *fuck*.

"Help her," he managed through a dry throat. "Fuck. Make it stop!"

Silence met his words.

An unacceptable reaction.

"She's in agony." Gabriel's jaw clenched around the words, his hands curling into fists. "Fix. It." As soon as he finished speaking, he realized the solution, his Seraphim mind taking over and misting him as far away from Hydria as possible.

Only, it took him to the one place he shouldn't have gone—home.

Where two messenger Seraphim were waiting for him in his living room.

Apparently, there was a deadline after all.

Of right fucking now.

CHAPTER NINE

SETHIOS

"WHAT THE HELL JUST HAPPENED?" Lucian demanded, entering the room about five minutes too late. He'd been so focused on that Eliza chick that he hadn't witnessed Gabriel's intense reaction to Clara's power.

It seemed experiencing emotions after a lifetime of disregarding them had been a bit too much for the Seraphim to bear. Or, more specifically, it'd been the "agony" he'd felt from the blonde Ichorian in the corner.

Sethios studied her while Balthazar brought Lucian up to speed with a quick summary of the events. "Gabriel imbibed some of Clara's blood, thereby inheriting her empathetic abilities. He didn't seem to enjoy it."

"He said he needed an empath to test his emotional levels. I assumed that meant he wanted someone who could read him, not someone he could literally drink power from." Lucian turned thoughtful. "I wonder if all Seraphim can do that."

"Caro couldn't," Sethios murmured as he went to his haunches before Clara, a strand of familiar energy catching his eye.

"Stas can't manipulate vision, yet she has obviously bitten Wakefield," Balthazar added, his words painting an unwelcome picture in Sethios's mind. He chose to ignore it and follow the enchanted lines weaving an invisible trail across Clara's svelte form. It wasn't an essence many would recognize or even be able to identify, but he had a lot of experience playing with spells such as these.

They were his father's favorite creations, after all.

This one was crudely done, as though he'd thrown this compulsion on her in a hurry or perhaps without much care. Maybe he'd anticipated someone seeing it and undoing the persuasion. "Has Astasiya seen Clara since you imprisoned her?" Sethios wondered out loud, his focus on those loose strands around her.

"No, why?" Lucian asked.

"Because I think my father left her a present to unravel." It would be just like him to compel someone as a training gift. Sethios paused for a moment, considering the opportunity to teach her, but decided against it. He wanted to know what his father had persuaded this girl to do before he endangered his daughter with the task.

Just a few more strands, he thought, untying the proverbial bow with his mind. *And... done.*

The girl shrieked in response, the scream harsh enough to make his ears bleed. He nearly commanded she shut up, but words were streaming from her mouth in a rapid fire of insults and accusations that all seemed to blend together. None of it was meant for him but was directed at the two Elders behind him.

"How could you?" she demanded, her voice breaking as she lost herself to a sob that had Balthazar immediately kneeling before her. "I would never do that! You know I would never do that! God, and the excuse. Issac. Are you kidding me? Aidan was my father. My family. I would never... I would never!"

Sethios moved out of the way as the mind reader

reached for the girl. He didn't want to be in the middle of whatever the fuck this was.

Which turned out to be the right move because Clara punched Balthazar half a beat later. Then she cried out in horror, another scream parting her lips.

The Elder massaged his jaw, his brown eyes narrowing up at Sethios. "What did you do to her?"

"I removed Osiris's compulsion," he replied. "I don't know what he persuaded her to do, but it's gone now."

"You can do that?" Lucian sounded intrigued.

"Not typically, no. This seems to have been done on purpose. I think he meant for Astasiya to remove it." Given the female's reaction, he was glad he'd handled this instead of his daughter.

Someone cleared a throat from the doorway, causing Sethios and Lucian to turn.

Alik stood with his arms folded across his chest, his hip propped against the door frame. "I assume this means Clara wasn't actually our mole but was framed as one." He didn't phrase it as a question so much as a statement. "Which means we have an even bigger problem."

"Unless Clara can tell us who did this," Lucian pointed out.

"She doesn't know," Balthazar murmured, his palm against the girl's cheek. She'd quieted a little, perhaps because he'd engaged his ability to manipulate emotion. Sethios had never actually witnessed that talent before, but he could see its usefulness in this situation.

"What does she know?" Lucian countered.

"That everyone she loved betrayed her," Balthazar growled. "That we chose to believe a cruel trick over decades of friendship."

"She admitted guilt," Alik drawled. "And she provided reasons."

"Reasons I said were asinine," Balthazar countered. "She's never been romantically inclined toward Wakefield. We all know that. We were just quick to assign guilt because we wanted a solution to the problem."

"Jonathan received a call with the location we gave her," Lucian said softly. "Mateo tracked the phone records."

"It wasn't me!" Clara shouted. "Why would I give that monster anything?"

Sethios considered asking what all this meant, but he had enough on his mind in regard to Caro and wherever the hell Gabriel had fucked off to.

"My services are no longer needed here," he said, heading for the door. "Call me if you have a prisoner I can actually play with."

He didn't wait to hear a reply, his steps already carrying him out of the room—after Alik had moved out of his way—and down the hall.

The female Guardian stood waiting at the end, her friend long gone after whatever Lucian had said to her. Sethios gave the woman a nod, then left the hut and went to find Astasiya. They needed to have a chat about her dreams. Gabriel would come back eventually. If he didn't, Sethios would send Leela to find him.

I'm done wasting time, angel, he thought at Caro. *If you don't want to reply to me, that's fine. But I'm going to find you. Even if it means crashing the council chambers and dragging you home.*

The more he considered that plan, the more he liked it.

What would they do? Rehabilitate him, too?

He nearly laughed.

If they couldn't fix his father, they certainly couldn't fix him. And neither of them could be killed. So why not?

If only I had my wings, he mused. *Then I could mist right in there and grab you.*

I miss you, she whispered back at him, causing him to freeze on the beach.

Caro? Was that really her, or a memory loop sent to taunt him?

Shh, she hushed him. *They'll hear you.*

Who will?

I'm not supposed to be here. I have to go.

Go where? he demanded.

Nothing.

He growled low under his breath, fed up with this game of hints and no solutions. *I'm done with this,* he said. *It's time to do things my way.*

With brute force.

Anger.

And a hell of a lot of blood.

He just needed a location for the rehabilitation facility, and he knew just whom to get it from—the only Seraphim currently on this fucking island. *Leela.*

CHAPTER TEN

GABRIEL

THERE WAS a reason Gabriel preferred to live just outside the main Seraphim boundaries—privacy. That didn't exist within the water veil encircling the primary cluster of South Pacific islands.

The barriers were built to keep mortals out. Ships and planes were diverted away from this area by technological and magical suggestions that essentially kept this place a secret on the globe. No mortal had ever discovered it.

Well, no mortal alive, anyway.

Gabriel had once heard a myth about the Bermuda Triangle from a mortal at a bar. He supposed the Seraphim region was a similar concept, only real and entirely undocumented. His kind ensured it stayed that way.

Once through the misty walls, a city of advanced tech and prosperity was revealed over hundreds of islands. They all varied in size. Except for the principal one at the center.

The central city was built into a dormant volcano that the Seraphim kept well under control. It housed all the primary business functions of their world, including the council chambers.

Gabriel drifted along on a breeze, choosing to fly instead of misting directly to their door. He needed time to rid himself of Clara's power. Fortunately, he wouldn't experience much of a reaction here, surrounded by unfeeling Seraphim. The problem was more that it made him feel. Sort of. Or he thought that might be the cause of this strange fuzzy sensation in his chest.

Was he feeling nostalgic? No. That couldn't be right.

Worried? Maybe.

His brow furrowed. *What is that nagging feeling? And why do humans put up with this bullshit?* It dragged him down, making him long to avoid his destination.

Maybe this was what dread felt like—that negative pull that had him wanting to return to Hydria, not head farther into Seraphim territory. He'd never experienced it quite like this before.

Typically, he just did his duty and left. It was quicker and more efficient than this floating along in the clouds.

Yet something about the wind in his feathers felt rather pleasant.

Why do I avoid this? he wondered, rolling onto his back to drift along. *It's... soothing.* His lips curled down. *Did I just call something "soothing"?*

"Fuck," he muttered, rubbing a hand over his face and gazing blankly up at the dazzling sun. It was closer to noon here. Maybe. His concept of time today blurred from all the traveling and his lack of sleep. He didn't actually require rest, but it helped with establishing a routine. However, his routine of late was nonexistent.

With a sigh—a noise he had probably never made in his life in this manner—he dove through the clouds and headed toward his destination.

This empathy gift wasn't leaving him anytime soon. So he'd use it to his advantage instead and see if any of the council members were showing signs of emotion that he could use against them. Because this conversation was going to be a painful one, indeed.

Gabriel marveled at the golds and silvers of the main island on his approach. He'd never noticed just how sparkly it all was, the sunlight illuminating it and giving the metal structures a majestic appearance. Tall palm trees and other vegetation decorated the scene, adding to the enchanted atmosphere.

There were trees on top of buildings and inside them because the Seraphim had built around the natural landscape. Branches poked out through the myriad of glassless windows, the city climate one that kept everyone comfortable despite the humidity. It was another magical antidote that Gabriel had never really considered yet viewed in an entirely new manner now.

This truly was paradise.

Although, no one really acknowledged it.

The living conditions kept everyone comfortable, and comfort increased productivity.

Which was the purpose of living within the barrier—to keep the Seraphim world thriving.

The community was completely self-sufficient, using solar energy, water power, and a variety of other advancements to keep the world around them flourishing. Human nature had grown over the millennia, but they had yet to reach even a tenth of the potential here.

Of course, it helped that Seraphim were ethereal beings with inherent powers. The humans were actually partly created from Seraphim genetics. Or at least influenced by them. That was why Osiris's abominations were resurrected with enhanced talents—it all came from the bloodlines.

Gabriel's pocket buzzed as he landed just outside the

massive coliseum dedicated to the council. *Turn left, then right*, the message read.

Of course Vera would choose now to finally reply to him. She likely knew about his summons and had anticipated him arriving just outside the coliseum's entrance.

He narrowed his gaze in irritation, then remembered his surroundings and blanked his expression. This empathy shit was going to be a problem. The last and only time he'd inherited a power in this manner, it'd taken several hours to wear off.

Damn it.

Stowing his phone, he followed the directions Vera had just sent him and found her waiting outside a cafe with her vibrant navy wings fluttering around her. Her eyes were bluish green in this form, but they shifted to a glimmering silver as she turned corporeal.

It was an uncommon trait among the Seraphim. Gabriel's irises remained light green no matter his form. Leela's remained turquoise during her transition. Stas's stayed green. *I wonder what pigment—*

He blinked, forcing the thoughts of colors from his mind. It was entirely irrelevant and unimportant to the situation at hand. Fuck, next he'd probably start analyzing all the possible plume hues.

Gabriel nearly rolled his eyes, then realized that wasn't helpful either.

Enough.

"Are you here to confess?" he asked, his voice flat and void of emotion just like it should be.

She snorted. "Not exactly." She pressed a petite palm to his cheek, and energy flared between them.

He tried to step back to avoid the impact, but it was too late. A series of memories unfurled inside his head, each one a new explanation that left him gasping out loud.

"Remove them. It's the only way," Gabriel said, his voice void of emotion. Yet he felt the ache in his heart, the pain of having to make this choice.

She's better off, *he promised himself.* At least she isn't drowning.

However, as the memory began to change, Gabriel wondered if they'd made a mistake. What if he found out via other means? Would he break all his oaths to rescue her?

"The loop will help," Vera promised. "I'll do what I can to regulate it for you all."

"I know you will," Gabriel replied. "Do what you need to do. Make me forget."

The council had found Caro hours after Osiris had left her at the bottom of the Atlantic Ocean. They'd saved her only to put her in a different sort of cage, one where they would do their best to reform her.

But her ties to Sethios could never truly be broken.

Even a hundred years in that reformation chamber wouldn't be enough to destroy their bond.

He'd bring her back.

He'd have to. There was no other alternative.

As the memory of his mother's captivity slid from his mind, another came to him, the one of Vera delivering the news of the council retrieving Caro from her water prison.

A debate had followed. To save her now could dismantle everything they were working toward, not just in regard to Osiris but also in safeguarding Astasiya. She was too young and therefore susceptible to their influence. If the Seraphim found her now, everything Sethios and Caro had given up would have been for nothing.

No, they had to let this play out. Reformation wouldn't hurt. It would just put Caro in a state of limbo, her mind constantly monitored for any and all signs of emotion.

Another Seraphim would be there to bring her back, to reprogram her under the mentality of her true purpose—to live a life of practicality.

She'd grown up in that environment. Then Sethios had changed everything. He would just have to do that again.

"It was the best way," Vera whispered now, drawing Gabriel back to her.

Next, she showed him the memory of altering Leela's mind as well, removing the knowledge of what the council had done, while adding in little changes that protected her from discovery.

No one knew they were searching for Caro.

Vera had orchestrated everything, morphing the loop within his mother's mind to ensure the regular blasts went unnoticed.

"But she keeps undoing them," Vera muttered, stirring Gabriel from his thoughts. "Your mother is a lot more powerful than she realizes. She continues to access that back door because she sees it as a connection to her bonds. I have to shove her out every time so the others don't notice what I've done."

"Why are you showing me this now?" Gabriel asked, his voice a rasp of sound from the electricity humming through his head, reweaving paths that had been magically altered by the Seraphim beside him.

"Because you already know they have Caro. Adriel informed you of the council's decision to rehabilitate her, and you agreed to it."

Another memory slammed into him, one showcasing his father's golden hair and fiery red wings—both traits Gabriel had inherited from him.

He'd arrived at Gabriel's house in the South Pacific only hours after Gabriel had left Astasiya with the Davenports.

And it was just minutes after Vera had flashed in to warn him about Caro's fate.

Adriel had flatly told him about Caro's choice, including her bonding to Sethios, creating a life, and then hiding that life. Then he'd ended with a short "She will be rehabilitated and cured of her fractured mindset."

Gabriel had dully stated that it was the right course of action.

And that was it.

He'd sealed his own mother's fate.

Then Vera had returned to remove the memories—with Gabriel's permission.

"Use that," she said urgently, glancing down at her wrist where a bracelet blinked with purple lights.

Ah, a frequency jammer, he thought. *So she wanted this conversation to be private.*

"We only have thirty seconds before the surveillance equipment around us resets. The audio and visual will begin to record again. You have enough to work with. Don't let me down."

Gabriel stared at her. "What other memories have you altered of mine?" Because he sensed there were more. Many, many more.

She flashed him a secret little smile. "Who says these are even real and I haven't just made it all up?"

Always mischievous. Not at all like a typical Seraphim. That was why she and Leela were such close friends—neither of them favored the stoic nature of their kind.

"You pledged fealty to Astasiya." That wasn't something he could sense, yet he felt the truth of it inside. Likely because he now possessed the memory of watching it happen. However, it was when Astasiya was a baby, not seven. Which meant he had other holes in his mind from that period of her life.

Unless all of this was a lie.

He frowned.

His sister would be able to feel the existence of a fealty pledge from Vera. Just as she would be able to feel his loyalty to her if she searched deep enough.

Gabriel considered Vera, weighing the chances of it being a mental trick or a reality. He could ask her how the council hadn't discovered her change of allegiance, but the same question could be tossed right back at him. They had no idea he'd pledged fealty to his sister because they hadn't yet met her. The moment they did, they would sense the ties between them and would realize he'd given her his loyalty, not the council.

However, without a previous cause to investigate his behavior, no one had noticed his shift yet. That could very well be the purpose of today's discussion.

Given his bizarre behavior of late, they'd probably looked into his essence more and found the shift inside him. In which case, they would outlaw him from Seraphim society—a punishment he would happily accept.

Except Vera had spent ample time around the council over the last twenty-five years. It was surprising to him that no one had noticed her lack of a loyalty pledge to the higher Seraphim.

Unless she'd used her gifts to alter their memories of discovery.

The only one who could confirm the pledge was Astasiya, and he didn't have a way of asking her about it right now. Besides, she'd require coaching to even be able to sense the bond. And there just wasn't any time left with the council requesting his presence now.

"If it's all just a mental trick, then my fate is decided either way," he added. "I'll just have to choose to trust you."

"A wise choice," she replied, her irises shifting to blue-and-green orbs as her feathers sprouted around her. "Good luck, Gabe," she whispered, her bracelet releasing a small beep before she misted out of sight.

He swallowed, then glanced at the massive structure behind him.

He'd meant what he said. His fate was already decided. If her manipulation proved to be a lie, he'd end up in a rehabilitation chamber beside his mother.

However, if the memories were genuine, he now had a very real card to play.

Chapter Eleven

SETHIOS

"You can't just waltz in there, Sethios. The wards will incapacitate you, and you'll end up defenseless on a shoreline." Leela stood with her hands on her shapely hips, her blonde hair pulled back into a ponytail.

Sethios had found her in Balthazar's house doing fuck knew what since she was alone here. He hadn't bothered to ask, his first and only question being about Caro's location.

Astasiya and Issac had followed him. Now they sat on the couch in the living area, watching Sethios battle with Leela's logic.

Battle and lose, he thought, irritated. "I can't just sit here, Leela. We know where she is. Just mist me into her cell, and I'll take it from there."

"Yes, that requires me to know her cell." She rolled her eyes at the notion. "Oh, and as I've said three times now, get you past the barriers. Which is *impossible*. You're not an inducted member of society. The wards will fire defensively. They may not kill you, but they will break you."

"Gabriel is taking care of it," a voice chimed in as dark blue feathers appeared in his peripheral vision. "He's meeting with the council right now," Vera added, her body turning corporeal in an instant. "Also..." She touched Leela's head, causing the female to jolt.

"What are you doing?" Balthazar demanded, his gaze locking on Leela as he stepped into the house with Lucian right behind him. He started toward Vera, but she held up a hand—the one not touching Leela—to halt him. Her authoritative aura had both Elders pausing beside the couch.

"Why didn't you tell us the council has Caro?" Sethios asked her, spoiling for a fight. "And what the fuck are you doing here now?"

"We told her to erase our memories of it," Leela breathed, her blue-green eyes rimmed with tears. "Oh, Vera."

"Yeah, yeah. Almost done."

"She can manipulate memories?" Balthazar asked, his eyes narrowing.

Vera grinned at him. "You're not the only one who dabbles in mind play, sweetheart."

His brown irises swirled with suspicion as he looked at Leela. "We have met before."

Sethios glanced between them, his brow furrowing. Then he shook his head. "Tell me about Caro, Vera. Now." He underlined each word with persuasion, causing the memory-manipulating Seraphim to sputter in annoyance.

"She was born in—"

"Tell me where she is right now," he rephrased, not wanting a historical summary of Caro's being, but her current location.

"In a Seraphim rehabilitation chamber that you can't reach, so don't even think about trying."

"I could compel you to take me to her," he growled, his patience long gone.

She shrugged. "Fine. But it'll kill us both."

"We'll regenerate."

"Yes. In our own rehabilitation chambers," she drawled, rolling her eyes in a similar fashion to Leela moments ago. "Use reason, Sethios. Let me explain. If you still feel like persuading me to take you to Caro after that, then we'll go to war and see which of us is stronger in battle. But keep in mind, you are significantly younger than I am. And I was able to incapacitate your father long enough for your daughter to save you."

"I want to hear what she has to say," Astasiya said softly before Sethios could react.

His jaw tensed, annoyance thick in his veins.

They'd wasted so much time while his angel suffered. Now that they knew her location, he wanted to save her. It physically hurt not to go to her. But one look at his daughter had him nodding. Because a tender part of him —one that existed only for her and Caro—understood the practicality surrounding her request.

"Speak quickly," Sethios gritted out through his clenched teeth.

"Caro's mission twenty-five years ago was to find and deliver an edict to Osiris. She failed and never reported back. The council never attempted to locate her because of her concealment line—they knew it was futile to even try—but they did meet to discuss whether or not to wake up her mother. However, the Fates' prophecy regarding Astasiya changed that debate."

"So all this happened twenty-five years ago?" Sethios asked.

"It happened soon after Astasiya's birth, when you and Caro bonded," Leela whispered, her eyes wide with what was likely a new remembrance, thanks to Vera's tampering. "The council realized Caro wasn't going to bring the child back with her—which we all know was the real reason for her mission—and they met to discuss their options in locating her. Only, the prophecy changed."

"Yes," Vera confirmed. "I witnessed everything and reported back to you all."

"Then you told Vera to remove the memories," Leela added.

"I *what*?" Yeah, that sounded like utter bullshit to him. "Why the fuck would I do that?"

"To protect Astasiya," Vera replied. "The council didn't wake up Chanara to find Caro. They woke her up to locate your daughter."

His lips worked without words. He had no recollection of any of this. Because, apparently, he'd asked for it to be wiped from his mind.

"You didn't want to risk the council finding out what you both knew about Chanara," Leela further explained. "We knew Chanara would go after Caro when she failed to find Astasiya. That's why you played Osiris the way you did. Almost seven years after the council ordered Chanara to be woken up."

"The requisite time that it takes to wake up an ancient sleeping Seraphim," Vera concluded. "You always knew Osiris would find you. It was a matter of when, not if. And we all used that to our advantage."

"Your sacrifice was even more powerful than you realize," Leela whispered, awed. "The council has been trying to locate Astasiya through Caro because Chanara has continued to fail. I mean, she was able to find Caro, but never your daughter."

"The rune," Lucian interjected. "It doesn't just block Ichorian gifts."

"Correct." Vera grinned at him. "Originally, it was intended to only block Ichorians because of a prophecy from

Skye. But when we learned of Chanara's awakening, Caro made a few updates to hide Stas from her own bloodline."

"So you removed the memories of the decision to wake up Chanara, and the subsequent plans that followed, so the council wouldn't know about the protective rune," Lucian translated for the rest of the room. "That's a brilliant strategy. But how did you orchestrate Osiris finding them?"

"Via Gabriel and Ezekiel. As I said, we all knew it was inevitable. And he provided the perfect cover as well to essentially distract the council. Astasiya disappeared while Osiris had Caro, which left Caro unable to say what happened to her daughter that day."

"Because you altered her memory of Gabriel's arrival," Sethios said, making it a statement more than a guess. It was the natural solution. Otherwise, the Seraphim would have just discovered the affiliation during the interrogation process. If the Ichorians and Hydraians had mind readers, so did the angelic beings who had birthed all of humanity.

"I altered all her memories of Gabriel," she confirmed. "The council has—or rather, *had*—no idea he was involved in any of this. Until now."

"But how could they not even suspect him?" Astasiya asked, her tone riddled with confusion. "He's my brother. Who else would have taken me that day?"

"Because he's never given them reason to question his loyalty," Vera replied. "When the council informed him of their intentions to rehabilitate his mother, he gave them his consent, stating it was a necessary maneuver after everything she'd done. The member from the council—his father—didn't suspect any other reason to question Gabriel and left him alone to continue his mission of monitoring the CRF's developments."

"He purposely took that assignment so he would have

an excuse to be around humans," Leela said. "No one has paid any attention to him. He played it all perfectly."

"Until his cover was blown this week by having all the abominations at his house. Owen was hard enough to hide. Everyone else, well, he pretty much gave up." Vera shrugged. "He knew the council would call him in, which they've now done. And I tried to return as many memories as I could, but I held back the information on Chanara. I needed him to be genuinely surprised to see her. No one ever told him about her awakening, so I had to keep it that way."

"So you've been playing with all our memories," Sethios drawled, both amused and irritated. Mostly irritated. Sure, he'd agreed to it, or had maybe even suggested it. But that didn't mean he had to fucking like the consequences of it. "What else have you altered, Vera?"

He knew better than to take the Seraphim at her word. She was always hiding some caveat or another.

"I created the memory loop that Stas and Gabe have been seeing in their dreams. I also sent you the vision earlier today to get you all moving."

"So it was a memory loop. She's not still drowning." Astasiya sounded relieved, but her expression turned incredulous. "And you did this to keep us all from finding Caro." Not a question, but a statement.

Still, the Seraphim confirmed with a "Yes. It was the only way to ensure Gabe didn't try to save her from the council—which was his idea, by the way. He needed to remain off their radar to keep your location hidden."

"Because they've never suspected him of helping," Astasiya clarified.

"Correct," Vera agreed. "There's never been any

reason to suspect he had anything to do with your disappearance."

"Family loyalty isn't a concept among Seraphim," Leela elaborated. "We are created as a result of the Fates assigning us a fornication partner and date. It's not necessarily romantic, nor does it foster adequate relationship building."

"A solid control mechanism," Lucian inserted thoughtfully. He hadn't moved from his position by the couch, but the other Elder had disappeared into the kitchen. He was likely still listening to every word while busying himself with something else.

Probably food.

If Sethios had learned anything over the last week in Gabriel's house, it was that the Hydraians were always fucking eating.

"As you said," Lucian continued. "It makes forming bonds or relationships difficult when everything is dictated by a governmental structure. It ensures your loyalty remains to the hierarchy, not to anyone else. Therefore, they would have no reason to expect Gabriel to help his mother."

"And not reacting at all to Adriel's news of her rehabilitation—other than to agree to it—only further confirmed his lack of involvement," Leela agreed.

"Why are you telling us this now?" Astasiya asked, the skepticism in her tone one Sethios knew very well because it was the same tone Caro had often used on him. "Why not a week ago?"

"It wasn't the right time yet," Vera replied.

"The right time was when we started looking for Caro last week," Astasiya argued. "Instead, you pushed us along with visions that led my brother and father directly into Osiris's trap."

Her concern warmed Sethios in a manner he'd not felt in his very long life. Having a daughter had awakened certain parts of him he never knew existed. And it seemed she wasn't done altering his world outlook.

I wish you were here to see her, Caro. She's truly magnificent. Just like you, he thought, so incredibly proud despite the troubling topic at hand.

"Perhaps, but what would you have done?" Vera countered, arching a brown brow into her dark hairline. "Gone to the council and demanded her release?"

Astasiya didn't reply, just narrowed her green eyes.

She has my eyes but your fiery spirit, angel, he thought, his heart aching at the sight of his daughter's stubborn side showing. *We created a masterpiece.*

Vera snorted at Astasiya's look. "That's not how our society works, youngling. They need a rational reason to comply—which is something Gabriel is about to give them. If he uses the memories I supplied him with, anyway."

"Unless the empathy impacts him," Balthazar said, walking in with some sort of fruity alcoholic beverage in his hand.

"What empathy?" Vera asked.

"The ability he imbibed from Clara," Balthazar explained, his focus on Leela. He handed her the drink, his eyes glimmering with knowledge. "Rum and punch. Seems like something you would like."

The Seraphim had gone pale, her fingers wrapping around the glass as she replied, "I'm more of a wine girl."

"Liar," he accused. "You like fruity concoctions. Mimosas, too, if I remember right."

She blanched, then glared accusingly at Vera.

"What do you mean, he imbibed an ability?" the other woman asked, acting as though her best friend hadn't just flashed her a murderous look.

Right. Sethios was done with this back-and-forth game. He'd lost his patience hours ago, and he no longer had any more fucks to give. It was time for Vera to give him all the specifics and stop wasting his time with frivolous details.

"He sliced Clara open and licked the blade, which gave him the ability to feel emotions. Or that was our observation of the results, anyway," he replied quickly. "Now give me back my memories."

He didn't word it as a request but as a compelling demand.

"The only reason I'm not fighting you on this is because I know it's going to hurt," she growled, pressing her palm to his head. "Enjoy."

CHAPTER TWELVE

CARO

SOMETHING WAS HAPPENING. Caro couldn't define it, but she felt the agony associated with the change coming from someplace deep within.

She followed the thin strand, curious to determine the source of the intrusion. One moment, she'd been entirely fine. Floating. Alone. The next, that sting had punched through her heart and twisted her insides into a knot she couldn't seem to untie.

What is that? she wondered, tracing the glimmering cord. Part of her recognized that it wasn't real. A ghostly ribbon of unknown origins. It truly wasn't practical to follow that cord. However, she supposed ending the pain proved to be a reasonable excuse nonetheless.

Caro swam along, searching, searching, searching.

Such an alarming nuisance. She'd been at peace, surrounded by sunlight and nothing, just waiting to be. Then this thing in her chest had to start aching.

She found the wispy essence, the ends intangible. Because they didn't exist, of course. Not in a physical sense, anyway. Her spirit recognized them, not her body.

An odd sort of experience, one that defied her logic. Which was precisely why she followed the path. It served a suitable purpose to determine the origin and report back on the bizarre sensation.

Report back to who? she asked herself. When was the last time she even spoke to another being outside of the figments in her mind?

She pondered the latest figment, a rich, deep baritone that constantly infiltrated her thoughts. Caro rather liked his voice, something that alarmed her slightly. Because she shouldn't like anything. What purpose did enjoyment serve? None at all, really.

Yet she found herself waiting for him to speak and missed him when he fell quiet. He told her strange things about their daughter.

Daughter. She puzzled over that phrase, curious as to what that meant. She'd procreated, but the memories were fuzzy.

Hmm. She pushed them away, chasing the pain into her core to locate the source.

And fell headfirst into a reality that made little sense to her.

She spun around in a circle, pausing at the heat from the fireplace. No sun. Instead, the moonlight glistened off the snow outside. Her lips parted at the sight. So beautiful, so—

"Caro?" that deep male rumble came from behind her.

"I'm almost done," she heard herself say.

She frowned, not understanding how she'd spoken without actually moving her mouth. Then she turned to see herself on the couch beside a handsome dark-haired male. He held a tiny child in his arms.

However, it wasn't a typical infant hold.

He had her upside down, his big hand gently cradling the baby's face a few inches above his thigh. Her lower half was stretched out across his lap. The child slept soundly, which was rather bizarre because that didn't appear comfortable at all. Unless she was a stomach sleeper.

Caro crept closer to see what the other woman was doing. *Me*, she thought. *What I'm doing.*

How very strange to observe herself in this manner, but she was too fascinated by it to question the abnormality. Instead, she watched as the magic flared from the fingertips caressing the child's lower back.

A rune, she realized, her eyes widening. *I'm creating a rune.*

"You've turned it into a heart," the male mused.

"Yes, I'm disguising it," she replied, a smile in her voice. "It seemed appropriate with her being our little heart."

The man's lips pulled into a breathtaking grin, one that gave Caro momentary pause. *I recognize that look.* It stirred a foreign warmth inside her, one that seemed to spread heat through each of her veins.

This was much better than the pain that lurked inside her.

"It will still protect her against Ichorians, just like Leela's original mark intended. But now it'll conceal her from my familial line, too." *Has my voice always been so soft?* Caro wondered, listening to herself speak. "We'll have Vera shift our memory to only remember that part, not the concealment aspect."

"We'll need to do the same for Gabriel," the male murmured.

"Yes," Caro agreed. "And Leela, too." She sighed, the enchantment flickering as she sealed the rune with a final swipe of the branding pen. It was a tiny needlelike object that oozed skin-altering ink. She set it to the side and met the male's gaze. "It's done."

"How long will it take for her to heal?" The male's

tone held a touch of concern to it, one that sent another wave of heat through Caro's insides.

"A few hours at most."

"Should we bandage it?"

"No. But we should keep the area clear." She glanced at the stairs. "We should put her in the bassinet and let her sleep it off."

"She won't wake until I release the compulsion," he replied, carefully rotating the small child in his arms to cradle her properly. His green eyes smiled down at her, his pride radiating through the bond. "How is something so tiny destined for such greatness?"

Caro followed his gaze, her heart giving a small pang of longing. She didn't quite like the pain that little look caused. Yet she found herself creeping forward, needing to see the child more clearly.

So beautiful, she thought.

"Because we created her," she heard herself say. With a frown, Caro glanced at the woman and found her staring directly at her. "She's ours."

Ours?

The memory faded away, lifting up into the bedroom, to the male stripping off the woman's dress and laying her on the mattress while the baby slept soundly in an adjoining nursery.

What are you doing? she asked herself, confused by the shift. *Where's the ceremonial robe? What child are you creating now?*

Because it was clear that their intention was to mate. Yet it seemed they were doing this for self-fulfillment, not for practical means.

Why would I do such a thing?

A moan spilled from her own lips as the male licked a path downward to the apex between her thighs. Caro's legs clenched as though it were happening to her as well—which, she supposed, it was.

How strange a sensation to watch something happen from outside her own body yet feel it deep inside.

Her stomach tightened as the woman on the bed writhed, the male devouring her in a cyclone of ecstasy and strength.

Oh, she thought, her spirit burning with the remembrance of just how that felt. *Oh, I like that.*

It caused her knees to quiver, her body flaring with a yearning she hadn't experienced in such a long time. *Yes. More.* She closed her eyes, pretending to be the female on the bed. With the moans and pants so familiar to her ears, she could almost be her, could almost feel his teeth against her sensitive folds and his tongue on her clit.

Her back bowed, the rapture spilling out of her on a tidal wave of sensation.

She screamed his name... *Sethios...* and climaxed so hard she swore she died.

But as she opened her eyes, she found herself beneath him, his dark eyes swirling with adoration and sensuality as he slid inside her, taking her to new heights and forcing her to forget the impractical nature of it all.

For just a few moments, she forgot her own existence. Stopped thinking about how this couldn't be real. And just experienced his tenderness and love and *pain.*

His teeth were in her neck, drinking from her, showering her in goose bumps and spearing through all her defenses. She cried out, tumbling headfirst into another oblivion as he drove into her, taking her with a force that hurt in a beautiful way, one that touched her very soul.

This was her life.

Her purpose.

Her meaning.

She loved this man. This Sethios. This male who had shattered all her beliefs and had broken through the harshest of her resolves.

Caro clung to him, weeping, her time with him too short. The sacrifice they would make would change the future of the world. But what if they couldn't come back from it?

She would never voice that fear, the knowledge of what was to come.

Because her mother would find her when she failed to locate Astasiya.

Caro would endure rehabilitation.

And she would survive.

That was her purpose, her one secret, that she never gave up. With Sethios forever etched into her very soul, the council couldn't separate them. They would try, and they would fail. She would return to him. Always.

"I love you," he whispered to her, his lips a caress against her ear. "I will forever love you."

"I love you, too," she breathed. And this time it was her. Her voice. Her heart. Her body. Her soul. She'd fallen into the memory, enraptured and ensnared and never letting go.

His eyes burned into hers. "Come back to me, Caro."

"I'm right here."

"Come back to me, angel."

She frowned. "I'm here."

"I miss you."

It didn't make any sense. How could he miss her? He was inside her. Making love to her. Only, everything began to blur, the memory slipping from her fingers and surrounding her in a cage of literal glass.

She frowned. *Where am I?*

Wires hooked into her arms, legs, around her chest. A

soft beeping sound echoed outside her chamber. The room was dark. Cold. Smelled of antiseptics and sterility.

Caro shivered. This wasn't where she wanted to be. She desired the warmth of Sethios's body. His touch. His tongue. His voice.

She closed her eyes, striving to return to him, but the ice of her surroundings infiltrated her mind, suffocating her beneath a wave of harsh reality.

Reformation.

That was what this glass pod meant.

There was no sun here. No peace. It'd all been a figment in her mind, a ruse meant to lull her into a false sense of calmness while they reprogrammed her from the inside.

But a memory had awakened her, one so powerful it had shattered the chains locked around her mind and shoved her into full awareness.

How long had she slept in this thing?

She took a physical assessment of her atrophied muscles and prone form. It was all she needed to do to know she'd been here for a while.

Caro strived to remember her last true memory, but the past however many years or decades clouded her judgment. So she clung to the one fresh in her mind—the one where she knew this would be her fate and had done everything in her power to ensure it.

For Astasiya.

Where was she now? Was she safe? Had their plan worked?

Fuck! Sethios raged into her mind, jolting her inside her glass pod. *I hate this, angel. I fucking hate this.*

Hate what? she asked him, startled by his outburst.

You ignoring me.

She frowned. *I'm not ignoring you.* Which was fairly obvious by her replying to him now.

Then whatever the fuck this is. You talk to me for half a second and disappear. When I find you, I'm going to ensure you never stop speaking.

There's some irony, she thought at him, snorting. *If I remember correctly, you commanded me not to speak when we first met.*

He fell silent at that, causing her lips to curl down even more.

Sethios?

Caro?

Where did you go?

I could ask you the same fucking question. Are you really there, or is Vera messing with my mind again?

Why would Vera...? Caro trailed off, her eyes widening as a thought nagged at her. Something about the memory manipulator being inside her mind. But she couldn't quite identify the source of that recollection. *Wait, where are you?*

Hydria, he muttered, his tone indicating how he felt about that.

With the Hydraians?

Yes.

That seemed counterproductive to their goals. *Why are you in Hydria?*

Because our daughter is here.

Why? she asked again. Why would Astasiya go to Hydria? Unless... *Is it finally time?*

Are you really here?

No, I'm in a pod, she replied, confused by his question. *Answer my question. Is it time? Wait, are you free from Osiris?*

Her heart began to pound at the memory of what his father had done, how he'd erased her essence from Sethios's mind right before her eyes.

You remember me? she asked, tears blurring her already darkened vision. *You're okay? Safe? Astasiya is safe, too?*

Oh, angel, he breathed, his voice a caress that had her heart picking up speed and causing the beeping around her to increase in volume.

Because she was fully awake and shouldn't be.

A Seraphim would be by soon to check on her.

Oh, no... they'll put me back in stasis! She didn't have time for an emotional reunion. She needed to think. But wait... *Tell me if it's time.* Because if it was, then she'd prepare herself for a fight. If not, she'd—Caro swallowed—she'd allow them to return her to rehabilitation.

It's past time, angel. I've been looking for you all week.

She frowned. *That's not a very long time, Sethios.*

You have no idea.

Rather than correct him, she focused on what his words meant. *I can free myself.* She didn't need to go back.

You can?

She didn't understand his question until she realized what she'd said. *I mean, I'm allowed to free myself.*

So she needed to work on her strength, which was a problem in this pod. Her limbs were thin and unused, her body incapable of misting with all the enchantments surrounding her in this equivocal tomb.

Her lips pursed as she considered what to do. Then an odd sort of tingling began in her lower leg, a warmth she hadn't experienced before. She investigated it with her mind, trying to determine the source and its purpose.

Half a beat later, she gasped. *I'm healing myself.*

What do you mean? Sethios asked. *What needs to be healed?*

My body. My muscles are all nonexistent from having lain here for... how long was I here?

It's been almost eighteen years since Osiris found us, he whispered.

117

Oh. That explained her physical condition. Although, she couldn't remember how or when the Seraphim had found her.

She wasn't going to waste precious seconds now trying to recall it. Caro needed to heal and prepare for what came next because the moment they realized she was awake, they would return to subdue her once more, and she needed to be ready.

How are you healing yourself, angel?

My dormant power, she breathed. *It seems to have finally come to life.*

The one the Fates said you would eventually need?

Yes. She'd once told him the story about her lineage, how the Fates always chose a pairing based on the potential powers of the progeny. They'd predicted she would one day need to know how to heal. Whether it'd been for this purpose or another remained to be seen.

Why would they help you when they're the reason you're in rehabilitation?

The council is the reason for my current situation, not the Fates, she replied, her focus divided between speaking and healing. *The Fates merely predict. The council chooses what to interpret and how to interpret it.*

She wiggled her toes, the action shooting spikes up her legs and causing her to wince. Not a great sensation, but it implied her gift was working as expected.

How clever of the Fates to allow her this small defense. Did that mean they favored the outcome of her escape? Were they playing a game of their own?

Caro's brow furrowed as she considered what it could mean. They were essentially owned by the council, their hive mind one very few Seraphim were allowed to touch. She'd never considered what that meant for their existence until this very moment. Perhaps they despised the method by which they were used. Yet that would imply some manner of feeling, which didn't exist within this world.

Shaking her head, she decided to ponder it another day and put all her mental effort into expediting her healing because the beeps were growing more rapid outside her glass prison.

She couldn't see well, the darkness of the room around her glass tomb void of any external lights. However, her enhanced sight allowed her to see just enough in the dark to understand her surroundings.

It was a smaller room with one door, her pod, a series of machines, and nothing else. Not even a chair.

She'd never been inside the rehabilitation center, but she imagined this was similar to where the ancients slept. Small, neat quarters with equipment meant to pump nutrients into the body to keep it well nourished.

What they didn't do was aid the body in physical recovery. However, that wasn't really necessary with how quickly Seraphim could regenerate.

Angel?

Yes?

Just making sure you're still there, Sethios said, his voice oddly relieved.

Where would I go? she asked him. *I'm stuck in a glass pod. This is the longest we've spoken since Astasiya rescued me.*

Caro paused. *Our daughter rescued you? From Osiris?* That'd been the expectation all along, but to hear that it'd actually happened sent a spark of life through Caro's veins. *They battled? Did he perish?* She frowned then. *Did I miss everything?*

You haven't missed anything, he promised. *But yes, they fought. Vera helped. She saved me, and we've been trying to figure out how to find you since. We thought you were drowning in the ocean.*

What? Why? I haven't been in the water for... well, I'm not sure how long, she admitted. *I'll think about it more after I free myself.*

Her mind seemed unable to multitask, perhaps a result of being in stasis for so long. She didn't feel all that well, her body still mending itself and her mind a swarm of chaotic thoughts and memories that didn't appear to want to stay put in any sort of logical order.

Rather than piece it all together, she concentrated on moving her foot. Sharp pricks shot up her lower limbs, rivaling the ones in her arms as she twitched her fingers and hands. *Almost there*, she thought, her muscles beginning to flex and shift as she rebuilt the ligaments and strengthened her joints.

Seconds turned into minutes, Sethios's presence in her mind and heart an anchor that helped her remain conscious.

Every few beats, he'd say her name, and she'd reply with his own, both of them reminding the other that this was real, that she hadn't fallen back into that dreadful coma.

Her throat worked on a hard swallow, her heartbeat a regular cadence in her ears, and that beeping had reached a crescendo.

No one came, making her wonder how closely the Seraphim monitored her vitals. Perhaps she needed to unplug a few of these cords.

She considered them as her arms moved inside the tiny box. There was a tube connected to one side that pumped oxygen into the container. She didn't want to mess with that. She rather liked breathing. A memory told her why, but she shoved it away, not wanting to think about drowning right now.

Instead, she focused on the electrical wires that seemed to be hooked into her chest and head. Those needed to go regardless, so she might as well undo them.

She tugged the first one out of her temple and cried

out in pain at the metal dislodging from her mind. Sethios's voice reverberated through her thoughts, his words unintelligible over the agony shooting up and down her spine.

"Fuzz!" she shouted, her voice a rasp of sound that didn't match the anguish behind it. *Oh, ow, ow, ow.*

Sethios replied, but she couldn't understand him.

And oh, she had another one in her other temple.

Might as well yank it out now and just recover from both.

She screamed as the needle released her on a violent tug, electricity humming through her skull. Tears streamed from her eyes. Her mouth worked soundlessly over words.

Agony shredded her in half, but then her new gift kicked in, and a warm sensation stole through her mind, soothing the pain with a kiss of healing heat.

She wept with gratitude, her body shaking from the onslaught of the unexpected torment. Caro should have anticipated it, but in her haste to escape, she hadn't considered the repercussions.

No, not exactly that.

She had just chosen not to acknowledge them because there was no practical reason to dread them. The needles had to be removed to free herself, consequences be damned.

After a few soft words to Sethios, promising him she was fine, she started on the other needles lodged in her chest. They all came with their own variety of excruciating results, but nothing compared to the metal probes in her mind. Those were taking the longest to heal, the Seraphim having used advanced technology to quite literally control her brain.

That explained so much about her lost time.

Fortunately, they had no harness for her soul. Which

was why her spirit had been able to force her into a wakeful state despite the rehabilitating machines attached to her physical form.

Almost there, she whispered, more to herself than to Sethios.

Then a burst of light blinded her, the door to her room being thrown open by a Seraphim with a shock of white-blonde hair and startling blue wings.

Chanara.

CHAPTER THIRTEEN

GABRIEL

THERE WERE SO many colors in the coliseum—a fact Gabriel had never noticed until today. He was simply awed by it all, the fluttering of wings a cacophony of sound that he found to be rather pleasing to the ear.

His lips threatened to curl, his heart warming to the sensation.

Then the absurdity of the thought kicked him in the gut. He was surrounded by Seraphim, all studying him for a reaction, and he was two seconds away from *smiling*.

Pull yourself together, he chided himself. *Admiring the way the sun plays off all the plumes decorating the open-aired auditorium isn't practical or useful.*

Except it was rather beautiful.

Stop it.

His father cleared his throat from the second row, his red wings tucked behind him in his backless chair.

In this room, everyone remained ethereal except for the one under scrutiny, which left Gabriel standing alone in the center in his corporeal form while everyone else misted in their seats.

Hundreds of Seraphim encircled him, all sitting at varying heights in a myriad of rows ringing the auditorium floor. Above him was a pure blue sky. No clouds. Just the sun illuminating the cascading colors of feathers fluttering in the air.

"Would you like to make a statement, Gabriel?" his father asked by way of beginning the proceedings.

"I'll wait until I've been formally accused," he replied in as flat a tone as he could manage. He would prefer to learn what they knew about him first rather than unceremoniously give up information.

His father nodded, respecting his logical path forward. "Cavalina," he prompted, waving at the air before them.

A series of images appeared in a cloud of mist, all projected through the female Seraphim's violet gaze. She was from the recollection line—a Seraphim family that could collect and retain information and then present it visually before a crowd. The female essentially served as an evidence bank for debates.

Photos streamed across the room, breaking out into tablet-sized images that flew upward to each council member to roll before their eyes like a floating television screen.

Gabriel watched the show with a bored expression, not surprised at all that they showcased the Hydraians and Ichorians at his estate. He'd given up trying to hide them all over a week ago. This fate had been inevitable since the day Sethios and Caro met.

Gabriel hadn't understood the purpose of her mission, had felt it was dangerous and unproductive, until he'd learned about her pregnancy from the Fates. That was the day his perception of the council shifted. He no longer trusted their guidance, and that, unfortunately, included his own father.

Osiris had been a problem for millennia. Why send Caro twenty-five years ago to deliver a pointless edict?

Because they needed her to create Stas. So why not just tell her that? She was a dutiful Seraphim. She would have played her part without all the lies and deceit.

Which was how he knew there had to be a missing piece to all of this.

They wanted to use Stas in some way that Caro never would have agreed to allow, even with her faithful obedience.

That'd been the reason he'd pledged fealty to his sister, something he had no doubt the council knew now.

His father would be able to sense it with a simple prod through their bond. But his expression and aura gave nothing away.

The entire room was eerily silent when it came to emotional reactions. No anger. No disappointment. Just an air of nothingness.

Seraphim found no cause or logic behind emotions.

Gabriel had always thought he agreed. However, Clara's power had awoken him to a new method of understanding, even when it came to evaluating himself.

He did care to an extent. It was why he'd aligned himself with Stas. Why he'd helped Sethios and Caro twenty-five years ago. Why he tolerated Ezekiel. Why he felt a nagging annoyance earlier when he thought Vera had betrayed them.

Gabriel *felt*.

It wasn't the same as a human, or anywhere close to the Hydraians, but in his heart, he was intensely loyal to those he considered his.

His sister.

His mother.

His allies.

They were all under his umbrella of support, and with

that came a level of sensation he never truly comprehended until today.

"Your loyalty is no longer with us," his father said, his tone robotic. "Where does it lie?"

"With Seraphim Astasiya," Gabriel replied, not bothering to hide it. "She required my fealty to survive. I therefore pledged it."

Silence.

The Seraphim weren't sure how to interpret his response, which he'd anticipated.

"*An unknown power is surfacing. She will possess the strength and will to destroy us all unless certain measures are put in place to curb her inclinations,*" he quoted out loud. "I provided some of those measures."

"Who delivered that prophecy?" his father asked, his brow slightly crinkling.

"Prophetess Skye. I believe the 'us' applies to the abominations roaming the earth. Therefore, if Astasiya is the one who will finally rid the planet of Osiris's plague, then she has my loyalty."

Whispers broke out around him, but he kept his gaze on his father. It would be Adriel who determined Gabriel's fate because he was his creator and the oldest of his line. While the council might vote, it was Adriel's words that mattered most.

"Is this the prophetess you speak of?" Tulan, the original Seraphim of Darkness, asked.

He sent one of his rotating images down to Gabriel, the photo one of a dark-haired female with ice-blue eyes being carried by Ezekiel across the beach. The image alone confirmed Gabriel's property had been under surveillance as early as last week. It was honestly surprising it'd taken them that long to notice the activities at his villa.

"Yes. That's Prophetess Skye," he confirmed. With a

flick of his wrist, he returned the image to Tulan, who proceeded to pass it around the room in a series of clicks.

Louder murmurs broke out through the room.

Then his father cleared his throat. "Are you aware of who she is?"

"An Ichorian Osiris has held prisoner for a century," Gabriel replied.

"No. She's a lost Fate," Tulan corrected him.

Gabriel's lips nearly curled down, but he caught them in time to stop the infraction. "She's not a Seraphim."

"Not all Seraphim have wings," his father said, his expression hardening. "Particularly those who are in exile."

That was news to Gabriel. He'd never met a featherless Seraphim. "Osiris has his wings."

Tulan clasped his long fingers in his lap, his formal blue robes fluttering around his bare ankles. "Osiris is an original Seraphim. His mist cannot be removed."

"Yes. Younger Seraphim are susceptible to the castigation," Adriel confirmed. "Older Seraphim are not. In Skye's case, she was of an age where removing her ethereal essence suited the crime."

"Why have I never heard of this?" Gabriel asked. *And what crime did she commit to earn such a harsh action?* he wondered.

"You haven't heard of the practice because you're not privy to council matters," Tulan replied. "How we punish, and why we punish, are our decisions, not yours."

"We are losing sight of our topic," Silvia stated matter-of-factly. The dark-skinned female craved order in all things as the Seraphim of Justice. "He has pledged allegiance to a young Seraphim. The suitable reprimand is outlawing him from society."

"Except he did it to help her remove Osiris and his

abominations," Adriel interjected. "I believe that's cause for discussion."

"He should have brought it to the council before acting cavalierly on his own," Silvia replied. "That demonstrates a lack of care for our laws and should be handled accordingly."

"What if he fixes his pledge?" Tulan inquired, his beady eyes thoughtful.

"I can't," Gabriel replied, not wanting to waste time. "I will not remove or reevaluate my pledge until her birthright is fulfilled." His wording was precise and adequate and perfectly planned. They would assume he wanted to help her kill Osiris. And that was exactly what he desired them to think.

"Explain your reasoning," his father said, playing right into his hand.

"As I reported several decades ago, Osiris funded the CRF project. That project and its proxy leader, Jonathan Fitzgerald, have officially been dismantled—a task Astasiya helped see to fruition. However, the task before her is far greater, and as a result of her involvement with the CRF, he now knows of her existence."

He allowed that information to settle before adding, "She's going to require all the assistance available to guide her in the prophecy's path. To withdraw my pledge could be detrimental to the future."

More murmurs followed his proclamation, but he kept his focus on Adriel, who continued to give nothing away with his light green eyes.

The only emotion in the room seemed to come from Gabriel. Either his borrowed empathy was waning, or the Seraphim truly felt nothing about the task or his accomplishments.

That didn't surprise him, even though he felt a small

twist in his gut at all he'd done for these beings without even an ounce of gratitude.

"Where is Astasiya?" Tulan asked. "She should have arrived with you, as per the edict."

"She declined your invitation for a meeting," he replied flatly.

That garnered a bigger reaction from the crowd, in the flavor of gasps and louder whispers.

His lips threatened to twitch. He swallowed the sensation instead.

"What do you mean, she 'declined' our invitation?" Silvia demanded. "One does not deny an edict."

He nearly pointed out that Osiris denied each and every one of their edicts without a single reprimand, other than to let him continue to flourish on Earth and corrupt humanity.

"She's a new Seraphim who does not yet understand our ways," Gabriel replied.

"Then teach her," Silvia replied, her tone curt.

"She will still refuse to adhere to your command," he promised.

Silvia's eyes widened. "Why?"

Thank you so very much for asking, Seraphim Silvia, he thought, pleased. "Because you have her mother in a rehabilitation chamber."

It was fortunate Vera had provided him with the memory of his father's visit. His plan before had required him to feign confidence. Now there was nothing fake about his proclamation. He *knew* they had her.

"While I might agree with the reason behind her mental reprogramming, Astasiya will not," he continued. "She's been raised by humans, and her mentality does not align with our way of thought."

This caused a few of the Seraphim to glance at one another, a trickle of surprise clouding their auras.

Ah, so they can be shocked. Thank you, Clara, for allowing me to witness it. Because without her gift, he would have mistaken their reactions as mere questionable glances. But his inherited empathy allowed him to see through the action and understand the true purpose.

His father's aura radiated a hint of curiosity.

Meanwhile, Silvia appeared annoyed.

And Tulan was just Tulan—as stoic as usual.

They all sat on the second platform in a row, making it easy to read them. Those on the lowest tier weren't council members but workers like Cavalina.

Rows upon rows stretched upward in amphitheater-seating-style, with the weakest bloodlines at the back and the oldest and strongest toward the front. From what Gabriel understood, Osiris had organized his Conclave meetings in a similar fashion.

"Are you suggesting we release Caro?" Silvia asked, her thin black brow reaching her equally dark hairline. It was probably the most expressive face he'd ever seen from the millennia-old woman. She'd recently awoken before his birth—after a seven-century-long "nap." And it wasn't her first time sleeping off her ancient existence, either.

"If you want Astasiya to learn and accept our ways, then yes. She needs a mentor, and Caro is suitable for that as her mother. That is, assuming she's fully reformed." Gabriel added that last bit as a test, curious about his mother's mental state. He suspected she fought the process, perhaps not outwardly but inwardly. Although, her overall lack of communication with Sethios indicated she might have lost that battle.

More glances were exchanged. Silvia pursed her lips.

But his father remained inquisitive, asking, "Do you feel Caro can aid Astasiya on her destined path?"

"I do," Gabriel replied. "As I said, Astasiya was raised with a mortal mindset. Family is an important value in her life."

"And where were you while she was being raised by humans?" Silvia inquired.

"In New York City following my mission to monitor developments at the CRF." It was the truth. He just didn't mention the part about his frequent visits to Montana to check up on his little sister.

"Did you know her whereabouts during your time with the CRF?" The direct question came from Tulan. Always astute and paying attention. Part of his gift rested in the art of deception. So lying to him wasn't an option.

"I did," he admitted.

"And you didn't come forward with this information?" Silvia demanded.

"I was never asked about Astasiya, only Caro," Gabriel pointed out.

"You knew what we desired," Silvia accused.

"As Tulan recently pointed out, I'm not privy to council matters." A strange sort of bubbling sensation clawed at Gabriel's throat after he finished speaking, his chest rumbling a little as a result. It took him a second to realize that he wanted to laugh at his play on words. His lips nearly quirked up, but he forcibly swallowed the inane reaction and maintained a bored facade.

Or as bored as he could with his humor rioting inside.

He'd indulge in the chuckle later, once this situation ended.

With his luck, it would be after his empathy died, rendering the need useless.

Silvia wasn't impressed, but the others within her row

were all studying Gabriel intensely. There were thirty-nine of them in total, making up the strongest circle in this theater hall.

Seraphim of Justice—Silvia.

Seraphim of Darkness—Tulan.

Seraphim of Warriors—Adriel.

Seraphim of Violence—Rubeen.

Seraphim of Mind—Stahr.

He looked at each of them—most of them the originals of their lines, or the second-in-command because their originals were lost to slumber. All of their names and abilities came to him in a flash, his early childhood spent memorizing them all and their gifts. He was destined to take his father's seat, which sat two spaces away from an empty chair.

That particular spot hadn't been filled for thousands of years because it belonged to the Seraphim of Life and Resurrection. *Osiris*. He had no others in his line to occupy the position in his absence.

Only Sethios.

And Sethios didn't yet have wings.

But Astasiya did.

The Seraphim needed her, of that Gabriel was certain. What he didn't know was why. She served a greater purpose than Osiris, one the council had known and refused to share. He felt it deep within that they were hiding something. Which was the only reason they were considering him now, not issuing an edict for him to bring Astasiya to them with force, if required.

They wanted her to come to them willingly. Just like Osiris wanted to recruit her willing participation.

So what is it that she can do that has all of you utterly obsessed with her? he wondered. He'd witnessed some of her power when she battled her grandfather, but she hadn't been anywhere near winning that sparring match. He'd gone easy on her, had spent more time showboating and testing her than actually trying to hurt her.

Granted, it'd been an impressive show for one so young.

However, the Fates must have predicted something far grander for her. Something… terrifying.

Yes.

He could see the fear in some of the Seraphim around him. Subtle, but there. A hint of anxiety floating on the wind.

Gabriel inhaled the pungent aroma, confirming the accuracy of his assessment with Clara's talent.

They fear her.

Perhaps, then, the prophecy wasn't about the Hydraians and Ichorians but about them all. Seraphim included.

Yet how was that possible? Seraphim couldn't perish. Unless Stas would one day determine the true origin of life. Specifically, *Seraphim* life.

He played Skye's words over in his head once more, his gut tightening with the realization of just how dangerous his sister could grow to be.

"Are there any additional questions?" Adriel asked, his inquiry for the council, not for Gabriel.

"Would you be willing to submit yourself to rehabilitation?" The higher-pitched feminine voice came from behind him.

Dara, he recognized. *Seraphim of Fertility and Genetics.*

She was Leela's mother.

Rather than turn to look at the female, he said, "Not at this time."

"What about after you've completed your mission assisting Seraphim Astasiya?" his father pressed.

Gabriel considered his response before saying, "If it is a necessary measure at that time, I would take the recommendation under advisement and follow protocol if I felt there was an adequate flaw in my soul's programming."

He chose the words carefully because he would only agree to such an action if he truly believed it was necessary.

Which would likely never happen.

But as his kind focused primarily on logic, not emotional well-being, they would take his statement as truth and agree with the rational reply.

"Would you agree to realign your fealty with your elders?" Tulan inquired. "After the prophecy is fulfilled, I mean."

If they required a blood vow from him, he would reject it. So instead, he said, "I would discuss the appropriate alignment of my fealty at that time, yes."

He suspected it would stay with his sister. But that all depended on the future events—events the council was hiding and trying to manipulate.

Was that why they punished Skye? Because she refused to assimilate to their protocols? Did Ezekiel know of her true heritage?

The questions pelted his thoughts while the Seraphim around him fell completely silent, their inquiries seeming complete.

That was how these trials always went—quick and efficient. They'd gathered the majority of their evidence before calling him here. This part of the discussion had merely been about what truths he was willing to reveal.

His father glanced around once, then nodded with finality. "As there are no other clarifications, the council will convene on a proper course. You are temporarily dismissed, Gabriel. We will call you back when we have our final edict."

"Thank you, Adriel," Gabriel replied, using his father's given name as a sign of respect to the family line. He bowed deeply, then took his leave, aware that this might be the last afternoon he was permitted to roam inside the Seraphim city walls.

He glanced around.

Then shrugged.

He'd rather spend the time packing up his minimal belongings because it seemed Hydria was about to inherit a new seraphic resident.

His wings flickered to life around him just as an alarm flared about a hundred yards to his right. Seraphim took to the sky in a flurry, their defensive training igniting in an effort to protect the council.

Only, the threat wasn't outside the gates.

But inside.

In the form of a naked, blue-winged Seraphim with furious blue eyes.

Gabriel relaxed his plumes and arched a brow. "Mother," he greeted. "Would you like to borrow my shirt?"

"Take me to Sethios." Her voice was a rasp of sound, confirming she'd only recently awoken. And given her bloody state, he suspected it wasn't with the council's permission.

Rather than question her, he held out his hand.

It seemed he wouldn't be packing after all.

And Hydria wasn't going to gain one seraphic resident, but two.

CHAPTER FOURTEEN

CARO

TALK TO ME, angel, Sethios said, his mental tone holding a touch of concern. It was a warranted reaction, considering the fiery essence standing in the doorway.

My creator is here, Caro whispered to him. *When did the council wake her?*

She searched her own mind for the answer but came up blank. The last however many years or decades blurred together in a sea of sunshine and nothingness.

Because the council had put her in a rehabilitation pod.

A part of her had always known that would happen, yet she couldn't identify where the sense came from. Some memory, perhaps, that failed to form. Not surprising, given her current situation. Seraphim were notorious for wiping the mind during the reformation process.

It was a miracle she remembered Sethios.

Or, at least, certain things about him.

Such as the fact that they were bonded.

Other aspects were fuzzy. Hopefully, they would clear in time.

We'll make new memories, angel, he promised.

Her thoughts must have gone to him via their connection. Rather than try to turn it off, she held on to that link while looking at the woman who had birthed her.

The winged Seraphim blinked back at her and then stepped into the room in her corporeal form, her white dress dancing around her knees. "It isn't time for you to wake yet," she informed flatly. "I'll fix it."

Caro said nothing.

"Fixing it" required opening the container, which meant all she had to do was wait. And the calmer she appeared, the better. She would need the element of surprise for this to work. Mostly because she wasn't yet sure how strong she would be after all this, and her mother out-aged her by a few millennia.

But Chanara wouldn't expect her to react. It was entirely impractical to fight the conditioning process.

Unfortunately for her mother, Caro wasn't feeling all that practical at the moment.

She wanted out of this hell.

To escape.

To fly.

To *feel.*

Goose bumps pebbled down her arms and legs, her limbs tingling with the anticipation of having a purpose. She'd lain here to the point of atrophy, her mind nearly reprogrammed to forget her entire existence.

Parts of it still glimmered in the shadows—dark specks on her otherwise white conscious. But it was enough to pull her focus, to force her into action. Because something existed outside these walls that she cared about.

Sethios.

I'm here.

I know, she breathed, her heart skipping a beat. She

could see him in her mind, his striking green eyes, those alluring dimples when he smiled. Yet her past with him blurred in and out, a blink of time that she understood one moment and forgot the next.

She turned her healing power upward, seeking the fractured strands of her mind, wishing to piece them back together.

But movement in her periphery gave her pause.

Her mother was preparing the tools necessary to force Caro back into a peaceful slumber.

It would be so easy to allow it, to succumb to the numbness once more.

But a tug at her soul grounded her in the present, reminding her why she needed to fight.

Caro's purpose wasn't to exist inside a pod. *I'm meant for more.*

Yes, Sethios agreed. *You're mine.*

She nearly snorted. Yet his words filled a void inside her, sending warmth through her veins that mingled with the prickling sensations of her limbs. It made her feel alive. Renewed. Reborn.

"Yes, thank you. I need Adeline, please," Chanara said.

"She will arrive in five minutes," a deep voice replied from the air around them.

Chanara must have hit a speaker button to communicate, or perhaps had paged a telepathic Seraphim.

Adeline would be used to return Caro to her slumber, her knack for dream states well known among her peers. If she arrived before this glass container opened, it would be a problem.

Fighting her mother was one thing.

Taking down a Seraphim known for inducing comas with a thought was entirely another.

Breathe, Caro told herself, calming her racing heart. She needed to appear unthreatening. That would encourage her mother to open the pod and begin the preparation while they waited for Adeline to arrive.

Seraphim do not feel.

Seraphim do not react.

Seraphim accept rehabilitation as a corrective measure.

Caro chanted the words through her head, needing to embody and temporarily believe those statements.

Sethios growled in response, and she hushed him through the bond. *I need to focus.*

If you leave me again, I'm going to compel Vera to mist me to you. Fuck the wards. Fuck the defenses. I'm coming for you, angel. Whether you're ready or not.

Heat slithered through her at the thought, making it difficult to freeze him out. But it was the only way for this to work.

She closed her eyes, stole several deep breaths, and pretended to rest. Her mother would assume she'd exhausted herself by pulling out the cords, that Caro had just fallen back into a light slumber while waiting for the Seraphim to fix her pod.

One, she counted, doing her best to focus on the numbers and her deep breaths. *Two. Three.* On she went, her mind utterly consumed by the task and holding her absolutely still as the clasps began to unfasten around her.

When she hit forty-seven, a hiss of air touched her ears.

At sixty-five, the glass shifted.

And at eighty-nine, her mother's fingers brushed her pulse.

Now, Caro told herself, reaching for her maker and grabbing her by the neck. Chanara huffed in surprise, the noise silenced as Caro took them both to the ground in a flurry of limbs and unpracticed movements.

But her body quickly remembered how to operate, her muscles entirely healed. The only part of her left to recover was her mind, which would take more time.

She'd work on that later.

For now, she had to kill her mother. Not permanently —everlasting death was impossible for a Seraphim—but temporarily. Her grip around her mother's neck tightened, her thighs clamped down against Chanara's midsection to hold her on the ground beneath her.

Neither of them could mist, the facility heavily warded and underground.

And their seraphic gifts weren't of a warrior nature.

Caro had years of sparring training under her belt, her desire to learn defensive maneuvers a practical course that aided her now. Her maker had focused on intellectual lessons, not combative experiences.

Bet she wished right now that she'd at least taken a defense class.

Her blue eyes began to roll, her pale face turning a purple shade. But Caro didn't let go. She kept counting.

She was over two hundred now.

Nearing three.

That meant Adeline would be here any minute, perhaps any second.

Seraphim were always punctual.

When she reached three hundred nineteen, she released her mother and jumped to her feet, searching for anything that could be used as a weapon. But all that existed in this room was monitoring equipment tied to her pod. Not even a scalpel.

She'd have to use her hands, then.

She knelt once more, took her mother's head into her hands, and twisted at an angle meant to snap her neck.

The crack reverberated through the too-quiet room.

Then everything went silent once more.

Caro leapt back up to her feet and went straight for the door, refusing to waste time. It was unlocked, making it easy for the Seraphim to walk in and check on the pod victim inside.

They built this facility with the mindset that the pods would hold the prisoners steady. Therefore, additional measures weren't required.

Which was why she found the hallway vacant and the stairwell at the end unlocked and unguarded.

She tested her weight and found her footing light as she scaled the stairs upward, her body rejuvenated, thanks to her freshly awakened gift. But the sun gave her pause as she reached the ground level, her eyes unaccustomed to the brilliance.

Her gift triggered, mending whatever she required to see, and then she was moving once more.

Did you just kill Chanara, angel? Sethios asked softly.

Yes. She didn't bother pointing out that her mother would be fine in an hour or so. Sethios would already know that.

Without your knives?

Yes, she repeated.

Hmm.

She frowned at that hum inside her mind. *What's wrong?*

I'm just intrigued, he admitted, a warm note in his voice. *We'll play later.*

I just broke out of a reformation pod, and you're talking about playing.

Does that surprise you?

She considered it. *No, actually it doesn't.* While her

memories still hadn't fully formed or returned to her, her instincts guided her thought process.

A pair of glass doors was all that separated her from the outside.

She ran for them, bursting outward and ready to take off, when a myriad of alarms went up around her. Caro spun in a circle, then engaged her misting ability, preparing to leave the primary islands.

Only, a familiar sight about a hundred yards away gave her pause.

Gabriel. She started toward him in her angelic state, using her wings to propel her forward. They ached from disuse, her magic triggering again to begin healing and taking away from the work in her mind.

It was all too much. She needed somewhere safe to fully recover. A place where she could sleep off the headache forming behind her eyes.

Her son said something to her about a shirt. She ignored him and said, "Take me to Sethios." Her voice was surprisingly strong for her lack of use over the last however many years.

"I'd rather him meet us elsewhere," her son replied as he pulled out a small device from his pocket. He studied the screen, his fingers moving over it in rapid succession before he returned the item to his jeans. "Let's go."

Is Gabriel still on our side? she asked Sethios, confused by his behavior.

Unless the council changed his mind in the last few hours, yes.

Council? She knew he meant the High Council of Seraph, but wanted more details.

He received an edict to meet with them. He intended to more or less trick them into freeing you.

But they didn't free me, she replied. *I freed myself.* Did that mean she couldn't trust him? *What if—*

Fire encircled her, the heat lashing out at her skin and causing her to draw a hiss through her teeth. She misted away from it, only to be engulfed in a fiery net that stirred a scream from her lungs.

Caro! Sethios cried out in her mind. *Send me a visual. Show me where you are.*

It was a demand that forced her compliance, her eyes opening to capture the buildings around her, all mingled with burning embers that seared her retinas.

The persuasion left her in an instant, her mate immediately sensing the pain he'd caused. He didn't apologize, his mind whirring through hers as he tried to find a way to reach her, to help, to take down those harming her.

She fell to her knees, her lungs burning with the need to grasp clean air.

But in the next breath, it all disappeared.

The warmth.

The fire.

Everything.

She opened her eyes and blinked at the sight of Gabriel in full warrior mode, taking down a horde of Seraphim in one swipe of his sword.

They bellowed, cries of pain gracing the air, but he was on a warpath, his destructive side engaged. It wasn't a proper sword that he'd wielded, but a weapon made of *power*. He'd called it to him using the talents from his paternal side.

Awe swept over Caro at watching her son annihilate the others without a single misstep. *I created him*, she thought, her eyebrows lifting. *The Fates mandated this.*

Most Seraphim were over five hundred before their bodies were considered viable for procreation. Caro had been significantly younger when the call came for her to mate with Adriel. She'd followed through on the edict because it was the expected response.

Never once did she question the purpose, but seeing him in all his battling glory now, on the heels of her new talent awakening inside her, she began to wonder if the Fates had orchestrated all of this for a reason. Some purpose beyond the council.

"*Enough*," a deep voice bellowed as Adriel appeared, his red wings splayed around him in a cape of pure energy.

The fighting ceased, but Gabriel didn't lower his sword. Instead, he faced his father with an expression unlike any she'd ever seen from her son before. Fierce emotion radiated from him—a palpable anger that threatened to burn everyone alive.

Father and son stared each other down, their warrior spirits testing each other as they floated in ethereal form.

"Banish us if you have to," Gabriel said, his tone underlined with authority. "But I will do what is necessary to see the prophecy fulfilled. And right now, I need Caro's help with Astasiya."

What's wrong with Astasiya? Caro demanded through the link.

She's fine, Sethios promised. *Why?*

Gabriel just said he needs my help with her to ensure the prophecy is fulfilled.

He's using that as a reason to convince the council to free you, Sethios replied.

She considered that. *Oh. That's a practical move.*

Yes, he agreed.

"You choose the prophecy over your loyalty to me? To your home? To your council?" Adriel asked, seemingly unbothered by the power his son wielded before him in the form of a vicious sword.

"It's my loyalty as a Seraphim that drives me toward

this decision. It's the only path for me to take, Adriel. Even if it means that I need to go through you." Gabriel shifted his grip, his stance boldly hostile. "Decide."

"I could have you stripped of your wings."

"You could try," Gabriel countered. "And you would lose."

"I'm the original warrior, *Son*. You can't dethrone me."

"It's not my goal to dethrone you, *Father*. I merely wish to see this prophecy through. Is that not why the Fates created me?"

So he senses it, too, Caro thought. *He senses that the Fates are playing the council.*

What do you mean? Sethios asked.

It's all too coincidental. I gave birth twice in a century— something that shouldn't be possible with Seraphim only being able to procreate every five hundred years or so. I also created two of the most powerful progeny in existence today. But I, too, was birthed with a purpose. It's all aligned, only I don't think the Fates told the council the real reason for our existence.

I'm still not following, angel, he whispered into her mind. *Are you suggesting the Fates have tricked the council somehow? That you all weren't created to take down my father?*

I don't know. But there was something nagging at her mind, some puzzle she hadn't quite pieced together yet. However, she sensed she was on the right trail to a bigger revelation.

The council thought they were all destined to destroy Osiris.

But what if that wasn't the purpose at all? *What was the prophecy again?* she asked, trying to remember and coming up blank. *What are we destined to do?*

Astasiya is prophesied to be the one to destroy us all, meaning the Ichorians and Hydraians because it was Skye who voiced it.

Caro frowned. *Something about that feels… We're missing something.*

A flash of energy yanked her out of her thoughts, drawing her back to where Gabriel squared off with Adriel about ten feet off the ground. Several other Seraphim had joined the lead warrior Seraphim's side, but her son didn't appear fazed. If anything, he looked impatient.

"I've fought my way up to second-in-command, Adriel. I'm more than capable of doing it again." He twirled the sword as another appeared in his opposite hand, the dueling blades blazing with angelfire.

Power oozed off of Gabriel, his birthright showing in the smoldering green of his irises. He wouldn't back down. And in this state, only Adriel would be able to defeat him.

Unless the other older Seraphim arrived, which Caro suspected might be the point in this delay.

She quietly tested her ability to mist and found it fully intact once more, her body having healed automatically from the ropes of fire that had threatened to bind her to the earth.

"The council has not yet reached a verdict," Adriel replied. "Until that point, Caro should return to reformation."

Gabriel shook his head. "Your decision is the one that matters. So deliver your verdict, Adriel. To do otherwise is just a waste of time, of which I have little to give. Things with Osiris are escalating, and I've left Astasiya unprotected. She may be able to take care of herself, but she still requires my guidance. And that of her mother, too."

He's magnificent, Caro thought, pride flourishing inside her at the sight of her son refusing to give his father an inch. He was still so young, and yet he appeared positively ancient in that moment.

If Adriel felt similarly, he didn't show it. Instead, he took his son's measure, his mint-colored irises flaring with knowledge and power. "You will convince Astasiya to answer our edict," he said. "Once that happens, we will discuss your future with the Seraphim."

"You're not exiling him?" a feminine voice demanded as Silvia appeared in a flurry of soft yellow feathers that were a stark contrast to her darker complexion.

"Not yet. He has four weeks to comply with my edict. If Astasiya does not appear before the council by that point, then we will reconvene to discuss our verdict."

"And Caro?" she pressed.

Adriel glanced down at the woman in question, his expressionless face giving nothing away. "She will accompany him in an effort to guide the infant Seraphim appropriately. We'll discuss her fate in four weeks as well."

Gabriel nodded, his swords dissolving into the air. "Then we had better get started." He misted to Caro's side, his hand grabbing hers. "I'll deliver an update in four weeks' time, either with Astasiya or alone."

He didn't wait for confirmation, his power wrapping around her in a protective cloak of energy and forcing her to move with him through time and space.

Caro?

I'm fine, she said. *Gabriel is misting me, and I don't appreciate the sensation.*

That I understand, he replied, his words stirring amusement inside her without a source. There was some memory tied to that—a memory she couldn't yet access. *I'm coming to you, angel.*

Coming to me, how?

You'll see, he whispered. *Be ready.*

Chapter Fifteen

Sethios

"Take me to Caro." Sethios held out his hand. "Now."

Vera narrowed her silver eyes at him—eyes that turned blue green as her feathers sprang to life. "I hope this hurts."

"It will," he promised. "But it's worth it."

Her lips twitched then. "Yes. On that, perhaps, we agree." She pressed her palm to his, whisking them away from Hydria to the location Ezekiel had texted her moments ago.

For whatever reason, Gabriel wanted them all to meet at Ezekiel's place, not in Hydria. While Caro and Gabriel had fought the council—or whatever had just happened—Sethios, Vera, and Leela had chatted about how to proceed.

They'd agreed that Astasiya should remain in Hydria with her friend and Issac while Sethios assessed Caro's mental state.

From what he'd gathered thus far, her memories weren't fully intact. So while she understood the bond, she didn't seem all that engaged with it. Almost as though she'd forgotten that she owned his heart.

He would happily remind her of that fact the moment

he saw her. And if she put up a fight, he'd enjoy taking her back to the beginning of their relationship with a few carefully crafted commands.

The misting subsided, revealing a black night sky littered with stars. It was similar to the late-night hour in Greece, only his feet were now covered in snow.

He frowned, his stomach beginning to churn as his body caught up with the teleportation effect brought on by his "flight" with the Seraphim. It always left him queasy. "Where are we?" he asked, his voice strained as he fought his body's need to vomit.

Ugh, he hated how weak this made him feel. One day, he'd master it. Hopefully when he grew his own wings.

"About an hour east of Reykjavík," Ezekiel replied as he traced to his side in the middle of what appeared to be a field of absolutely nothing.

His best friend waited a beat, then nodded. "Right, we need to go for another hop." This time he grabbed Sethios and whirled him through space to the final destination—or what he hoped was the final destination. At least Ezekiel's ability didn't stir up the need to retch everywhere. Perhaps because the duo had traveled together in this manner for years.

They materialized inside a warm home beside Skye in the kitchen, where she removed a whistling kettle from the stove. "Tea?" she offered without looking at them.

"Yes, please," Ezekiel said, his voice soft and holding a touch of emotion in it.

A few decades ago, Sethios would have called him on it. Tonight, however, he left the assassin to his unrequited love problem.

It wasn't necessarily that Skye didn't love him back so much as she couldn't return his affection. She just seemed incapable of the emotion, her mind constantly lost to the troubles of the future and unable to remain in the present for long enough periods to *feel*.

Vera misted into the small dining nook of the kitchen, her eyes narrowed. "Thanks for the directions."

Ezekiel lifted a shoulder. "Gotta keep you on your game, Seraphim."

"And if I hadn't been able to grab that memory fast enough, you would have, what, left me to freeze in the middle of Iceland?"

"Southern Iceland," he corrected, pulling a beer out of the fridge to toss to her. "And I'm sure you would have found a warmer place to wait for further instructions."

"Are we still in Iceland?" Sethios wondered out loud. He owned a home here that he hadn't visited in quite some time. Actually, he possessed several properties. Or used to, anyway. He'd have to look into them later to see what sort of conditions they were in or if they even still existed.

"Yeah, Northern Iceland. I just had to make sure you weren't being followed by anyone." Ezekiel opened a cupboard to pull out some sugar and set it on the counter beside the mugs Skye had arranged. She had little tea bags in each, her focus on the water she poured into them.

Sethios frowned as he counted them all—eight cups. *Ezekiel, Skye, Vera, me, Caro, Gabriel...* "Who else are we expecting?"

"Oh! That reminds me," Skye replied, moving to the oven to catch the dial right before the timer sounded. She slid on a pair of gloves to pull a pepperoni pizza from the oven. "No one touch that. It's for Jacque."

Sethios and Vera shared a look while Ezekiel disappeared without a word.

"Jacque's in Hydria," Vera said.

"Is he?" Skye blinked big blue eyes up at the ceiling, then she cocked her head to the side as though listening for something. After a beat, she shook her head. "He'll be here shortly."

Sethios shrugged. The woman could see the future. Who was he to argue with her expectation?

"I need to prepare your room," Skye went on to say, glancing from Sethios to the clock. "And later, I'll draw Caro a bath." She left them staring after her from the kitchen.

He arched a brow at Vera after the dark-haired seer disappeared from view. "Why will Caro need a bath?"

"She's not bathed in several years because of her reformation status, but the Seraphim keep the pods relatively clean. Perhaps Caro and Gabriel had to battle their way out?"

Are you okay? he asked his angel.

She didn't reply, causing his heart to skip a beat. *Caro?*

Nothing.

A demand lined up in his mind just as a commotion came from the living room. A familiar scream had him running toward the source, only to come up short at the sight before him.

Not only was she naked, but she also had one of Ezekiel's knives in her hand—one he recognized because of the trademark handle.

"Angel?" he asked softly, confused by why she had the blade pointed at his best friend.

"You betrayed us!" she accused, only seeing Ezekiel.

Ezekiel had both his palms up in the air in a placating manner. "Darlin', I did exactly what we planned."

"That wasn't the plan. None of this was the plan!" she shouted back at him, making Sethios's eyebrows draw farther downward.

What do you mean, angel? he asked her mentally.

But she ignored him. Just like she refused to look at him now.

Gabriel materialized beside her, his shirt torn and decorated in bloodstains that matched his red feathers. They disappeared as he turned corporeal, his focus falling on Caro. "She grabbed Ezekiel's knife mid-transport."

"Of course she did," Sethios replied, both impressed and completely baffled as to why she'd done it. He took a step toward her, only to freeze as she hissed over her shoulder at him. "Caro, it's me."

"Lies," she said, her blue eyes wild with fury. "It's all lies!"

"What the hell happened?" Sethios demanded.

"Yeah, I'd like to know that, too," Ezekiel added as he took a step away from Caro. She growled at him in response, causing him to freeze.

At least she seemed physically fit. Every part of her was just as he remembered her—toned legs and arms, flat stomach, beautiful tits, supple waist, long blonde hair to the middle of her back, and a face crafted by God himself.

He wanted to hold her, to kiss her, to tell her how much he'd missed her.

But she seemed completely oblivious to him. As though he meant nothing to her. Like she'd forgotten every key part of their bond.

And all that drove her was a furious need to hurt Ezekiel.

"Why do you think we're lying?" he asked her, his voice pitched low, his tone meant to soothe.

"You're not here," she said through her teeth. "And you gave us up to Osiris."

Ezekiel's eyebrows hit his hairline.

"She needs her memories," a singsong voice informed them from the head of the stairs. "Vera, if you please.

Then Sethios will facilitate her bath. Oh, but stand behind her, or else she'll hit her head on the way down." Skye skipped off down the hallway at the top, leaving them all glancing at each other.

"My memories," Caro said, looking around the room and narrowing her gaze at the brunette leaning against the wall. "*You.*"

"Right." Vera cleared her throat, pushing upright and starting toward her. "I have a lot to undo."

"Don't touch me."

"Afraid I have to," Vera said, glancing at Sethios. "A little help here?"

"And you want me to do what, exactly?" he asked.

"Compel her to stand still and not fight me."

He snorted. "No."

Annoyance muddled her features. "Do you want me to fix this or not, Sethios?"

"You created the mess. You clean it up," he tossed back at her. Except, as soon as the words left his mouth, another memory tickled his thoughts—one that reminded him of the day he and Caro had asked Vera to wipe their minds.

He muttered a curse under his breath.

"All right," he said, not at all pleased by what he had to do but understanding the need for it. "Caro, drop the knife and don't move or mist." He threaded the compulsion through his words, earning him an enraged growl from the now frozen female.

The blade fell to the carpet at her feet, the last of her fight draining from her currently steady limbs.

He walked up behind her and bent to retrieve the knife.

She growled again, making him smile.

This reminds me of how we first met, he whispered into her mind. *You couldn't move then either.* He drew the tip of the blade up her leg as he returned to a standing position.

"I'm keeping this," he informed Ezekiel as he twirled it between his fingers and then slid it into the pocket of his jeans. Then he stood dutifully behind his angel, ready to catch her just in case she fell.

His lips twitched at the accidental pun in his mind—*his angel falling*—she'd fallen long ago into the pits of hell with him by her side. The heat emanating from her now seemed to confirm their position together.

But it was the simmering anger that really captured his attention.

You're making me hard, angel, he told her, aware that she wasn't responding to him at all. *Should I take the knife back out and play? You're already naked for me. Maybe we'll find a window to fuck against, see if that jogs your memory.*

Release me, she seethed.

Never, he vowed, clasping her hips to drive his point home. *You're mine, just as I'm yours.*

I will kill you for this.

You've promised that before, he reminded her, bending to press a kiss to her shoulder. *I'm still waiting.*

Remove this spell and I'll deliver your fate.

Once Vera is done, I'll consider it, he replied, glancing at the memory-wiping Seraphim. "She's ready."

Vera flashed him an incredulous glance. "She looks ready to murder us, not comply."

"She can't break my hold," he murmured, his grip tightening on her hips. "And if she does, it'll be me she tries to kill, not you."

There will be no "trying" about it, Caro replied darkly.

He chuckled. *I've missed this side of you, angel. It's like I need to teach you how to feel all over again.*

I feel just fine, thank you.

Yes, anger. Which I can easily turn into something so much hotter, he replied, kissing her neck this time before nibbling on her ear. *Keep taunting me, angel. See what happens.*

How are we connected? she demanded.

You don't remember? he asked, frowning.

She fell silent.

His teasing mood fled, his focus falling on Vera. "Fix her mind. She's losing sight of who I am to her." He could feel the uncertainty in their bond, the way it wavered between them, her knowledge of their mating undeniable one minute and gone in the next breath.

"So you can offer demands without compulsion," Vera said as she moved to stand in front of Caro. "Fascinating."

"Do you prefer to be persuaded? Because I'll happily comply."

"No, you won't," she murmured, lifting her palm to Caro's cheek. "This isn't something you want me to rush— not with how much I've altered within her mind." She closed her eyes, her voice growing softer with each word as she added, "I had to hide her memories not only from her but also from others of my line and all of Seraphim kind. This won't just hurt her, Sethios. It'll hurt me as well."

He wanted to say he approved of that reciprocated pain. However, it would be a lie. Now that he had all his memories back, he'd realized the sacrifices they'd all made —Vera included—in protecting Astasiya.

And for that, he would forever be grateful.

Which was why he kept his mouth shut and merely nodded, his way of informing her he understood what needed to be done and would do what he could to help. He slipped his arms around Caro's waist, hugging her from behind and holding her as Vera went to work on her mind.

His angel screamed, the sound radiating through the bond and engulfing his entire being. It wasn't out loud, but internal, and soul-destroying. Her suffering nearly undid him, leaving him shaking and causing tears to spring to his eyes. But he took everything she had to give, his persuasive grasp resolute.

She would not move until this was done, no matter how much she yelled and cried. And he'd accept her anguish as punishment.

He closed his eyes, wincing at the shrieks echoing inside him, at the pure agony setting their connection on fire.

She blamed him.

She hated him.

She loathed her existence.

She mentally wept.

She shattered.

She rebuilt herself, then fractured again.

Over and over it went, each sensation slamming into him as though it were his own. He *felt* Vera meddling with her memories, picking them apart and piecing them back together again. It was worse than what she'd done to him, the amount of weaving and unweaving so substantial that it was a shock Caro had even been able to function.

And it wasn't just the memories, but her time in reformation, too.

He overheard the chanting, the rules, the edicts that Seraphim were not supposed to feel or care or consider anything other than logic.

Fuck, it was cruel. How could beings exist without so much an ounce of humanity or remorse inside them? Not all decisions were driven by reason. Emotions mattered. Which he showed her through the bond, telling her how much he loved her, how much he missed her, how much he wanted her to come back to him.

She shut him out.

Then let him in again.

Then slammed the door in his face once more.

It was a mental dance that left him shaking against her, his arms holding fast, his body her anchor in a world she didn't want to return to. *There's no choice, angel*, he whispered, his voice agonized by the pain straining their link. *You're coming back to me. Then we're taking them all down.*

Because this experience showed him something very important—a fact all of them had danced around for years.

The Seraphim were just as big a problem as his father. Perhaps even worse because they had a society littered with harsh rules and stoic edicts.

They'd created Osiris. Left him to do whatever the fuck he wanted on Earth. And now wanted to use Astasiya to remove the bastard.

A twenty-five-year-old *girl*.

Mated or not, she was still a child in the grand scheme of the universe. They all were when compared to the ancients on the fucking council. And they wanted a young female to take down one of the oldest beings known to time?

She's expendable to them, Caro whispered, their connection more alive now than it'd ever been. Or at least, it felt that way after years of being separated.

He released her from his persuasion and turned her in his arms, finding her eyes filled with knowledge and *history*. It was all written there in her expression, the love they'd once had, the bond they'd held sacred, and the inevitable heartbreak they'd both endured.

They want to use her because she's expendable, she reiterated, drawing him back to his thoughts on the council and their intentions. *She's a soldier to them.*

Yes, he agreed. *We all are.*

Her knees buckled, but he caught her with ease and lifted her up into his arms. Vera sat in a chair a foot away, her eyes closed.

"Is it done?" he asked her. She didn't answer, causing him to frown. "Vera?"

"She's resting," Gabriel said from the other side of the room. He'd taken a seat as well, and Ezekiel was nowhere to be seen.

"How much time has passed?" Sethios asked, noting the sunlight outside—a rarity in Iceland during the winter season. That indicated it was close to noon.

"Several hours," Gabriel confirmed. "Skye said your room is upstairs and two doors down on the left. Jacque and Owen are staying across the hall. I'm sleeping here." He stretched out on his back along the four-cushion couch and tucked his hands behind his head. "We need to talk tomorrow" was the only other thing he said before his eyes fell closed.

Yeah, Sethios imagined there was a lot everyone needed to say. But his first priority was taking care of the now dozing woman in his arms. She'd tucked her head against his shoulder, her blonde hair tangled and unwashed. That didn't stop him from pressing a kiss to her forehead. *I've got you, angel*, he told her.

I know, she replied, sighing against him.

He took a moment just to study her, amazed that he *held* her.

She was here.

His Caro.

His life.

His heart.

In his arms, against his chest, warm and fragile and beautiful and strong. Such a conundrum. He felt her vulnerability, her exhaustion and exposed mind, yet power emanated beneath the surface, his warrior refusing to stand down even in her weakest state.

I love you, Caro.

I love you, too, she whispered, the fatigue in her mental voice rivaling the one exuded by her body.

He carried her upstairs and to the bedroom Gabriel had indicated was theirs for now. Inside, he found a warm bath already poured, the scents of eucalyptus strong and encouraging.

Laying Caro on the bed, he stripped out of his clothes and hid the blade in the nightstand. Then he lifted up his angel and took her to bathe.

She didn't stir, not even when he used a shower head to wash her hair. It wasn't an easy task, her body dead weight against his, but he took his time, cleaning her thoroughly and combing her hair afterward. Then he tucked her into the sheets and slid in beside her, determined not to let her go ever again.

You're mine forever, Caro. When you're awake, I'll remind you of what that means. For now, sleep well.

CHAPTER SIXTEEN

ISSAC

"CLARA ISN'T THE MOLE."

Balthazar's statement reverberated in Issac's head as he considered what that meant. When he and Lucian said they needed to have a conversation with him and Astasiya, he hadn't known what to expect. With everything going on, the commentary could have been regarding anything. But this proclamation hadn't even made his list of possibilities.

What did it say about him that the female he once adored like a sister hadn't even graced his thoughts?

That you have a lot on your mind, Aya replied softly. *We all do.*

"How do you know she's not the mole?" she asked out loud.

"Sethios somehow undid the compulsion around her." Lucian stood with his arms folded across his chest, his gray T-shirt stretching across his pronounced biceps.

He'd been channeling his grief over Aidan's death by spending more hours working out rather than sleeping. Amelia had expressed her concern to Issac that her big brother wasn't grieving properly. He was starting to agree with her. And not just because of the dark bags beneath Lucian's emerald eyes.

"He said it was crudely done, and he suspected that Osiris had left it for you to dismantle as practice," Balthazar added.

"Has Clara been able to give us any leads on who the mole might be?" Issac asked.

Both men shook their heads. "But now that we know it was all a ruse, we can use it to our advantage," Lucian replied. "We've left her in the cell, albeit with much more comfortable accommodations. As far as everyone else is concerned, she's still guilty and not to be spoken to."

"Alik knows. But no one else." Balthazar ran his fingers through his dark hair, fixing what the outside breeze had done to his artfully messy strands. "We'll tell Jay when he has less on his mind."

"So that means the person reporting to Jonathan is still roaming among us," Aya said, frowning. "Or has the culprit tried to flee?"

"Jacque's the only one not on the island right now, but he's with Owen and your parents at Ezekiel's undisclosed location." Lucian didn't sound pleased by that. "But everyone else is still here."

"Who do you suspect?" Issac asked. "Originally, you insisted on testing Nadia, Clara, and Tristan."

"We also suspected Ezekiel. Ash and Jacque were mentioned as well." Balthazar's tone held a lack of emotion, which was uncharacteristic of the mind reader. Perhaps he didn't want to let his opinion show either way on the topic.

Lucian's eyes narrowed. "We know it's not Jacque or Ash."

"We also knew it was Clara," Balthazar reminded him. "And it wasn't her."

The two Elders shared a long look, the tension between them palpable.

Issac cleared his throat. "Right. We made a mistake. Let's fix it by finding the culprit."

"One hell of a mistake," Balthazar muttered.

"And we'll spend the next several decades or centuries making it up to her," Issac vowed. "But first, we need to find the real guilty party so we can move forward. Until that point, we're stuck in this perpetual cycle of blame, and it's not healthy for anyone."

"He's right." Aya's green eyes blazed with power. "What we need right now is to be able to trust each other, not point fingers unnecessarily. So tell us who you suspect, and we'll go from there."

"That's the problem—only those in the inner circle knew about our test," Lucian said, his expression turning pained. "Someone would have had to orchestrate Osiris compelling Clara to paint her as the villain."

Issac considered that before saying, "Unless she was always the scapegoat." It would make sense to have that playing card lying in wait to be used at precisely the right moment. "Osiris's compulsion isn't always immediate. And now that we know he's the creator of all Hydraians and Ichorians, it's possible he's left persuasive strands in all of us, for him to tug on as he needs to."

"Which means he could have compelled her months or years ago, and only recently called in that strand, as you call it." Lucian lifted his hand to his square jaw to scratch the light dusting of blond hairs growing along his chin. "Do you think our real mole is also being compelled?"

"It's possible," Issac said. "But whoever it is must have called him to let him know that he needed to activate his tie to Clara."

"What I'm trying to understand is the link between Osiris and John," Aya said. "If Osiris compelled Clara to act as a scapegoat, then he's actually the one in charge of the mole, not John. And if we're right about that person being in the inner circle of knowledge, then Osiris let John die."

Lucian's eyes took on that faraway gleam they always did when his omniscience kicked in, his mind working through the various puzzle pieces to arrange them into a neat answer for them all to hear.

That look reminded Issac of Aidan, how he used to lose himself to the millennia of knowledge he kept stored in his head, never forgetting a single detail. It was why everyone considered the duo omniscient. They had lived through so much that they literally knew everything.

"Osiris sees us all as pawns in a war he intends to wage with the Seraphim," the Elder said slowly. "I can't imagine he was thrilled by Jonathan taking down some of his most valuable assets."

"Osiris and Aidan were rather close," Issac replied, recalling all the moments he'd witnessed between the two men over the last few centuries. "And he was fond of Anya as well."

"Jonathan also destroyed the CRF," Balthazar added. "He blew it up. I can't imagine Osiris appreciated having all his experiments taken down in the process."

"So John was no longer useful to him." Aya leaned into Issac's side, her voice soft. "Rather than try to save him, he allowed us to remove the problem from the chessboard and also triggered Clara to take the fall for the leak of information."

"He would see her as an ideal pawn—she can only sense emotion, not control it." Lucian's pragmatic nature had taken over, his tone no longer irritated, just flat and to the point. "She's expendable to him. Which means his real mole is far more valuable."

"Jacque is valuable," Balthazar said. "As are Ash, Tristan, and even Nadia."

"It's not Tristan," Issac replied, confident. "He's my best friend."

"He also didn't know about your test." Aya radiated certainty through their bond, confirming she agreed with Issac's assurance of Tristan's innocence. He wrapped his arm around her, giving her a subtle squeeze to show his gratitude. She and his progeny weren't friends. But her loyalty to Tristan meant a great deal to him.

"So we agree it's someone who knew about the test," Balthazar said.

Lucian nodded. "Yes. Unless Osiris has a spy in our midst who isn't visible to our senses."

"Technology?" Aya suggested. "Or do you mean a Seraphim?"

Issac frowned, her questions igniting a flurry of potentials in his mind. "Hold on. I think you might be onto something there." He started to run through all the facts, piecing together everything they knew.

Clara's phone records had indicated she'd spoken to Jonathan on numerous occasions. So they'd all suspected she'd called Jonathan to tell him about the wedding on the beach. They also assumed she'd warned him about the assault on the CRF headquarters. Just as she supposedly called to inform him of the location they'd given her—a false location that only a handful of people knew about.

But they'd tracked all those suspicions through one thing.

Technology.

His heart skipped a beat.

There was only one person on this island with the ability to control technology. That person also happened to be involved in all the planning, knew about the tests, and could have provided the details back to Jonathan for him to act.

Only, Aya's comments about the culprit really working for Osiris gave him pause.

"We all agree that the guilty party reported everything to Jonathan, such as the wedding details and the pending assault on the CRF headquarters. But we also believe Osiris didn't appreciate Jonathan's actions." The jigsaw pieces in Issac's head were refusing to marry together. "The mole couldn't possibly have been reporting to both because Osiris's objectives differ from Jonathan's destructive goals."

They all fell silent for a moment.

Then Aya said, "Maybe John was the go-between. Osiris doesn't strike me as being easily contacted. So maybe the mole was feeding information to him via John."

"And Jonathan chose to act on the details rather than pass them on," Issac added. "Which earned him a proper death sentence."

Lucian and Balthazar hummed in agreement.

"So our mole has been working for Osiris this whole time but reporting through Jonathan," Issac continued. "The question is whether or not he's been compelled or if he's been betraying us all for decades."

"He?" Lucian arched a brow.

"Mateo," Balthazar said. "That's who he suspects."

Issac was only mildly irritated at the mind reader for speaking his thoughts out loud. They had bigger problems. Particularly if Issac's suspicion proved right. "He was in the inner circle, and he has the means with which to manipulate everything. Such as the technology around us. He's also the one who provided Clara's phone records, and he was the one in charge of the radios at the CRF—"

"The radios that failed," Balthazar added.

"Yes. And he would be the only one capable of sending updates to Jonathan undetected because he manages the technological infrastructure of the island." The more Issac thought about it, the stronger his suspicions became.

"That could also explain why he wasn't able to access classified documents at the CRF," Aya murmured. "It was his idea for me to go back to the CRF, remember? He wanted me to gain access to John's computer."

"So you would agree to become a Sentinel." Issac swallowed a furious curse. It all made sense. He'd orchestrated everything, guiding them in the appropriate direction to play right into Osiris's hands. "Osiris was intrigued by you that night of the Conclave. He wanted to see what kind of supernatural you would become. And so he drove you to the CRF, where Jonathan could keep an eye on you."

"Osiris provided us with just enough information to keep us moving forward, but at the pace he preferred." A respectful note underlined Lucian's words. As a master strategist, he would find this all fascinating.

"Where is he now?" Balthazar asked.

The four of them frowned.

"I haven't seen him since he left Gabriel's house the other day," Issac said. "He's staying with Nadia at the fledgling house, right?"

Lucian's expression hardened. "With Eliza, yes." He took a step toward the path, leaving the others on the beach behind him.

"Wait!" Aya called after him. "If he's really the mole, then he's still feeding information to Osiris. Shouldn't we use that to our advantage? He thinks he's free of suspicion, right?"

Issac and Balthazar shared a look. Concern etched a path into the mind reader's brow. Amelia had been right.

This was far worse than Issac had realized. Lucian never acted without thinking through a plan, and he'd clearly been on his way to act on the information without considering an appropriate course.

He just wanted blood.

Mateo's blood.

Fortunately, Aya's words had given him the clarity he needed to reconsider his rash decision.

The Hydraian King slowly turned toward them, his face devoid of emotion. "How shall we use it?" he asked Aya.

"I don't know. Maybe we use him to find Osiris? Or trap Osiris?" She frowned. "I... There has to be some way to gain the upper hand with this knowledge."

"We can use him to feed Osiris false information about our plans and whereabouts," Balthazar suggested. "Or we can wait for the right opportunity to present itself. Regardless, it is an advantage we didn't have before."

Issac nodded. "Yes. Osiris has always been ten steps ahead of us. Maybe it's finally our turn to be a few steps ahead of him."

Lucian faced them fully, his eyes glimmering with knowledge and power. "I have an idea."

CHAPTER SEVENTEEN

CARO

Caro awoke in the dark.

No lights.

No sound.

No life.

The pod. A scream threatened her throat, but she forced herself to swallow it. If she allowed them to know she was awake, they'd use their abilities to force her back into lasting slumber, to listen to the mantra on repeat about Seraphim and their purpose in this world.

She didn't want that.

She wanted warmth, love, *feeling*. Seven years of emotion had destroyed her. She would never be stoic again. Too cold. Too boring. Too inanimate.

She desired heat, passion, *life*. She needed to breathe, to fly, to love.

Her heart thudded loudly in her ears, echoing off the shell around her. All glass. A room of white and sterility. The basement of a perpetual morgue.

When the Seraphim pulled her out of the ocean, she knew this had been her fate. She'd accepted it only to hide the truth—a truth she'd forgotten because of Vera's help. However, she recalled it now, the reason for all of this.

Astasiya.

Caro's heart stopped. Knowing the name was fine, but all the secrets they'd vowed to hide were rioting in her mind. Even the memory of Vera removing it all.

Oh, no… they know!

Her chest pounded back to life, her lungs filling with a gasp of air she hadn't meant to inhale. But if they knew, then she had to fight. She couldn't let them have Astasiya. Not yet. It wasn't time! It wasn't—

"Caro." The familiar voice gave her pause.

Sethios?

Something sharp touched her collarbone.

"Angel." The cold edge drifted along her skin. "Do you remember the last time we were in bed together? You pressed a knife to my throat that morning before kissing a path downward to my cock."

Warm lips met her ear, his voice whisper-soft. "I promised to return the favor later that day, but things didn't go as planned. Shall I return the favor now, sweetheart?"

Her blood heated at the prospect, her nipples pebbling on instinct. *This isn't real*, she told herself. *It's another trick, one to teach me not to feel.*

Oh, it's very real, Sethios whispered back into her head. "Allow me to prove it," he added out loud, the razor point drawing downward to her breast to circle a stiffened peak.

She flinched as he pressed the tip into her sensitive skin. The subtle scent of iron tickled her nose, confirming he'd made her bleed. Then his mouth sealed over the wound, causing her to hiss at the pleasure-pain sensation he elicited with his tongue.

Her thighs clenched, her body awakening beneath his familiar assault. She inhaled deeply, his woodsy cologne filling her nostrils and making her want to weep. *You're here*, she breathed. *Unless—*

His teeth sank into her breast, lighting her blood on fire with his bite. She arched into him, her eyes flying open to reveal the darkness around them.

But it wasn't the darkness of her pod.

They were in a bedroom with windows displaying a beautiful night sky.

She tried to process her surroundings, to remember how she'd arrived here, but a pull of his mouth had her eyes falling closed once more and a moan spilling from her lips. The sensation felt so fresh and new and *right*.

How long had she gone without this? Without him? Her memories were raw, broken pieces that drew jagged lines across her heart.

No.

She didn't want to think about them right now.

She was here, with Sethios, in bed, and he was drinking the essence from her veins and sending fresh waves of heat through every fiber of her being. Yes, that was more important. He mattered most. This bliss. This embrace. This experience.

"Kiss me," she begged. "I need you to—"

He silenced her with his tongue, his mouth demanding and true and exactly what she needed.

Peppermint filled her senses, followed by his woodsy scent. *Pine*, she thought. *No, cedar. Maybe both.*

It didn't matter.

It was *him*. Her Sethios. Her love. Her impossible man, the one who infuriated her and enamored her in the same breath.

He grounded her, made her feel alive, created the air inside her lungs, and forced her heart to beat.

She wrapped her arms around his neck, holding him to

her as he settled firmly between her thighs. They were both naked. Both aroused. Both entirely lost to the flame reigniting itself between them.

It'd been so long. Too long. An eternity.

Her body craved his.

Her soul yearned to reconnect.

I need you, she told him. *I need* us.

But he didn't give her what she desired. Instead, he broke their kiss and started a path downward, the knife still in his hand as he drew the sharp tip along her sternum, creating a path for his tongue to follow.

No blood, just a fine red line. It stung, but his mouth kissed away the prickling sensation.

It was such a Sethios thing to do. She reached down for his dark hair, her fingers threading through the strands as she tried to yank him back up to her. He smiled against her lower abdomen, then whispered, *Release me,* into her mind.

She obeyed because he left her no choice, and she growled in response.

"Mmm, I have missed that fire," he said, his lips caressing her mound on the way to the apex between her thighs. "Almost as much as I've missed this." His tongue parted her folds, drawing a sharp gasp from her throat.

And then he reminded her of just what he could do with his mouth.

This was the man who had tempted her to fall from grace. He'd forced her to feel, to love, to *enjoy*. These were the sensations Seraphim weren't supposed to value. The reformation process had claimed this act to be impractical and not a worthwhile endeavor.

Well, it certainly felt worthwhile now.

Electricity hummed along her skin, raising all the hairs down her arms. Everything vibrated. Her stomach tightened. Her toes curled. Her body shook. Words fell from her lips, pleas she didn't recognize, and Sethios bit down.

She erupted on a scream, ecstasy flooding every inch of her being and shattering her hold on reality. She burned. She quivered. She *felt*.

Oh, glorious feeling!

She'd spent too long in a pod without this, wasting time listening to stoic mantras on repeat in her mind.

But this... this was real. This was thriving. This. Was. Existing.

The taste of her own bliss met her tongue as Sethios kissed her, forcing her to embrace the pleasure he'd just forced upon her spirit. She accepted the kiss, returning it in kind and wrapping her arms around him as she did before.

He allowed it.

He settled between her legs.

And he thrust forward to join their bodies as one.

It hurt, her body unaccustomed to accepting his, but she welcomed the sweet ache, each pump of his hips a reminder of who they were together. As a unit. As *one*.

This was her Sethios, the one who had taught her how to truly fly, and he was returning her wings once more. Freedom had a taste, and this was it.

He'd found her at last.

Had returned her to the world of sensation and rapture and true survival. She thanked him with her hips, meeting his pace in a brutal coupling underlined in adoration and mutual respect.

She never wanted to stop.

Only, the flames inside her were reaching a boiling point all over again, inflaming her bloodstream and eliciting sharper quakes through her already trembling form.

"Sethios," she breathed, burying her face in his neck.

"Bite me," he said, his usual compulsion missing from the words. He wanted her to choose this, to reignite their bond, to stoke the sizzling inferno already smoldering between them.

It was her welcome back to reality. His way of ensuring she knew this was all happening in real life, not just inside her mind. He wanted her to feel that snap of their connection, to experience the power lurking within his blood.

She accepted the challenge, her incisors piercing his skin to drink the ambrosia from his veins.

He growled, his hips pumping faster, harsher, *violently*.

She felt his need, his pent-up rage at not being able to have her all these years, and the intense buildup of yearning from too long without her.

Memories spilled through their connection, ones of torment and aching, where Osiris had tested the limits of their relationship. The visions physically hurt, causing her to wince at the torture he'd endured and the residual anguish of the trials he'd faced.

"Don't," Sethios whispered. "Don't, Caro."

"It's not me," she replied softly, his pace slowing as the events continued to unfold between them. He pressed his face into her throat, his body shaking from the onslaught of exquisite agony.

His father had tried to force him to perform with other women, but he hadn't been able to comply. Even when compelled, his body wouldn't work, which created the worst kind of pain for Sethios.

He'd despised the string that had kept him from being able to perform. Only to be allowed to remember her for an excruciating moment afterward—a moment where he'd hated himself so much more than he ever could have hated her, because he couldn't believe he'd forgotten her so easily.

And then Osiris would take it all away to begin again.

She felt it all, saw each horrible moment flash between them, his agony a palpable force that threatened to destroy them both.

Her heart fractured at the trials he'd endured. But it mended when she experienced his love and adoration. She understood that it hadn't been him doing those things— it'd been Osiris.

"Don't let him exist between us," she said, threading her fingers through Sethios's hair to pull him away from her neck. Tears glistened in his green eyes, his purgatory a whiplash to her senses. "I forgive you, Sethios."

"You shouldn't."

"But it wasn't you," she stressed, cupping his cheeks. "I refuse to allow him to alter our bond. If I can come out of reformation and still love you, then you can pull yourself out of this historical loop and remember how to love me."

She undulated her hips beneath him to prove a point. He was still hard inside her, his body raging with the need to copulate and destroy.

It'd been so long. He'd gone without any form of pleasure all these years, living in a perpetual state of agony he hadn't fully felt until this moment. It was brought on by their reignited link and his soul confessing everything to hers in a whirlwind of minutes.

She'd absorbed the brunt of it, returning the favor by blasting him with her own memories. Except hers were all isolated to a box. She'd only drowned for a few hours before her mother had found her.

And then Vera had altered Caro's mind, demolishing all her links and bastardizing her familial bonds with harsh, looping sequences.

It'd all been unraveled upon her arriving here—wherever they were, surrounded by darkness and snow. She didn't care where he'd taken her, just that she was with him, that they'd survived and were finally together again.

"Remind me who we are to each other, Sethios," she whispered. "Forget the past. Forget the pain. Forget it all. Just exist with me. Teach me how to feel like you did that first time. Make me enjoy it."

He'd already blown her mind once since waking, but she knew he could do better. With his blood flowing through her veins, the results would be cataclysmic, and that was just what they both needed to survive.

"Take me, Sethios."

"Angel," he breathed, his lips whispering across her cheek to her neck. He adored her with his mouth, his touch featherlight against her skin. She had no idea where the knife had gone, lost somewhere in the sheets, but if she found it, she'd draw blood.

"More," she demanded.

"Patience," he returned.

Her throat vibrated with annoyance. She'd been patient for far too long. "No." She wrapped her legs around his waist, her thighs tightening to a death grip. "Fuck me." Those two words from her mouth had always excited him.

His cock pulsed inside her, his body shuddering in response. "*Caro.*"

"Fuck me. Now."

"Who taught you those dirty words?" he mused against her ear. "I thought you preferred *fuzz.*"

"I prefer *you*," she countered. "Now stop delaying and give me your cock, Sethios. Make it hurt. Make me bleed. Make me *yours.*"

"Fuck, Caro," he whispered, shuddering all over again.

175

"You don't sound like a Seraphim who needs to learn how to feel, sweetheart." He slid almost all the way out of her and drove back in, causing her to cry out in both surprise and delight. "It's like someone already gave you a lesson in ecstasy."

"Several," she moaned. "But I need more."

He repeated the action of slipping out all the way to the tip and slamming back into her. "Are you addicted to me, angel?"

"Yes," she hissed, arching into him. "You're mine."

"Damn right I am," he agreed, his mouth finding hers and silencing them both as his body began to really move once more.

Their dance was one destined for the stars, creating a new history underlined in survival, blood, and forbidden affection.

Caro allowed him to plow the reformative thoughts right from her mind, her spirit rejoicing in the connection reverberating between them.

She felt his guilt and sorrow melt away, replaced by a hunger to sate them both. His heart beat with hers. His breaths mingled with hers. His soul married hers.

Tears pricked her eyes at the beauty of it, the rapturous torment overtaking them and forcing them into a new beginning. She gave up trying to process it all and just allowed it to consume her.

Sethios kissed her.

She kissed him back.

His body moved; hers moved.

It was a timeless mating, a coupling underlined in the purest of emotions, and she reveled in it all.

He whispered into her mind, telling her how much he'd missed this, reminding her of their love, and promising her a future of eternity. She returned the words in kind, her cheeks wet from crying, her body strained from the pending release.

Everything tingled inside her.

She misted.

She turned corporeal.

She misted again.

Sethios smiled against her neck, then bit her again. She cried out, her nipples tender and hard against his muscled chest. "More," she begged. "Give me more."

He didn't hold back, unleashing all his power on her, all his pent-up fury and need, all his broken emotions and love.

She clung to him, her nails digging into his shoulders, holding on for dear life as he ravaged her to an utter completion that stole the breath from her lungs. His name was silent on the air, her oxygen depleted from the force of his thrusts, her essence suffocating beneath the onslaught of his exquisite torture.

He followed her over the edge, his shudders violent and drawing more pleasure from her already replete form.

It seemed to go on forever, the euphoric tide carrying them out to sea and refusing to release them. She'd happily drown all over again if this was what it felt like. Exhaustion pulled her under, sending her into a blissful sleep, bathed in the heat of Sethios and the reminder of who they were to each other.

In that moment, nothing else mattered.

Only that they existed.

Together.

Forever.

Tomorrow, they would face their future. For now, they would just… be.

CHAPTER EIGHTEEN

GABRIEL

GABRIEL STRETCHED out his wings and rolled his neck, his body sore from lying in the same position for too long. After Vera had finished with Caro's mind, she'd started on his, and it'd left him with one hell of a headache.

He never wanted anyone to alter his brain ever again.

At least it was done. Well, assuming Vera hadn't hidden any other little nuggets away for a later time.

Gabriel scowled at the prospect, then frowned even more upon realizing he'd just expressed annoyance with his face. Odd. He'd slept off the remainder of Clara's emotive abilities. So why were his lips moving in such strange ways?

He straightened them, but his brow furrowed right after. *Stop,* he commanded himself. His forehead didn't listen, and his damn lips twitched downward once more.

"Fuck," he muttered, rubbing a hand over his face.

"You hear them, too?" Owen asked, skipping down the stairs. Jacque met him at the bottom, having teleported from the top. Both men were freshly shaved and showered and wearing an odd sort of glow.

Happy, Gabriel translated. *Wait, why the hell do I recognize that?*

"I'd be grumpy, too, if I overheard my mom getting

pounded like that," Owen said, nodding as though commiserating with him.

"What?" Gabriel asked. Then he shook his head. No. He didn't care. None of this mattered. He needed to talk to Skye. "Where are Ezekiel and Skye?"

"She's building a snowman outside," Jacque replied. "And Ezekiel's helping." He glanced at Owen, and the two of them grinned like loons.

"You sent the photos to Jay, right?"

"Yep," Jacque confirmed, his lips popping on the end of the word. "I figured he could use the smile during everything."

"A whipped Ezekiel." Owen whistled. "Never thought I'd see the day."

Gabriel waved them both off, done with their frivolous conversation. He needed to ask Skye about her origin, then be on his way. To where, he didn't know yet. But somewhere private. All this bonding and blood drinking and general working had altered him fundamentally, and he wanted to return to his former self.

He pulled on his boots and stomped outside to find Skye dancing around her snowman while more white flurries fell from the moonlit sky. Gabriel had no concept of the time, his nap having taken longer than he'd anticipated.

As the couple outside hadn't noticed him, he announced his presence with a lingering question from his mind. "Where did Vera go?"

"She mentioned something about packing," Ezekiel replied without looking at him. "I think she's moving to Hydra."

That made sense. She'd played a dangerous game by altering all their minds to hide her involvement. Now that she'd undone the memories, the council would more than likely find out. Once they did, they'd see that her loyalty no longer remained with them but with Stas, and she'd be excommunicated.

Or worse, he thought, looking at Skye.

Her blue eyes focused on him half a beat later, her dark lashes dropping as she blinked. "Oh. Yes. It's time to discuss."

"Time to discuss what, darling?" Ezekiel asked, his soft tone underlined in indulgence and reverence.

Why am I noticing inflections in voice now? Gabriel wondered idly, irritated by the change. He didn't want to notice such things. Unless they could be useful in some way. He started to consider the prospect, only to be interrupted by Skye.

"My missing wings." Her singsong voice matched the dreamy quality of her eyes as she gazed upward at the dark night. "I sometimes dream of them." She twirled around with her eyes closed and sighed. "Freedom mattered more to me than my wings."

"The council told me they removed them as a punishment. I didn't realize that was possible."

"There's a lot they don't tell you," she replied softly, her sapphire gaze landing on him. "You believe they work with the Fates, that they keep us sequestered away from the others to protect us." She smiled, but it held a touch of sadness. "Is it considered a partnership when there's no choice in who you serve?"

Gabriel considered that. "No. It isn't." Then he looked at Ezekiel. "Did you know she was a Seraphim?"

The long-haired assassin lifted a shoulder, his trademark leather jacket crinkling with the movement. "I knew she came from your world and that she wasn't an Ichorian."

"And you never thought to mention that?"

"I asked him not to," Skye said. "It wasn't time yet. But now you finally know, and we can truly begin."

"Truly begin what?" Gabriel asked, his eyebrow twitching with the urge to arch. He ignored the sensation, keeping his face bored.

"The future, of course." She walked over to her snowman to twist the carrot nose just a little. "Now it's perfect. Let's go inside, Ezekiel. I'm starting to shiver."

He pulled off his jacket to wrap it around her shoulders, then led her toward the front door. Gabriel followed because he didn't know what else to do.

"What does the future hold?" he asked, wanting more information.

"Change" was all she said before shaking the snow from her dark strands and rushing over to the fire. Ezekiel watched her with an indulgent smile that had Gabriel wanting to slap some sense into him. He was too busy mooning over the girl to help clarify her cryptic statements.

How she'd brought such a formidable male to his knees, Gabriel would never understand. He'd never allow a female to leash him in such a way. It just served no practical purpose. And he liked his independence.

He also enjoyed controlling his senses and emotions. It helped him focus on what was important—like finding out what the hell Skye meant by "change."

"What kind of change?" he asked as she bent to tend to the fire glowing in the living area.

Owen and Jacque had either teleported somewhere or had stepped out through the back door of the house because they were no longer here. Gabriel would have to bring them up to speed when they returned. Just like his mother and Sethios, who were still upstairs.

"The needed kind," Skye said, straightening and wrapping Ezekiel's jacket tighter around her. "We've been controlled for so long. It's time for everyone to choose their own freedom." She faced him, her eyes clearer than usual. "Did they tell you what I was punished for? Why they removed my wings?"

"No."

She nodded. "There were two destinies; I wasn't sure which path you took. You picked your mother over your father. A wise choice."

He didn't need her confirmation to know it was the right decision on his part, but he dipped his chin nonetheless. "Why did they remove your wings?"

"Because I didn't conform," she replied. "They group the Fates into circles to predict certain outcomes. And I refused to focus on the outcome assigned to me. So, my wings were removed. But what they didn't realize was I'd chosen my path with a purpose. Wingless Fates are scarcely monitored because they can't mist. I used that to my advantage to flee."

Her lips curled down, her blue eyes shifting to Ezekiel.

"Unfortunately, my chosen destiny morphed when Osiris learned of my unprecedented escape. And so, I ended up in his captivity." She shrugged then as though unbothered by the twist of fate. "I will be free. One day."

"You're free now," Ezekiel insisted.

She blinked at him. "Am I?"

"Are you saying I'm keeping you here against your will?" he countered.

She considered him for a moment, her shoulder hitching upward again. "You mean to protect me. I understand and value that protection."

"If you want to go somewhere else, you can." He stepped forward to cup her cheek. "I'll take you anywhere you want, Skye. Just tell me where you want to be."

Gabriel suspected that she wanted to be somewhere

away from him and the leash that came with knowing him. He'd been the cause of her imprisonment with Osiris. Perhaps not by choice, but it was all linked to Ezekiel's obsession with her.

"I like snow," she said softly, leaning into his touch. "It's cold. I sometimes feel it."

Their dynamic confused Gabriel. One moment, he swore the female hated Ezekiel. The next, she looked at him as she did now with such gratitude and affection in her gaze that he almost understood how she'd melted the cold assassin's heart.

What would it be like to have someone look at me like that? Gabriel wondered idly. Then he frowned at the very idea. And scowled even harder at the fact that he was *frowning*.

Clara's power had bewitched him, forcing sensations to grow inside him that he had no business feeling.

He didn't want someone to look at him like that. He didn't want anyone. He was fine alone. Content, even. *Fine.*

A growl threatened to lodge in his throat, his annoyance at this asinine conversation enough to drive him mad. Which only upset him more because he shouldn't be feeling anything. None of it. Not anymore. He no longer possessed Clara's emotive ability, yet everything around him seemed to roar to life beneath a new light. He was picking up actions and tells that he was better off ignoring.

Like how Ezekiel smiled secretly for Skye.

How she seemed to fall into his gaze and smile back.

How their bodies gravitated toward one another as though pulled together by some unknown divine inclination.

Gabriel shook his head, spinning away from them. He had nowhere to go except back to the couch. Or maybe he could mist back to Hydria for a bit. Find Clara. Demand answers.

His eyes narrowed. *Yes. Yes, that's what*—

Skye sucked in a breath, the harsh sound pulling him from his thoughts and forcing him to face them once again. She had Ezekiel in a death grip, her knuckles white against the fabric of his shirt as she clung to him for dear life. Her blue eyes had gone white, her head tipped back at an odd angle.

Ezekiel held her steady, his hand still against her cheek, the other on her hip. He said nothing, his expression wary as he watched her.

And then she started speaking, the tone oddly flat and lacking the soft quality that usually caressed her voice.

"The Seraphim of Resurrection has created a new life. Power. Blood. A combination of abilities unlike any this world has ever seen. The daughter of a supreme being and one of his abominations. With her, he will create more. And more. And more..."

Ezekiel met Gabriel's gaze just as Skye jerked herself out of her reverie, her sharp inhale reverberating around them.

"The High Council of Seraph knows," she breathed, her voice hoarse. "They're going to kill her, Ezekiel. They're going to kill the baby!"

Gabriel pulled out his phone, dialing Leela. She answered on the first ring. "How's Caro?"

"The High Council of Seraph knows about Lizzie's child. They're coming."

"What?" she asked. "How could they—"

The line went dead.

Chapter Nineteen

CARO

Caro drew the blade across Sethios's hip, the sharp edge slicing easily through his skin and leaving a trail of blood behind it that she followed with her tongue.

He tasted so good. Like home. She indulged herself in the flavor, memories of their short seven years together floating through her mind in a warm wave.

"I see you found the knife," he mused, his green eyes smoldering as he met her gaze.

"You tucked it into the pillowcase," she replied. "Which means you wanted me to find it." Or he would have hidden it more thoroughly.

He smiled. "You took it off of Ezekiel; therefore, you earned the blade more than I did."

Yes. Her mind held a version of events that had painted Ezekiel in a horrifying light. So she'd reacted accordingly, the confusion of Gabriel having taken her to the male she'd thought betrayed them all overwhelming her entirely. She'd jumped to several conclusions, including thinking Sethios was some sort of mirage.

Fortunately, all her memories were in the right order once again, putting her at peace for the first time in what felt like centuries. It'd only been eighteen years, according to Sethios. Yet it felt like so much longer.

She kissed his hip bone, her tongue touching the trickle of blood she'd created with the blade. His cock pulsed in response, making her smile. "This is the reason you wanted me to find the knife."

"One of many," he admitted, his fingers threading through her tangled strands. "Fuck, I've missed your mouth on me, Caro."

A tingle worked through her at the need in his voice. He'd just gone down on her for the third time—which was when she'd found the knife—and yet her body was roaring back to life all over again.

He made her insatiable.

And she very much wanted to return the favor.

She guided the blade across his lower belly, hard enough to make him bleed. He flinched and groaned in response, his grasp in her hair tightening as she slid her tongue along the scrape.

More, he growled into her mind.

Make me, she said, wanting to feel his power wrap around her in that intimate caress only he could give her.

"Suck my cock, Caro," he demanded.

She grinned at his directness, loving that he didn't waste time with unnecessary words. He knew what he wanted, and he took it. That'd always been the way with Sethios. And she happily gave him what he desired, her lips wrapping around his thick head and gliding down as far as her mouth would allow.

A guttural noise left his mouth, his body spasming from the onslaught of pleasure her tongue provided against his shaft. She grazed him with her teeth, drawing a hiss from his lips.

"Fuck," he muttered, arching into her.

She repeated the action, knowing he liked the danger of her potential bite. It was a game between them, a harsh dance of sensuality intertwined with unpredictability. He'd once told her he wanted to watch her go down on him just to see if she would bite.

She did.

Frequently.

But not today. She wanted to feel him come undone in her mouth too badly to prolong his sexual torment.

And he'd commanded her to suck, his words underlined in a healthy dose of persuasion that compelled her cheeks to hollow around him. She reveled in the energy coursing through her veins, the need pulsing against her tongue, and the connection thriving between her and Sethios.

It was perfection.

Made her feel alive.

Provided her with the history she needed to ground her in the present.

She set the knife beside them on the mattress and drew her nails up his thighs instead, needing to mark him and remind the world of her claim.

He cursed and his grip in her hair twisted, his hips pumping upward and forcing her to take him deeper. She hummed in approval at his dominant side coming through, her throat working to accept his thrusts as she continued to swallow around him.

"You're destroying me, angel." His words were gruff and riddled with agony, his body trembling violently beneath her, his mind lost to her ministrations.

She loved the warm energy flooding through her veins, the knowledge that while he might have compelled her to pleasure him, she was really the one in charge. Because she controlled the pace. Her mouth decided how hard to work.

Her tongue chose how to stroke him. And her teeth dictated how hard she bit into his sensitive skin.

He jolted as she clamped down just a little more, then groaned as she sucked the pain away.

He was close. She could feel it in the way he pulsated in her mouth, and also through their bond. His breathing shallowed, his muscular legs tensed beneath her fingers. "Swallow" was all he said as he exploded onto her tongue.

There was no compulsion in that single word, but she drank him down because she had no other choice. She needed this as much as he craved it, his taste an exquisite flavor that was all Sethios.

Warm. Hot. Male.

Oh, she'd missed the potency of this position, the way he gave in to her entirely with each thrust of his hips. She owned him completely. Just as he owned her. And it was the most amazing power exchange, filling her with renewed vitality and joy.

She drew out the moment, licking Sethios clean, indulging in every drop, until he lay replete beneath her. And then she crawled over him to straddle his hips, her heated center exactly where it belonged.

He grinned lazily up at her. "You look quite pleased with yourself, angel."

"I am."

He chuckled, then grabbed her hips and rolled her beneath him on the bed. "I still have more in me," he murmured against her lips. "I'm thinking another decade will suit us just fine." He kissed her with an intensity that stole her breath, only to growl as someone knocked on the door. "Fuck off," he said by way of greeting.

She would have chastised him for the rudeness, except she felt similarly.

"The council knows about Elizabeth's pregnancy," Ezekiel replied through the door. "And she's gone missing."

Sethios froze on top of Caro, causing her to frown. "Who's Elizabeth?" A jolt zapped her heart. "And why is she pregnant?" She'd felt Sethios's pain at what his father had done to him, how he'd attempted to coerce him into performing sexually when his body refused to allow it. But what if—

"She's our daughter's best friend," he said, cutting off her concern. "She's pregnant with Jedrick's child, not mine." Those last two words were growled down at her. "Osiris never succeeded. He couldn't. I've always been— and always will be—yours." He punctuated that statement with a kiss that left her panting upon completion, his smoldering irises holding an intensity that healed her heart immediately.

Until all of his words processed. "Who's Jedrick?"

"A Hydraian Elder. He actually goes by Jayson now, but I know him as Jedrick."

She frowned. "And he's... procreated?"

"Yes, with a genetically engineered Seraphim. My father created her to help him breed my replacement. Apparently, I've disappointed him as a son," Sethios drawled, rolling off of her to open the door. She quickly pulled the sheets up to cover her breasts, but he stood completely nude and uncaring before Ezekiel. "How long has she been missing?"

"About thirty minutes," Ezekiel replied, unbothered by Sethios's nudity. Their friendship transcended millennia. Caro doubted many secrets remained between them. "Stark called Leela as soon as Skye predicted the child's birth. She said the council intends to kill the child."

Sethios grimaced. "She saw that?"

"No. But she's a Fate. So if she prophesied the child's

birth, so did the others. And she knows the council will never allow the baby to survive."

"Wait, back up." Sethios narrowed his gaze at the male in the doorway. "Skye's a Fate?"

Caro frowned. "She's a Seraphim?" She'd never met the female but knew about her ability to see the future and predict destinies. Ezekiel and Gabriel had never mentioned her being a Seraphim. She'd just assumed the woman was an Ichorian, turned by Osiris.

"Yes. The council removed her wings when she refused to cooperate with their guidelines." Ezekiel went on to explain her punishment and how she'd used it to escape, which was when Osiris had learned of her existence and tasked Ezekiel with tracking her down.

Sethios folded his arms. "And you've known this since the beginning?"

His best friend nodded. "She asked me not to say anything. It wasn't the right time."

"But now it is," Caro said before Sethios could reply. "Because we've already started to figure out that the Fates are not actually working for the council but against them."

Both men stared at her.

Their blank expressions told her that maybe that wasn't right. Or perhaps they hadn't pieced it together yet.

"The Fates have provided prophecies that they've allowed the council to interpret without any sort of direction. Like the prophecy about Astasiya being the one to destroy us all—the High Council of Seraph believes it's in relation to Osiris's abominations. But what if it isn't?" Caro continued, telling them about her escape and her healing power awakening, how that couldn't be a coincidence.

"The Fates have given us the tools we need to survive,"

she concluded. "And I think it's because they want us to succeed."

"In what? Taking down the council?" Sethios asked.

"Yes," Skye said from the hallway. "To provoke change."

"You couldn't have provided that information forty minutes ago?" Gabriel's irritated tone came from behind Ezekiel, the three of them obviously standing in the doorway, but Caro could only see Sethios's best friend.

"I told you they want change," Skye replied.

"That's a broad statement."

"That is now better defined. You're welcome." She sounded so prim and proper, like a queen seated upon a throne accepting the gratitude of her people. "Ezekiel. They need to go now."

"They need to get dressed first, darling," Ezekiel replied.

"Where are we going?" Sethios asked, his arms still folded.

"Hydria," Gabriel replied. "Leela was shot in the head, but the Hydraian healer is helping her recover so she can tell us what happened."

Caro frowned. "How is she helping? We're immune to their gifts." Unless something had changed during her time in the reformation chamber?

"Vera etched a rune into Leela's skin to allow Hydraian gifts to work on her," Gabriel replied. "Jayson also took a bullet to the head. No other casualties, and both of them will recover. However, Skye says our assistance is needed, and given how close Stas is with Lizzie, I understand that need."

"Yes, your daughter has a penchant for putting her best friend's life before her own," Ezekiel murmured. "I suggest you go talk her out of waltzing headfirst into the council to demand her friend back."

"She would do that?" Caro asked, a hint of warmth touching her heart.

"Yes," Ezekiel and Gabriel said at the same time. Then her son added, "You have no idea what it's been like trying to keep her safe these last few years. It's like she courts death."

Ezekiel snorted. "No shit."

"Right. We'll be ready in a minute," Sethios said, his hand on the door.

"I'll meet you there," Gabriel replied. "I'll call you if you're needed."

"We'll be here waiting," Ezekiel drawled.

"We can build another snowman." A hint of childlike happiness touched Skye's voice. "I need a scarf."

"Of course, darling." He stepped out of the doorway. "Happy misting."

Sethios snorted. "Have fun with the snow." He shut the door before his friend could reply, then rummaged around to find his clothes.

Another knock sounded half a beat later.

Sethios opened the door with an arched brow. "Yes?"

"You might need these, mate." Ezekiel handed him a pair of jeans and a sweater.

Sethios frowned at them, then glanced at Caro. "I forgot you arrived naked."

"I didn't," Ezekiel replied, a smirk in his tone that earned him a growl from Sethios. "So possessive. Did you enjoy playing with my knife?"

Sethios shut the door again, not bothering to answer, and set the clothes on the bed. There was also a pair of boots and socks, both of which appeared to be in her size.

Everything smelled new, but freshly washed, suggesting

Skye had predicted the need for the clothing and had recently ordered it. Or perhaps she was just a similar size to Caro. She hadn't actually seen the woman to know for sure.

The two of them dressed in silence, Sethios wearing jeans and a T-shirt meant for warmer climates. As soon as they were clothed, he pulled her into a kiss and pressed his lips to her ear. "I'm not done fucking you yet."

"Should I take the knife with me?" She meant the question seriously. Not just because of his sexual threat, but as a protective measure.

"Yes." He nipped her neck, then ran his fingers through her hair, helping to unknot the strands. She'd need a proper brush later, but he managed to help with tangles. Besides, being entirely put together wasn't exactly a priority at the moment.

Although, she had hoped to be in at least a little better shape before seeing her daughter again.

She nibbled her lip, considering. "Do I look all right?"

Sethios's brow furrowed. "What?"

"Do I... Am I presentable?"

"You're always fucking presentable. But if I'm honest, I prefer you naked."

She narrowed her gaze at him. "I'm about to see Astasiya. I doubt she'd prefer me naked."

He chuckled. "That's how she met you twenty-five years ago."

"Sethios."

"What?" He grinned down at her, and she glowered back. After another chuckle, he kissed her cheek and said, "You look beautiful, angel. She'll think she's looking in a mirror when she sees you."

Caro blinked. "A mirror?"

"She's the spitting image of you, sweetheart." His

palms went to her hips, his green irises taking on a light sheen. "She's strong, just like you. A warrior spirit. She's grown into your figure—something I can't say I'm crazy about because it draws far too much male attention. And did I tell you she's already blood bonded?"

"*What?*" Mated? Her daughter? "She's only... only... how old is she?"

"Twenty-Five."

Right. He'd just remarked on their first meeting, indicating her age. Caro simply hadn't considered what that meant. "How the hell is she already bonded? To who? Is he worthy of her?"

"No one is worthy of her," Sethios retorted, sounding furious. But then a glimmer of respect met his gaze as he sighed, "But she could have done worse."

"Worse?" Caro didn't like the sound of this at all. "Was she coerced into this? Have they known each other long?"

"Longer than we knew each other before bonding," Sethios admitted softly. "And from what I can tell, he didn't coerce her. She seems to love him—a feeling that is clearly mutual."

"So he's... he's good to her?"

"Unfortunately," Sethios muttered.

"Unfortunately?" she repeated. "How is that unfortunate? You wish for him to be cruel to her?"

"Yes. Because then I could kill him." Sethios spoke the words with such seriousness that she knew he meant it.

Which caused her to giggle in response, a sound she hadn't made in... well, a very long time.

His eyebrows drew down. "Are you laughing at me?"

"Yes," she said, unable to stop herself from giggling again. He was angry that their daughter had chosen a worthy mate, only because it kept him from being able to kill the man touching her.

While Caro wasn't all that thrilled with the idea that her child—who was still a baby in her eyes—had grown up so quickly and found a partner, she could appreciate that her daughter had chosen well.

"It's not funny."

"No," she agreed, biting her lip again and holding back more mirth.

"Then why are you laughing?"

"Because you're upset our daughter found a mate you can't kill." She cupped his cheek, both amused and even more in love than she was minutes ago. "I want to see her. I want to meet this man who thinks he's good enough for her, too."

"You won't be laughing then," Sethios muttered, pulling her closer.

She smiled. "Perhaps not. Ready for me to mist?"

He stole another quick kiss, then nodded. "Yes. Let's go find our daughter."

A statement she'd been dying to hear for what felt like an eternity. It was finally time to see the result of their sacrifice. To see the woman her daughter had become. Caro realized in a breath that worrying over her own wardrobe or hair paled in comparison to the reality of being able to hug her daughter again.

Nothing else mattered. Only the reunion ahead.

"Hold on," she whispered.

"I'll never let go of you again," Sethios vowed.

Her lips curled, her eyes falling closed as her wings fluttered to life. She'd never felt more whole than in that moment, knowing they'd finally survived and were on their way to see the piece of them that'd been missing for far too long.

Except, as her wings began to pulsate, a strange sort of sensation settled over her. It tingled and vibrated, the energy an invisible strand that wrapped around her and held on. "Sethios?"

He didn't reply, his body tense.

Power rippled over them.

Electricity sizzled through the air.

And his limbs began to shake. He held on to her as tightly as he could, but the violent shudders appeared to be forcing him to release his grip. She threw her arms around his neck, igniting her mist, intending to take him with her, only he went ethereal at the same time. Wings twice the size of hers exploded from his back in a flurry of black plumes, tinged with dark blue at the edges.

She gasped, shocked by the display, only to swallow the sound as he sent them flying to an unknown destination.

Caro tried to ask him what he was doing, but they were moving too fast for her to speak.

It was almost as though someone had wrapped a cord around him and yanked him through space and time. She'd only been along for the ride because she'd clung to him. Her legs wrapped around his waist, her arms tightening around his neck, refusing to lose him.

He didn't hold her back, his agony at having no control over his actions vibrating through their bond. *It's Osiris*, he managed to grit out into her mind. *He's... he's compelling me to mist to him.*

How?

The day in Maine. I felt him unleashing his compulsion, but he distracted me by freeing Skye from his mental hold. I'd assumed the power I felt was from him releasing her. But I was wrong. He embedded a persuasive link in me so deep I couldn't even sense it.

She felt him trying to fight the compulsion, his mind frantically searching for the cord to sever it. But it was already too late.

White walls formed around them, their destined

location revealing itself inch by inch, until they found themselves in the middle of a large living area with windows overlooking a white sand beach framed by the bluest of oceans.

"Ah, you're here," a familiar voice said, sending a chill down Caro's spine. "And I see you found your lost Seraphim."

CHAPTER TWENTY

SETHIOS

SETHIOS'S BLOOD BOILED, his stupidity infuriating him. He should have seen this play coming from a mile away, but he'd been so consumed with finding Caro that he'd ignored the obvious.

His father was always several steps ahead. Of course he'd left behind a compulsion for Sethios to meet him somewhere in the future. He'd never just allow his son to exist on his own; he always needed to maintain some sort of control.

At least Astasiya was safe.

"Father," Sethios greeted, his arms still glued to his sides. "You can release me now."

"And risk you using your new misting ability?" He tsked, that strand of power tightening around him rather than loosening. "I need you to hear me out before you take off." He paused to study Sethios's wings, his chin dipping in approval. "I see you mostly take after me. That hint of blue must be a marker of your bond."

Sethios hadn't even looked at his feathers, too consumed by the fact that his father had bested him. *Again*.

"What do you want to say?" he prompted, wanting to

start whatever game his father intended to play. The sooner they began, the sooner it would end.

"Direct as always," Osiris replied.

"You say that as though it surprises you." Just as he mentioned it almost every time they met, like he expected some other outcome. Why would Sethios wish to prolong the torment? Best to rip the first layer off and get started.

"You never were a fan of my theatrics."

Sethios just blinked at him, unable to move anything other than his eyes and mouth. Well, his chest worked, too, since he was breathing just fine.

Caro was in a similar state, her body frozen against his with her arms locked around his neck and her legs around his waist. It would have been comical if it weren't so infuriating. His father could at least allow them to stand in a corporeal state, side by side, rather than glued together.

Fortunately, Caro didn't appear to be tiring of having to hold herself against him in such a manner. If anything, she merely vibrated with fury at having the evil incarnate at her back.

Osiris heaved a dramatic sigh. "Fine. As you've probably learned by now, Skye is a Seraphim. Which makes her one of the Fates. Did she tell you why she lost her wings?"

"She refused to conform," Sethios summarized. Technically, Ezekiel had told him, but Osiris didn't need to know that.

"Yes. When I learned of her deflection and escape, I sought her out as a valuable asset. Now you see the gift I've provided by allowing you to borrow her."

Sethios said nothing. He didn't consider it a gift to *borrow* someone. However, he understood why his father would perceive it that way.

"Did she see Elizabeth's future child?" Osiris asked.

There was no point in lying to the man since he'd been the one to ensure her genetics allowed for procreation. "Yes."

"And she explained that if she saw the birth, then the Fates did as well?"

Sethios wondered what he was getting at, which prompted him to reply again with the truth. "Yes."

"Excellent. You can turn corporeal now. I need your legs." He waved a hand, an invisible band snapping and allowing Sethios to return to a wingless state.

He frowned. "Did you remove my ability to mist?" Another thought immediately followed that. "Have you hidden this ability from me through compulsion?"

His father grunted. "Misting is a useful trait. Why would I keep that from you?"

"To ground me." *Literally*. Caro sent a similar thought through the bond as she slowly climbed off of Sethios and shook out her limbs.

Osiris considered the statement, then lifted a shoulder. "I suppose it is something I would do, but no. I merely threaded a command through your soul to return to me when you found your ethereal state. Skye had once predicted that it would be the same day Elizabeth went into labor. And I believe she was right."

"She predicted I would go ethereal today?" That implied she'd voiced that prediction before Astasiya had helped free Sethios... and Skye.

"She predicts a lot of things when forced to focus on specific destinies. Obviously, your future was one I needed to know."

"You knew I would escape," Sethios said, voicing his thoughts.

"Of course I did," he replied. "It afforded me an

excellent opportunity to test Astasiya, who proved to be just as magnificent as Skye predicted."

"But you didn't know about her," Caro interjected, her confusion palpable.

"Not until recently, no," he admitted. "However, I've since learned quite a bit about her. Such as she's the one destined to pose a threat to me and all of Seraphim kind."

Sethios and Caro remained silent, already aware that Osiris had misunderstood Skye's prophecy from all those years ago.

"I'll admit, I was extremely impressed that you both kept that from me. All this time, I thought I'd nullified the threat when I removed you from the equation. Then the council dragged you off to reformation, and I assumed it was a result of your failure." He shrugged again. "Of course, when Astasiya revealed herself to me, I started to understand the truth."

"And you made me bury myself in concrete as a punishment." Sethios's skinned burned with the memory of the excruciating sensation of hot cement touching his flesh.

"As both a punishment and a test of strength—one Astasiya passed beautifully. Not only did she fight better than I could have imagined, but she also managed to fracture my hold over you. Fascinating, really. Not even Skye could foresee that outcome. I mean, she failed to mention Vera's interference."

"Or she kept that detail from you," Sethios suggested.

"Yes, that, too. She has a penchant for twisting her visions. As do many of the Fates." He slid his hands into his charcoal dress pants, his white button-down shirt reflecting in the sunlight streaming in through the skylights above. "Did she mention what the Fates would do to Elizabeth's child?"

"They took her," Sethios said, feigning boredom. "I imagine they intend to raise the child within their rules since she'll be a genetically modified Seraphim. It's exactly what we didn't want for Astasiya." It also wasn't what Skye predicted. She'd stated the council would kill the child. Sethios hoped like hell that wasn't true.

"An intelligent decision for your progeny," his father replied, the compliment actually surprising Sethios. His father never praised his choices. "But your assumption is juvenile."

And there was the follow-up insult.

Sethios refrained from rolling his eyes.

"The council would never want the child to live," his father continued. "She's my creation, and they frown upon those."

"So you also think they'll kill her," Sethios said, displeased with the notion of such a meaningless death. Humans died early and young. Immortals did not —*should* not.

"Yes. And Elizabeth, of course." He uttered the words as if that outcome meant nothing to him. Which, Sethios guessed, it wouldn't. His father could just create more life —that was what he did.

"Why are we here?" Sethios asked. "Everything you've told us just confirms what we already know."

"Directness would be more suitable if used sporadically, not in every conversation tactic."

"The same could be said about dramatics," Sethios deadpanned.

His father dipped his chin. "Fair." He turned on his heel. "Follow me, then. No fighting me or misting."

Caro and Sethios exchanged a look, then their feet began to move of their own accord—compelled by Osiris. He led them through the downstairs of the beach house, alongside a myriad of windows. The home boasted opulence, the light coming in from above highlighted the gold accents, white framework, and sleek marble floors.

They wandered by a double kitchen with two islands, multiple ovens and stoves, and two sets of sinks.

"Are you planning to host a party?" Sethios asked, noting the lack of people and the abundance of space. They were moving through yet another living room toward what appeared to be a back staircase.

"No, I manufactured this home for the future owner."

"Future owner?" Sethios repeated.

"Keep walking," his father replied, leading them up the stairs to the second floor. Several bedrooms adorned the floor, each equipped with balconies that overlooked the ocean on one side and a vast field of exotic plants on the other.

They were clearly on an island somewhere. The turquoise colors of the water suggested the Caribbean. Perhaps a private estate in The Bahamas. It seemed like a place his father would favor.

Osiris continued onward to the fourth or fifth bedroom in the middle and opened the door to reveal a nursery. "This will be useful in a few hours," he said, causing Sethios to frown.

Then he opened the door directly across the hall from the nursery to where an unconscious Elizabeth lay in the middle of a large white bed.

Caro gasped at the sight of the very pregnant woman, her body angling toward her. "You can go to her," Osiris said, releasing Caro from his compulsion. "But don't mist her anywhere. She needs to remain here."

"Jedrick would probably disagree with that statement." Sethios folded his arms. "What the hell is this about?"

"Isn't it obvious?" Osiris asked. When Sethios said

nothing, he heaved another of his dramatic sighs. "I saved her from the council. Were you not listening to anything I've said? They would have killed her. I brought her here, to a warded home with all her favorite luxuries, to protect her. Obviously."

Sethios's brow furrowed. "Why would you be so magnanimous?"

Osiris snorted. "It's not about being magnanimous. It was practical to protect my lucrative investment. Particularly now that the CRF labs were destroyed. It will take me decades to create another being like Elizabeth, and given the recent events, I may not have that much time left. So I need to keep her alive, as well as her progeny."

"To prove she can carry a son for you? To replace me?"

"Well, that was my original intent, yes. But you've proven useful lately, particularly in the matter of procreation. Astasiya will be most valuable in our battle against the Seraphim."

"Assuming she agrees to help you," Sethios reminded him. "Kidnapping her best friend isn't going to win you any favors. Or did you not hear what Gabriel told you?"

The warrior Seraphim was seriously a genius. He'd created the dialogue surrounding Astasiya's willingness, which provided Sethios with the platform he needed to stand on and reprimand his father.

Elizabeth seems fine, Caro breathed into his mind. *She's just asleep.*

He probably compelled her, Sethios thought back at her.

Probably, she agreed.

"She'll never trust you after this," he said out loud, his words for his father.

"I took Elizabeth somewhere safe to guard her. I also barely wounded her midwife, thereby assuring she would be fully recovered before her labor started. These are all done in the best interest of her survival. Astasiya will understand that."

"Will she?" Sethios countered.

"Yes. You'll ensure she does," his father replied.

"Because you'll compel me to?" he guessed.

"I won't need to. You're going to call the Hydraians as soon as I leave and allow a few of them to arrive to help Elizabeth give birth in this heavily warded home, where she won't be found or discovered by the council. And after that, Astasiya will realize I am not the evil man she thinks I am."

"You dumped me in the ocean and forced her father to do unspeakable acts for nearly two decades," Caro said, her voice carrying a touch of anger in it. "You expect her to forgive you for that?"

Osiris didn't even hesitate. "Of course I do. She'll one day see that those trials were meant to strengthen you both, not torment you."

Sethios huffed a humorless laugh. "Right."

His father arched a brow. "Caro survived reformation. Do you know how many other Seraphim can claim the same? None. And do you know why she was able to survive? Because of your *tormented* bond. That pain you experienced the last eighteen years was what kept you glued to her. It was what made you fight for her, too. You may not see that now, but you will."

"And sinking me to the bottom of the ocean?" Caro prompted. "You claimed that was your way of removing the threat to your life."

"Initially, yes. But it also served as a way to strengthen my only progeny."

"Your definition of *torture* differs from mine," Sethios deadpanned.

"It tested the limits of your bond," he continued, ignoring Sethios's commentary. "Each day you became more resilient, remembering her faster than I could keep up with."

"You let me remember her."

His father smiled. "Sometimes, yes. Other times, no. You broke my compulsion through force of will."

Sethios tried to recall those instances; however, they all blurred together in a convoluted web of anguish. His father had forced his body through unspeakable acts—all of which he couldn't perform, and that had created an agony unlike any he'd ever felt.

"You did it as a punishment." It didn't matter how he tried to sugarcoat it now; Sethios knew the truth.

"When have I ever done something for one reason alone?" his father countered. "There are always multiple angles and benefits. You know that. And all of those experiences have strengthened you, not weakened you. They even helped Caro survive reformation."

Only his father would believe that torture could amount to a strengthening exercise. However, he wasn't necessarily wrong. The experience had empowered Sethios. It'd also enraged him. Nearly destroyed him. Made him hate his father even more. And about a dozen other results.

This is why Seraphim often slumber, Caro breathed into his mind. *Living forever can alter mindsets, erasing all semblance of humanity from the thoughts.*

I don't think my father was ever humane or sane.

True, she agreed. *But he's also not wrong. Our sacrifices have strengthened us. I feel now more than I ever have before.*

Sethios understood what she meant. It was as though they'd bonded all over again, on an even deeper level.

He could sense her every inhale, could almost hear the

beating of her heart, and could nearly read her mind. Not each individual word, but her emotions were very much tied to his. As though their souls had married one another on another plane of existence, creating a bond that was so much more intense than their initial mating.

Perhaps because they'd imbibed so much of each other's blood.

Yet they often did that during sex.

So maybe his father was right. Maybe he had somehow emboldened their relationship through his fucked-up trials.

Osiris smiled. "Your bond is going to prove most useful in the times ahead."

Sethios gritted his teeth, holding back a retort about how unlikely it was that his father would ever be able to use their bond to his benefit.

"Well, my task here is done. You'll both ensure Elizabeth survives her childbirth. Then I'll be in touch with next steps. We have a war to prepare for, something you'll better understand soon. Until then, I'll let you keep Skye. You're going to need her." He flashed them both an indulgent smile, then vanished without another word.

Sethios gaped at the vacant space, the compulsion surrounding him disappearing in a whisper of power. "That's it?" He'd persuaded Sethios to come here… to take care of Elizabeth and her baby?

Caro walked over to him, her frown matching how he felt inside. "I agree. That felt rather anticlimactic."

"He wants something," Sethios replied. "This can't be as simple as just bringing in a few Hydraians. He'll be back."

"Should we move her?"

He palmed the back of his neck, considering their options, and glanced at the stirring female. His father must have released her of the sleeping compulsion. "We might not have time," he muttered, noting the fluttering of her red lashes. "I think he means for Astasiya to come here. He knows she's loyal to Elizabeth. The moment she learns of her location and condition, she'll want to be here for her friend."

"Then we could mist Elizabeth to Hydria quickly," Caro offered.

Sethios shook his head. "Osiris wasn't wrong about the council. Skye said they know and would kill the child. They'll find her in Hydria. The one thing I think he didn't lie about was the wards around this property. He built it to protect her because he needs something from her."

"So you think we should stay here?"

He hated his answer, but he had to be honest. "Yes. I think she's safe here."

"And Astasiya?"

"I think she'll arrive the second she knows we're all here," he admitted. "Which will likely play right into Osiris's plans. But I don't think he wants to hurt her. Not yet, anyway. She's too valuable to him."

"He could take her."

"Yes," Sethios agreed. "But—"

A shriek sounded from the bed, forcing them both to move toward the writhing redhead. She wasn't fully aware of her surroundings yet, but the child inside her certainly was.

It seemed Skye was right.

The day Sethios learned how to mist was the same day Elizabeth went into labor.

There was only one thing he could say. "Fuck."

CHAPTER TWENTY-ONE

STAS

"Caro and Sethios should be here by now," Gabriel said, pacing the length of Balthazar's living room. "Something's wrong." He disappeared without another word.

"Yeah, that's helpful," Stas muttered, glancing at Issac. "Can I punch him again when he returns?"

"Absolutely, love." He wrapped his arm around her, giving her a slight squeeze. "Let's return our focus on Elizabeth. Where would the Seraphim take her?"

"She would be held somewhere near the coliseum," Leela said from the couch, her eyes closed as she recovered from the bullet wound she'd endured.

Lara sat on the ground beside her, sweating as she tried to help expedite the Seraphim's healing. While the rune Vera had created allowed Hydraian gifts to work on Leela, it seemed there was still some natural resistance. Or perhaps it was a result of runes canceling each other out.

Stas didn't understand how all that enchantment worked yet. Mostly because her brother had kept her in the dark for months on end rather than using their time together to bring her up to speed.

Yeah, Stas wasn't bitter at all.

Sure, she was being a brat. But the asshole had deserved it and far worse.

She'd undergone quite a few negative experiences while he'd kept the truth from her. Some of his reasons were legit. That didn't mean she was anywhere near forgiving him for the hell she'd gone through as a result of his choices.

"And there's no way to enter the islands without permission," Leela continued, her voice hoarse and softer than normal. "The wards will kill you."

"I thought they wanted to meet with me?" Astasiya replied.

"You, yes. Everyone else, no." She shivered as Lara touched her forehead, her body stiffening on the couch.

"That's not an option," Balthazar said from where he leaned against the wall.

He'd been abnormally quiet after settling Jayson onto the chair adjacent to the couch. He was still passed out from the bullet to his head, Lara having focused on Leela first. Luc—who stood beside Balthazar—had said Leela needed to recover first because her skills would be needed.

Stas agreed with that decision. "Leela and Vera could come with me, right?" Assuming Vera returned from wherever she'd misted off to. She'd disappeared almost as soon as she'd finished the rune on Leela's arm, saying nothing about her intended destination. She seemed to do that a lot.

Balthazar shook his head. "It's not a viable plan."

"Do you have a better one?" Stas countered, irritated.

His brown eyes smoldered with an intensity she'd never before seen in him. "I want Lizzie back, too. Don't treat me like an enemy, Stas. We're on the same side."

"Then give me a better idea." It would be more

productive than turning down the only plans she could think up.

"When I discover one, I'll share it," he replied. His tone was one she'd never heard him use. Yet the authority in his voice suited him in his Elder position.

Although, she didn't much care for his response. The longer they debated this, the more likely Lizzie would be hurt. And that outcome was unacceptable to Stas.

He's right, Aya, Issac whispered into her mind. *Going to the council won't help anything. We need a strategy.*

That could take days to come up with, Issac.

Look at Lucian, love, he encouraged her. *He's running through scenarios in his head. That's why he's so silent. Give him a few minutes to come up with an alternative. He'll tell us if you going to the Seraphim is the only viable plan or not.*

She knew he was right, that her mind had jumped to a rash conclusion, but she couldn't think of any other alternative. The Seraphim had taken her best friend. Gabriel had confirmed it by telling them about Skye's prophecy and her ties to the Fates.

Stas ran her fingers through her hair, frustrated. *I feel helpless.*

I know.

I hate this feeling.

I know, Issac repeated, kissing her temple. *We'll figure this out.*

She turned into him, her gaze finding his sapphire irises and holding on for dear life. "How do you manage to remain so calm?" The words were soft, meant only for him. But she knew the rest of the room heard her.

"Practice," he whispered, pressing his lips to hers. "And trust in those around me to determine a solution."

Trust wasn't Stas's problem. Concern was her issue. *What if we don't get there in time?*

As you age, you'll learn that time is relative. He cupped her cheek, his thumb running over her bottom lip. *The Seraphim took Elizabeth for a reason. If they wanted her dead, they would have killed her rather than going through the effort of kidnapping her.*

She hadn't considered that before, her mind immediately jumping to the worst conclusion.

However, she'd stopped herself from reacting without thought. An indication she was at least learning from her past mistakes. While she might not be able to die now, she could be taken captive and endure treatment much worse than death.

Issac kissed her again, his mouth a promise against hers. *We're going to figure this out, Aya.*

Thank you. Just being held by him made her feel a little better. No one here would allow Lizzie's disappearance to go unanswered. They just wanted to ensure the plan—

Gabriel reappeared, his light blond strands windswept and rearranged on top of his head. "Sethios and Caro are with Lizzie," he announced.

Stas gaped at him. "What?"

"Osiris took her," he went on to explain. "And he secured her in an estate on a private island in the Caribbean. It's covered in protective wards to hide her from the council."

"He knew they would come for her," Luc said.

"So it would seem," Gabriel replied. "Skye prophesied that Sethios would gain his wings the same day Lizzie went into labor. As a result, Osiris laced a compulsive spell through Sethios to force him to mist directly to the island the moment his wings appeared."

"Lizzie's gone into labor?" Balthazar said, pushing off the wall.

"Yes." Gabriel held up a hand. "There's more. They told Ezekiel—who relayed all this information to me—that they believe this is some sort of ornate trap meant to ensnare Stas. Skye says she can't see anything that confirms that threat, but she also didn't predict Sethios being compelled into Osiris's waiting arms either."

Luc nodded. "He likely left behind compulsions in her mind that keep her from commenting on his actions."

"Exactly," Gabriel agreed. "So this is all some sort of setup, but Caro checked the runes and said they're legitimate. Which means that regardless of his trap, it's a safe place for Lizzie to give birth."

"Safer than Hydria," Luc translated, his muscular arms tensed across his chest, his distaste of that proclamation clear.

"Your island isn't warded, something we can change, but we need more time than we currently have available."

"Gabriel's right." Leela sat up, her blue-green eyes alert and very unlike the healer beside her. "She'll give birth within the next hour or two. Which means we need to go. Now."

"Misting her back here could also put her at risk," Gabriel added. "And not just because of the missing wards. She's in a fragile state, as is her unborn child."

"Moving her isn't an option. We'll go to her." Leela was on her feet, her cheeks flushed with renewed color. She glanced at the worn-out female on the floor. "Thank you, Lara."

"You're welcome." Her eyes drooped closed, causing Stas to frown.

"Isn't she supposed to assist Leela with delivering Lizzie's baby?" she asked warily.

"We'll handle it," Balthazar said, walking up to Leela.

"There's no *we* here," Leela replied.

"There is absolutely a *we* here," he corrected. "You have your Seraphim fertility mojo. I have the medical training. And she's my best friend's wife. So you're going to have to deal and let me help, *Lee.*"

The Seraphim blanched. "Don't call me that."

"Oh, I'm going to be calling you a lot of names, sweetheart. Just as soon as we deliver a healthy baby together." He grabbed her hand and looked at Gabriel. "Tell us where to go."

Her brother looked her way. "You heard my warning about what they think is going to happen?"

"Yes." If Osiris wanted to trap her, then so be it. She'd escaped him once before. She'd happily do it again.

Except she was starting to think that he might not be her biggest enemy, that the Seraphim who wanted her best friend dead might pose a bigger threat.

"Then what you do with this information is up to you," he replied, then gave the location to Balthazar and Leela. "I haven't verified that yet, and it's a crude guess based on what Caro found outside while looking at the wards. She didn't have much time to survey the property, just long enough to confirm it was safe before returning to Lizzie."

"If they're wards meant to keep Seraphim out, I might have a problem," Leela pointed out.

Gabriel shook his head. "Caro said the protection runes thwart those who mean Lizzie harm."

"He used her blood to create the markings," Leela said, her eyebrows lifting. "He really did create the place for her."

"So it would seem," Gabriel replied.

She nodded. "We'll meet you there." She disappeared with Balthazar, leaving them all to discuss the next steps.

"I'll stay here and wait for Jay to wake up," Luc informed them. "As soon as he does, we'll have Jacque teleport him in."

"He's back at Ezekiel's house," Gabriel replied.

"Technology will fix that." Luc pulled his phone from his pocket, showed it to her brother, and returned it to rest against his upper thigh.

"Speaking of technology," Issac murmured. "Tristan is with Mateo."

What wasn't said out loud was that Tristan had volunteered to supervise Mateo and report back on his movements. Luc would understand Issac's context without him elaborating, something he proved by dipping his head once in understanding.

"If they stop by, I'll bring them up to speed," the Hydraian King said.

A lie, but one that would make the comments seem normal to everyone else in the room. It wasn't that they didn't trust Gabriel or Lara, but they weren't sure who else might be listening. With Mateo's penchant for technology, he could have placed bugs all over Balthazar's house without anyone knowing.

That part freaked Stas out the most—she didn't like that Mateo could be listening to everything she said. Which made her even more thankful for her bond to Issac and their ability to talk mentally.

I want to go to Lizzie, she told him now.

Yes, he said. *I knew you would.*

Am I being reckless for going? She knew he would tell her the truth, which was why she voiced the question.

You're aware of the potential consequences. It's quite possible Osiris will make an appearance. That said, I don't think he intends to harm you. He needs you.

But he might put you in a cage and use you to force my hand, like he threatened before, she replied.

Would you prefer me to stay here, then? he asked, looking at her.

She considered it and shook her head. *I want you there.* It would be the first time she'd seen her mother in eighteen years. Something about that left her uneasy. Mainly because of her nightmares. She wasn't sure how those would impact her when she finally saw her mom again.

We'll face it all together, Issac promised, lacing his fingers through hers. "We're going to the island."

Luc stared at him for a long moment, then nodded. "Better to walk willingly into the trap and learn the results than to wait around for a surprise opportunity. We'll arrive armed and prepared."

"I don't think it'll be needed," Gabriel said. "Sethios told Ezekiel that Osiris knew of his intentions to escape. He'd used the entire situation as a way to test Stas. Which I'm guessing he's doing again now. He doesn't want to hurt her; he wants to train her."

Stas bristled at the insinuation. "I'm not his to train."

"Something he'll learn with time," her brother replied. "I'll meet you both there. I need to have a conversation with someone here first."

She frowned at him. "Who?"

Rather than reply, his red feathers appeared, and he vanished into thin air.

"Now I get to hit him twice," she muttered.

"I'll enjoy watching," Issac replied. "Shall we?"

She responded by misting since, apparently, that was how Seraphim did things. They acted rather than explained.

Issac's chuckle hummed across her thoughts, his amusement at her version of a tantrum warming her a little inside. He always knew what to say and do to calm her. She wrapped her arms around him a little tighter, her opal wings fluttering in the ethereal state as she took them to the location Gabriel had mentioned.

When their feet met the white sand beach, she knew it

was the right place. Because she could feel the power reverberating around them, the wards enclosing her friend in a shield of absolute protection.

"He didn't lie," she said. "I can sense his magic all around this place. He's sheltering her."

"And you," a deep voice said as Osiris appeared beside them. "Hello, Astasiya. I was hoping you would come."

CHAPTER TWENTY-TWO

ISSAC

Energy flared around Aya as she faced her grandfather. Issac moved with her, his arm brushing hers as he stood right next to her.

"Osiris," she said, her tone flat.

"Granddaughter," he returned, his lips curling. "You knew I'd be waiting for you here."

"I expected it," she admitted.

"And you came anyway."

She lifted a shoulder. "You have my best friend. Of course I came."

"I'm protecting her," he said.

"I know." The nonchalance in those two words almost made Issac's lips twitch. He wondered if Aya realized how much she'd grown in her confidence over the last few months. She was facing the most powerful being in existence—the one who had created all of them—and she hadn't even broken a sweat.

Osiris studied her. "You approve."

"Of keeping my best friend safe? Always." She folded her arms. "But if you're planning to separate her from Jay or their baby, then no, I don't approve."

His brow furrowed. "Why would I separate them?"

"Because you want to use her to create your own progeny," she said.

"I wouldn't need to separate them for that."

"Then you underestimate Jay's possessiveness," Astasiya replied.

"I could make him watch, if I so desired, but that's neither here nor there. The time to create new life has diminished due to recent events. Trying to train a new progeny won't be possible. Which is why I've wanted to speak to you."

"You want to train me."

He dipped his chin in confirmation. "I do."

"And if I don't want to be trained?"

"Then you'll die," he replied simply.

Issac narrowed his gaze. "Choose your next words wisely, Osiris." A statement he never would have made a year ago, but Aya didn't exist in his life then. She did now. And this ancient being had just threatened her, something that could not be tolerated.

Osiris arched a brow at him. "Was that a warning?"

"Yes." A single word underlined in confidence. It didn't matter that this Seraphim possessed incredible power. He lacked family. Emotion. *Heart.* Those three items were ones Osiris looked down upon because he didn't understand them. However, Issac did. They weren't weaknesses but strengths. They created a defensive unit, one that would be used against Osiris should he try to harm Astasiya.

"Fascinating," the Seraphim murmured. "I've always respected you, Issac. You're bold and creative and loyal. And now you're proving to be protective of my most valuable weapon." He nodded slowly. "Yes, that'll do just fine."

"I'm not your weapon," Aya replied.

"Not yet," he agreed. "But you will be."

"Which leads us back to the training discussion. I'm not interested."

"Who else is going to teach you the full range of your gifts?" he asked, his tone chiding.

"My father," she offered. "My mother. Hell, Gabriel? Yeah, I'd allow him to teach me over you."

"You don't even know me, child."

"I know what you've done. And actions speak far louder than words."

"Actions," he repeated. "Such as freeing Skye from my compulsion and creating a compound with the sole purpose of protecting your best friend during her weakest moments? Or how about the fact that I let you free your father?"

"You didn't let me. We fought."

He chuckled. "Sweet child, that wasn't a fight but a training exercise. I don't wish to hurt you. I need you. Just as you're going to need me."

"I think I'm doing just fine on my own."

"Do you know what would have happened to Elizabeth had I not taken her when I did?" he countered, his dark brow arching upward again toward his bald head. "The council would have sent warrior Seraphim to Hydria to destroy her. No trial. No edict. Just a swift execution."

"She's a Seraphim," Aya replied, her eyebrows pulling down. "She can't die."

He gave her an indulgent glance. "She's not a pure-blooded Seraphim, Astasiya. But you're right; she might have survived. Which would have been worse for her because they would have responded by throwing her into a reformation chamber to be reprogrammed. And her child would have suffered the same fate."

Silence fell between them.

Do you believe him? Aya asked softly into Issac's mind.

I think there's a lot we don't know yet about the Seraphim. However, Skye told Gabriel that the council would kill Elizabeth and the child. He also said they removed her wings as a punishment for not complying with their assignments. Neither event paints a kind picture where they're concerned.

"There's much you don't understand. Do you know why I was exiled?" Osiris asked.

"You killed a Seraphim," a feminine voice replied as a blonde female appeared beside him in a flurry of pale blue wings. Her face gave her away immediately, her defined cheekbones and pert chin both traits she'd given to her daughter.

Caro materialized into her corporeal form, her focus entirely on Osiris. "Touch my daughter and you'll regret it," she added, her tone lacking all emotion.

"I'm beginning to see why my son is so enamored with you," the ancient male replied, blinking at her. "What Seraphim did I supposedly kill?"

"The name has never been mentioned, only the act."

"Convenient," he replied.

"Are you claiming innocence, Father?" Sethios asked, misting in on his other side, his black wings causing Issac's eyebrows to lift. Gabriel hadn't mentioned this development.

Black and blue wings, and yet I end up with pink feathers? Aya thought at him. *Seriously?*

Your feathers are opal, love.

They look pretty pink to me, she mentally muttered back at him.

Your parents are here with Osiris, and you're still fretting over some pink plumes, Issac mused, his lips threatening to twitch.

It's a good distraction, she admitted.

Yes, he agreed. And he imagined she needed it to keep her calm facade.

"Seraphim can't die," Osiris said. "How could I properly kill one?"

"You're the Seraphim of Resurrection," Caro replied. "You control life."

"I do," he agreed. "Life, but not death."

"So you're saying it's not true?" Sethios pressed, his tone expressing serious doubt. "That you were exiled for another reason?"

"One day I'll tell you my story," Osiris said. "The real one. Perhaps then you'll understand."

"Why not today?" Aya asked him.

"Because Elizabeth needs you, and I desire her survival." The stoicism in his tone reminded Issac of Gabriel. It was such a practical reply, confirming Osiris truly did have Elizabeth's best interest in mind.

At least for the moment.

"I only wished to see you for a moment," Osiris continued. "To express my desire to teach you. As I said, we'll need each other very soon. And I would prefer to ensure you're prepared for when that day comes."

"What day?" Sethios asked, his hands tucked into his pockets in the picture of ease. It didn't appear to be an act. As the male had spent thousands of years with his father, it made sense for him to know whether or not the ancient being posed an imminent threat.

That knowledge put Issac slightly more at ease.

But he kept his hands free just in case, his arm still touching Astasiya's.

"You'll see soon," Osiris said, his black wings springing to life. "I look forward to the future, Stas. Please give Elizabeth and her daughter my best."

He disappeared without another word, causing Caro to frown. "That's his second anticlimactic exit today."

"Yes," Sethios agreed, his gaze lifting to the darkening

sky. "It seems his goal for now is to convince Astasiya to work with him via pleasant methods. But that will change if she proves too stubborn for his manipulative games."

"I'm never going to work with him," Aya said at the same time Caro replied, "It will never happen."

The two females looked at each other then, Aya's green eyes widening a fraction as Caro's blue irises flared.

Mom, Aya thought, causing Issac's heart to skip a beat at the emotion underlining that single word.

Silence fell between them, Aya just staring as Caro stared back.

And in the next second, they were in each other's arms, hugging one another as though they feared the other wasn't real.

Love and affection poured through Issac's bond from Aya, followed by a deep-seated ache that was finally healing after years of agony. Visions of drowning flooded his mind, Astasiya reliving each one as she clung to her mother harder. Tears fell from her eyes, the reunion one of joy and sorrow and defined by their joint pain.

Issac cleared his throat, his own emotions rising at the sight of so much love flaring to life between a mother and her daughter. He looked at Sethios and found him in a similar state, his eyes glistening with unshed tears. They didn't fall, but the love was there. Pride, too.

And then he looked at Issac and it all disappeared in a heartbeat.

A darkness returned to the green depths of his gaze. His lips flattened. And power raged around him.

"You stood up to my father," he said. "Told him to choose his words carefully."

Ah, so they'd been watching the entire exchange. That didn't surprise Issac. They'd all known Osiris would be waiting for Astasiya, and her parents never would have allowed him to take her after all the sacrifices they'd made to keep her safe.

"Yes," Issac confirmed, unwilling to back down. "And I'd do it again in a heartbeat."

Sethios studied him in silence, his expression giving nothing away. Then, after a beat, he dipped his chin. "Good. Make sure it stays that way."

Caro giggled, causing Sethios to narrow his gaze at her. But the look lacked heat, unlike when he'd scrutinized Issac.

"Are you laughing at me again, angel?"

"Yes," she said, her eyes filled with tears from her reunion with Aya. She released her daughter just enough to hold out an arm. "Join us."

Sethios didn't hesitate, moving toward them and wrapping them both in his embrace. So many Ichorians believed this male lacked a heart, that he was just as cryptic and cruel as his maker. But in that moment, Issac witnessed the truth.

This man absolutely had a heart.

But it didn't belong to him.

It belonged to Aya and Caro.

They were his world, which made him just as dangerous as everyone claimed. Because if anyone ever touched either of those two females, he'd destroy them.

Issac understood then why his response to Osiris had mattered so much to Sethios. They'd just become allies. Two men caught up in the love of the women who made them whole, and would do anything to protect them, even take on the most powerful being in existence without blinking.

Sethios met his gaze then, his chin dipping once more in a gesture of respect—one Issac returned.

Aya meant everything to him.

He would do whatever was needed to protect her.

Even if it meant sacrificing himself.

Which was exactly what her parents had done all those years ago. They'd given up everything for her safety. And now they were together once more, a family reunited.

Take your time with them, love, Issac whispered into Aya's mind. *I'll update you on Elizabeth's progress.*

Thank you, she murmured back to him.

Always, Aya, he vowed, speaking their special version of love, the one only they seemed to understand.

Always, she replied, the single word a kiss to his mind.

He smiled and ventured inside to find Balthazar and Leela for an update.

It didn't take him long to locate them, Elizabeth's screams a beacon that led him directly to the second floor. One look inside the room confirmed Issac's future.

He and Aya were never having kids. Ever.

CHAPTER TWENTY-THREE

SETHIOS

A BELLOW from the house had Sethios pulling away from Caro and Astasiya, the hairs along his neck rising. "What the hell was that?"

Caro responded by grabbing his hand, her opposite arm still around their daughter, and misting them inside the room where Elizabeth lay still on the bed.

Jayson raged beside her, his eyes wild as he demanded they revive her.

"This is normal," Leela was saying.

"How the fuck is this normal?!" Jayson demanded, gesturing at the unconscious redhead. "Her heart isn't beating!"

Right. This was actually something Sethios could help with. "Caro died several times during childbirth. She's fine."

Caro nodded. "Yes. I survived. It's just the power exchange."

Jayson looked at them as though they were insane. Even Issac appeared alarmed.

Balthazar was the only one—aside from Leela—who seemed to accept the explanation. He merely bent over Elizabeth to check her vitals, then shrugged as her heartbeat began again. "What do we need to do?" he asked, looking at Leela.

"I need you to calm Jay down so he can help her bond with the child," she said.

Balthazar nodded, his focus falling on the still-raging Elder.

"Don't you fucking dare," Jayson said.

But Balthazar was already using his gift for emotions, the power flaring to life around them and almost instantly calming Jayson.

Sethios had never seen Balthazar use his talent before, other than the constant mind-reading. Emotional manipulation was a powerful tool, something that could be catastrophic in the wrong hands.

"Lizzie needs you," he said softly. "She needs to perform a power exchange with your daughter. Lie in the bed and hold her through it while remaining calm and lending her your strength."

"I could have used you about twenty-five years ago," Sethios remarked.

"You handled it mostly well," Leela commented.

"A compliment?" Sethios smiled at her. "Thanks, Lee."

"I said 'mostly,'" she replied.

Elizabeth came back to life on a scream that made everyone flinch. Jayson's crazed expression began to return, but Balthazar quickly pulled him back, telling him again to get into the bed and hold the girl.

"I'm never having kids," Astasiya said out loud.

"My thoughts exactly," Issac agreed.

I'm considering that a win, Sethios spoke into Caro's mind. *I'm not ready to be a grandfather.*

You weren't ready to be a father, either, she reminded him softly.

I'm still not ready, he muttered back to her. *But the idea of my child having a child? Fuck, Caro. No. She's still seven in my head.*

Caro's amusement touched his thoughts. *Then hopefully she doesn't have my genetics, because I defied all the odds by having two children in a single century. That's absolutely not the norm but may run in my bloodline.*

She uttered the words in that practical way of hers, the statements all underlined in realism. Which made them one hundred percent worse because she was right.

Shit. We need to talk to her about birth control. A conversation he couldn't imagine ever having with his daughter. *Actually, can I just kill Issac instead? That'll be much easier, and far more enjoyable.*

You can't kill him. He loves her.

Then I'll just castrate him. Problem solved. And still more enjoyable than a conversation about protection.

Caro giggled again, a sound he hadn't realized how much he'd missed until he heard it today. It was almost enough to make him forget she was laughing at him. Almost.

This isn't funny.

It's very funny, she corrected. *And there's no such thing as birth control for a Seraphim. But if it really worries you, we can ask Leela about Astasiya's fertility. She would be able to sense it.*

She said it wouldn't happen for another five hundred years, he grumbled.

She's probably right. Unless she inherits my procreation cycle.

Sethios groaned. *Stop saying that.*

Just informing you of the obvious.

I don't want to think about it.

You're the one who started this discussion in my head, she murmured.

You were supposed to let me kill him, he argued.

Caro turned and pressed a palm to Sethios's chest, her

blue eyes sparkling with mirth. *You don't want to kill him. You like him.*

I do not.

You do. She lifted onto her toes to press a kiss to his lips. *He showed his loyalty in front of Osiris. I felt your response to that. He reminded you of yourself.*

This bond is troubling, he replied, not really meaning it at all. *I can't keep anything from you.*

I could go back to the reformation chamber, she offered. *If you—*

He wrapped his palm around the back of her neck and yanked her flush against him. "Don't even think about it."

She smiled. "Then tell me how you really feel."

"I'd rather show you."

"Could you not, though?" his daughter asked, her voice a squeak beside them. "I... I don't think I want to see that."

Elizabeth screamed again before he could reply, sending both Balthazar and Leela into action. "Baby's coming," Leela said.

"I'm ready," Balthazar replied.

She gestured to Jayson with her chin. "Keep him focused."

"I am," the mind reader confirmed, his palm on the other man's shoulder.

"I'll be in the hall," Astasiya said, grabbing Issac by the arm to drag him with her. "We are never doing that."

"Please make that a demand," Issac murmured.

If she does, will it keep them from sleeping together? Sethios wondered.

"You're incorrigible," Caro whispered to him, lifting up to nip his lower lip. "But let's join them. I've already lived through this twice. I don't fancy watching it. And I'd like a proper introduction to my son-in-law." She frowned then. "That's the right term, yes?"

"I think we should just call him Issac. Son-in-law is weird."

She nodded slowly. "Yes. I like that more."

"He will, too," Balthazar said, intruding on what should have been a private conversation. But as they were only a few feet away from the bed, Sethios supposed it was fair game to interfere.

He wrapped his arm around Caro's shoulders and led her into the hallway toward their pale-faced daughter. Issac's palms cupped her cheeks, his voice low as he said, "She'll be fine, Aya. She's strong. You know she's strong."

"But she's not a pure-blooded Seraphim. What if this kills her?"

"We'll find a way to bring her back," Issac promised her. "However, I don't think it'll be necessary. She's a survivor."

"I agree. She'll be fine," Sethios said. They would all make sure of it. "I'm more concerned about Skye foreseeing her birth and the council's response to it. We can't keep her here indefinitely. Not with Osiris holding the master key."

"We also need to discuss the Fates," Caro added. "And how we believe they're working against the council."

Sethios nodded. "The High Council of Seraph has always believed the prophecy is in regard to you taking down Osiris and his abominations. But we think that's their arrogance talking, and the Fates just never corrected their interpretation."

He went on to tell her about Skye being a Seraphim, how they'd removed her wings, and why they'd done it.

Caro continued the conversation by detailing her realization that the Fates had predicted certain things to give them the upper hand. Such as her being born with a dormant healing ability that came to life when she needed it most. How the Fates had probably helped conceal their locations, perhaps by not predicting the rune on Astasiya's lower back.

"It's all theoretical, but Skye's commentary suggests we're on the right path," Sethios concluded. "Which means Osiris might be right about us working with him."

"So you believe the council is worse than he is," Astasiya summarized.

"I think there is all manner of evil in this world and that sometimes we have to align with our enemies to take down the larger of threats," Sethios replied.

"That will require the Hydraians to work with the Ichorians," Issac said. He'd moved to Astasiya's side, his arm wrapped loosely around her lower back. It was a gesture that seemed to claim her for all to see—her father included.

Another sign of his confidence and power. Sethios could make the man heel with a simple command, but he suspected Issac would fight back with the full force of his abilities. And Astasiya would help him.

Caro was right.

He couldn't kill Issac.

But he wouldn't admit to liking him either.

"My father encouraged a war between you all to test your strengths and remove the weak bloodlines," Sethios said. "He never admitted that to me out loud, but I know that was his intention. He's been preparing for this battle with the Seraphim for millennia. He's obsessed with it."

"While I can understand the theory, he's also instilled significant distrust throughout his supposed army." Issac's sapphire gaze blazed with intelligence. "The Hydraians will never stand side by side with the Ichorians who attempted to slaughter them. Just as the Ichorians have been bred to hate their offspring for being more powerful and immune to the blood-drinking requirements."

"Give them a common enemy, and they might fight," Caro said. "The Seraphim want to destroy all of them. It doesn't matter if they're Ichorians or Hydraians; to the council, they're all abominations that need to be destroyed."

"How do we fight an army that can't die?" Astasiya asked. "Even if the Ichorians and Hydraians work together, it'll be moot if the Seraphim will just survive."

"I think that's where you come in, love," Issac murmured. "The prophecy."

"*An unknown power is surfacing. She will possess the strength and will to destroy us all unless certain measures are put in place to curb her inclinations.*" Caro spoke the infamous words softly, reiterating them for all to hear. They'd never heard it from Skye's mouth but had it repeated back to them from Gabriel years ago. The prophecy had been forever ingrained in their minds and hearts.

"The measures we put in place were to ensure you valued humanity. But that doesn't mean the power inside you suffered. It just suggests you'll use it appropriately." Which, Sethios assumed, now meant she would direct her talents at the appropriate enemy, not the wrong one.

Of course, that required them to determine whom they were destined to fight—Osiris and his minions, or the Seraphim.

"You believe Astasiya has the power to destroy a Seraphim," Issac said, his British accent more pronounced with the weight of that statement.

"Yes." Sethios looked at his daughter. "You're a descendant of the Seraphim of Resurrection, which means you can control and design life, as you already know. Caro descends from a line of messengers with healing and concealment abilities. We're not sure how those markers have combined inside you, but the Fates ensured your creation for a reason."

Caro nodded. "I've always believed the council sent me to Osiris with that edict because they knew I would meet Sethios and thereby bring you into existence. They just misunderstood your purpose."

"This all works on the belief that the Fates are no longer aligned with the council," Sethios added. "So it's just a theory. But it's a theory that feels right."

"Yes," Caro agreed. "It does."

Astasiya blew out a breath, her body leaning heavily into Issac as he held her with ease. "This is a lot to take in." Her voice held a touch of exhaustion in it.

None of them had slept much over the last however many days. All the traveling had really warped his sense of date and time, not that it mattered. They were on the brink of a supernatural war.

"If this happens, our existence will become known to the humans," Issac said. "And with the CRF destroyed, new military agencies will be created to fill that void. Because it's safe to assume that at least some government officials are already aware of us through Jonathan's former contacts. Which means the mortals need to be factored into this equation. They're volatile and have a penchant for acting preemptively."

Approval radiated through the bond from Caro. *I do like him*, she mentally informed Sethios.

Yeah, yeah, he muttered back at her.

He felt her smile, but her lips didn't actually move until she started speaking. "The Seraphim have always viewed humans as a glorified experiment. They descend from our family lines—that's why those of you who have been reborn via Osiris's influence have unique abilities. They all tie back to the Seraphim familial lines."

Astasiya's blonde brows rose. "So humans are descendants of angels?"

"Not exactly." Caro fell into a contemplative silence for a moment before elaborating. "They evolved over millennia of natural cycles on Earth, but the Seraphim assisted in that evolution. I'm not sure of the full history, as that's not my specialty; I also wasn't alive then. But I know the ancients helped in some capacity via the bloodlines."

"That's not what I was taught in school," Astasiya replied.

Caro blanched. "They teach about Seraphim in schools?" She looked at Sethios. "They know of our existence now?"

"I believe our daughter was being sarcastic," Sethios replied.

Caro blinked. "Oh. Yes. Right." She shook her head. "Sarcasm isn't… my forte."

Sethios kissed the side of her head and pulled her into a half hug. "Seraphim don't understand humor." *Or pleasure*, he added into her mind.

She elbowed him. *I've grown into my emotions.* Her mental voice held a lethal undertone to it.

You have, he agreed, his thoughts warm as he pondered all the emotions she'd exuded earlier. *Do you still have Ezekiel's knife?*

You mean my knife? Yes. Yes, I do.

Good, he murmured back to her. *We'll need that later.* Then, out loud, he said, "I agree with Issac's assessment that the humans will soon be involved. It's inevitable. And they will add an unpredictable angle to the war. A lot of them will also die." A crude assessment, but true.

"Is there any way to avoid it?" Astasiya appeared even

more exhausted now than she had moments ago. "A war, I mean. Do we have to fight the Seraphim?"

He lifted his shoulder. "It remains to be seen. We're not even sure they're the ones we should fight."

"Skye said they would want to kill Elizabeth, but they didn't attack Hydria," Issac pointed out. "Perhaps because Osiris got to her first. However, it's all speculation at this point."

"I agree," Sethios replied. "We need to get over the hurdle in the other room and figure out how to help Elizabeth hide from both my father and the Seraphim. After that, we can focus on the potential fight ahead."

"And Osiris's request to train me," Astasiya added gruffly. "I've not particularly enjoyed his version of training so far. Pretty sure I'm not interested in learning more from him."

Sethios snorted. "Trust me, I understand that better than anyone you'll ever meet." He'd spent thousands of years beneath his father's tutelage. While many of his trials were practical in nature, none of them were easy or favorable to endure.

"We should—"

A cry of agony from the bedroom interrupted Caro's words and had them all turning toward the door. Astasiya was the first to move, the sound coming from her best friend.

She sprinted toward the commotion, only to freeze on the threshold at the sight before her.

Sethios was next at her back, his eyes on all the blood and mournful faces in the room.

Oh, fuck…

CHAPTER TWENTY-FOUR

LEELA

THE BABY WASN'T BREATHING.

Leela tried to calm everyone down so she could focus, but the others were too emotionally charged to listen.

Only Balthazar seemed able to understand her. His chocolate irises met hers, his chin dipping in confirmation that he could control the situation while she worked. She hadn't even needed to say anything to him; he just understood her—something she would need to evaluate more thoroughly later. Because it freaked her out how well he read her, in addition to everything else that had occurred since coming in to physical contact with him again.

He knows, she thought for the thousandth time. *But how is that possible?*

Vera had changed his memories of their time in Brazil.

He shouldn't *know*.

But he kept doing things that insinuated he did.

Like calling her *Lee* and offering her the exact drink they'd shared on the beach in Rio de Janeiro.

She mentally shook herself and stared down at the still infant in her arms. *You and I are going to have a conversation, little one,* Leela thought at her. *Starting with how not to freak out your parents.*

Seraphim babies never cried.

They were usually born aware and fully intelligent, marking them as supernatural and unique compared to human births. But Lizzie wasn't a typical Seraphim. She was created in a lab using technology and genetics that none of them understood or had proper access to.

Case in point—Lizzie had given birth well after her projected due date. Most Seraphim went into labor around week seven or eight. But not Lizzie. Which suggested some mortal genetics had impacted her gestational period.

Leela rocked the silent child, her fertility power igniting to provide the small being the nutrients she needed to return to them.

Seraphic souls couldn't die, only the body.

And this tiny form had endured quite a bit on her way into the world.

Come on, sweetheart, Leela cooed through her mind. *You're mostly healed. It's time for your spirit to return.*

Time seemed to tick by slowly, the others in the room growing more and more distressed with each passing second. Mostly because they were trying to calm the terrified mother on the bed. Jayson was still lost to Balthazar's emotional control. But Lizzie was beside herself with horror at having lost their child.

"She's going to be okay," Balthazar was saying. "Leela's confident, which makes me confident."

Warm praise, but again troubling in nature.

He shouldn't be confident in her at all.

They barely knew each other. In his mind, anyway.

Lizzie replied in gibberish, her statement lost over her sharp intakes of breath as she fought another wave of fresh tears.

"Did this happen to me?" Astasiya asked softly.

"No," Sethios murmured. "But your situation was different."

"Seraphim souls can't perish," Caro informed them all. "The body can die, but it'll regenerate."

Which was exactly what Leela had tried to tell them initially. Fortunately, they seemed to be hearing Caro.

Lizzie's breaths were evening, and Jayson was whispering words of encouragement in her ear. Either that was still a result of Balthazar's emotional control, or he'd finally regained his senses enough to do his job. Regardless, Leela was thankful because it gave her the peace and quiet she needed to nurture the child.

She closed her eyes, her mind seeking out the wandering soul of the infant in her arms. *Stop exploring, little one,* she mentally chided. *It's time for you to meet your parents in a corporeal state.*

Seraphim children were born with an intelligence unlike human babies. They were already aware and understood aspects of the world that many mortals didn't learn until they were in their teens or early twenties. It helped with facilitating their power transition at birth, which still needed to be done.

But the little darling had to be in her body for that.

Come on, sweetheart, she cooed. *I feel you nearby. Find yourself and show me those pretty brown eyes.* She'd seen them once initially, the alarm in them nearly breaking her heart. The poor tiny soul had felt her body deteriorating and had fled as a result. But she was mostly put back together now, confirming her seraphic birthright.

More minutes passed.

Then a sigh came from Leela as the heartbeat returned. *There you are,* she whispered fondly. *Show me those eyes, sweet girl.*

The child couldn't actually hear Leela's mental words, but she would sense the warmth and comfort in her essence. She was a fertility Seraphim, which meant she specialized in birth and fertilization. That also made her excel in the art of sex, similar to the fabled succubus. Only, Leela didn't require gratification for survival; she just liked it.

A snort came from behind her, Balthazar's hand finding her hip as he pressed his lips to her ear. "You and I are going to have a long conversation after this, Lee," he informed her, the words whisper-soft and meant for her ears alone. "How's she doing?" he asked in a louder tone, masking his previous statement under a guise of general curiosity.

She shivered and idly wondered if she could pretend she hadn't heard his statement. But a nibble to her earlobe told her that would be impossible.

Only Balthazar could turn a gory moment into something sensual. She was covered in blood and unspeakable fluids, and he somehow made her feel clean and real and powerful.

She shook her head and faced him, causing his hand to drop from her hip.

He met her gaze for a brief moment, a hint of knowledge lurking in his brown irises. Then he looked down at the bundle in her arms, his lips curling at the sight of two big beautiful eyes staring back up at him.

"Well, hello there, little LJ," he cooed. "I see you have your mother's eyes."

The child blinked.

He pressed a finger to her nose. "That's all Jay," he informed her softly. "But the cheekbones are definitely Lizzie." Dimples appeared on his cheeks. "You're stunning, little beauty."

A hint of understanding echoed from her eyes, her lips moving in a sucking motion. Leela giggled. "Yes, yes. You need to bond." She glanced up at Balthazar once more before moving around him and toward the waiting parents on the bed.

Lizzie's eyes were huge as Leela brought forward their child, her irises glimmering with more tears. But these were the happy kind, not sad ones. "Oh, she's alive!"

"I told you; she just needed to heal a little," Leela said softly. "But yes, she's very much alive, and quite a survivor, if you ask me." She smiled fondly down at the little one who made another sucking motion with her lips. "She's also impatient. You exchanged power during the birth, but she needs a little more."

"How do I do that?" Lizzie asked.

"She'll guide you," Leela assured her. "Can you help Lizzie sit up a bit? It'll assist with the process." The question was for Jayson, who promptly shifted on the bed to move the pillows around and give her the space she needed to properly nurture her child.

Already Lizzie's body was healing. Within an hour or two, she'd be back to normal. Assuming she repaired herself like a typical Seraphim. Hmm, but her gestational period had been a bit prolonged, so perhaps she'd need more time here as well.

Regardless, she'd recover quickly.

And bonding with her little one would help.

Leela stepped forward after they finished situating themselves on the bed, and slowly lowered the child to Lizzie's waiting arms. If she was alarmed by all the blood, she didn't show it.

"Oh, she's so beautiful," Lizzie said, awe coloring her tone.

"She looks just like her mother," Jayson replied, stars in his eyes as he stared down at his child.

Leela moved away from them, intending to give them a few moments of peace. But Balthazar stood right behind her, his warm body cradling hers and his hands finding her hips once more.

She shivered at the intimate touch. He was always bold, but this felt more like a claim. As though he knew he had a right to grab her. Because it was grounded in history and mutual affection.

I'm in so much trouble, she thought.

"Yes, you are," he replied out loud, causing her to freeze.

Did I say that out loud? Or did he just read my mind? It was then that she realized what she'd missed in the flurry of activity before. *The rune.* Vera had given it to her to facilitate the healing, but it'd allowed all Hydraian gifts to work on her. Which meant—

"I know everything," he whispered, his arms encircling her waist as he laid his head on her shoulder, watching as Lizzie and Jayson fawned over their child. "We'll talk later, Lee. For now, let's admire the life we helped bring into the world."

Stas and Issac stood by the bed on the opposite side, both of them enamored with the child. Sethios and Caro were beside them, their focus on their own daughter, a wave of memories swimming in their gazes.

Twenty-five years ago, they'd brought Stas into this world. And now she was all grown-up with a mate of her own. Leela imagined that both pleased and hurt them. They'd missed so much of her life. But they were reunited now to enjoy the future together. Whatever it might bring.

Leela didn't want to think about that now, so she did as

Balthazar suggested and admired the tiny being in Lizzie's arms.

The two new parents shared a look, Lizzie's expression almost dreamy from the power exchange her daughter had initiated. They were bonding as a unit, Jayson's energy added into the mix to help bolster their child's strength.

A happy new family filled with love and affection, born in a time of future war.

But this child would be more protected than any other before her. She had the Hydraian Elders and Issac as uncles, Stas as an aunt, and Leela as a guardian angel.

It hadn't been intentional. However, she'd bonded with the small child in her own way as she'd coaxed the soul back to her proper home.

Which meant Leela had tied herself in a way to the little spirit.

She'd never remove that tie.

It would forever remain between them, similar to how Gabriel had pledged fealty to Stas. But not quite the same.

"What do you plan to name her?" Stas asked softly.

Lizzie smiled. "Aidyn Lee," she replied. "Aidan saved us both. It's only fitting she carry his name in memory of his sacrifice. And Lee after Leela, for ensuring we all survived."

Silence followed her words, the emotions behind the names burrowing deep into all their hearts.

Leela's own heart seemed to stop beating, shocked at being honored in such a way. "No one's ever named a child after me," she whispered.

"Then I'm glad ours is the first," Lizzie murmured, smiling down at their daughter.

Aidyn Lee.

"A fitting name," Balthazar said. "Aidan would be honored."

"He would," Issac agreed, his tone a bit gruffer than usual. "Thank you for honoring his memory."

"We wouldn't be here without him," Lizzie replied, her voice soft. "It's the best way for us to remember him. It's also a strong name befitting our miracle. Our baby Aidyn."

More silence fell, the emotions in the room heavy.

Issac was the first to clear his throat, then he nodded and left. Stas followed him out, her hand against his lower back offering comfort.

Sethios and Caro were next to go.

Then Leela said, "Call if you need anything."

"We will," Lizzie replied, her focus entirely on their child.

Leela went to move, but Balthazar's arms didn't budge. She cleared her throat.

"We won't be far," he said, his words for Jay. "You know how to grab my attention."

"Thanks for calming me down," Jay replied.

She felt Balthazar nod beside her head. Then his arms fell, and his hand grabbed hers to pull her out of the room. Leela said nothing, following dutifully as he led them to another bedroom a few doors down.

A brief thought occurred to her, reminding her that she could mist, but one look from him had her squashing that inclination.

He sequestered them inside a room with a balcony overlooking the ocean, white furniture, and a large bed with blue sheets and a navy quilt on top. But rather than lead her in the direction of the mattress, he took her into the elegantly furnished bathroom. "Strip," he told her.

"You can't intimidate me," she informed him, obeying the command out of defiance more than submission. Being naked didn't bother her. She had a killer body, and she knew how to use it to subdue a man.

"I don't want to intimidate you. I want to take care of you and demonstrate my gratitude for what you've done for my best friend. Then I'm going to consider fucking you. And after that, we're going to talk. Unless you want Vera to alter my mind again?"

Leela stared at him. "I don't need you to take care of me."

"I know you don't, but I'm going to do it anyway."

"And there's no considering anything when it comes to fucking me," she added, ignoring his reply. "If I want to fuck, we'll fuck."

He smiled. "I can make you beg."

"You can try."

"Oh, Leela," he said, stepping into her personal space and kicking her bloody clothes aside. "I'm going to make you crawl, baby."

"That'll never happen." The words she spoke out loud didn't match the ones in her head, which were along the lines of, *Yes, please*. And the bastard heard them because of the altered rune.

It struck her then that Vera had to know what would occur after she altered the marking. Just as she'd clearly not warped Balthazar's mind the way Leela had asked her to.

He smirked. "You think what happened in Brazil was the best I can do? That was just an introduction. By the time we're through, you won't even know how to move without feeling me between your thighs."

Her body heated at the promise underlining those words. "Show me."

"I will," he vowed. "After I make you crawl."

She snorted. "Then it's all talk, *baby*, because I'll never crawl for you."

He smiled, his lips brushing hers in a sensuously bold move that lit her blood on fire. "Thank you, Leela."

She frowned. "For what?"

"For providing me with a new challenge," he replied softly. "Now get your fine ass in the shower. I'll join you momentarily. And we'll see how long your resolve lasts."

Chapter Twenty-Five

CARO

Sethios stood in a towel out on the balcony of their temporary room, his gaze on the stars above.

Caro joined him in the robe he'd left for her on the bathroom counter. They'd both showered in silence, kissing frequently and speaking into each other's minds but not doing anything other than existing together once again.

She wrapped her arms around his bare waist, pressing her nose into his shoulder as she just held him to her.

It felt nice. Warm. Right.

The peaceful roll of the waves along the shoreline below seemed to resemble the calm before the storm. She shivered at the thought of what was to come, the potential for devastation and war.

"Gabriel's still in Hydria," Sethios said softly. "Ezekiel's staying with Skye for now, but he'll continue to communicate via the phone he left on the nightstand."

"Ezekiel was here?"

"Yeah, he traced in for a quick chat while you were drying off in the shower." Sethios rested his arms over hers, his fingertip dancing along her skin. "He's going to try to learn more from Skye about the Fates but didn't seem too certain of his ability to coax information from her."

Caro sighed against him. "It's not in her nature to explain the future so much as to foresee it."

"We need her to be a little more detailed."

"Yes, but that doesn't mean she's capable of it," Caro replied, moving along his back and side to face him.

His arms immediately came around her lower back, his forehead dropping to hers as they held each other in a contented silence. She understood his need, as it rivaled her own, their bodies having missed the comfort of the other for far too long.

They stood like that for a long, long time, with no words spoken between them but enough emotion to drown out even the loudest of events.

His lips found hers, worshipping her in a way that made her legs shake. But he held her upright, his tongue a benediction in her mouth that ignited her entire being.

She encircled his neck with her arms, holding on, their bodies marrying in a way that rivaled their spirits.

Each stroke of his tongue against hers grounded her even more in the present, her reformation experience subsiding beneath the memories he evoked from her mind. All those years lost between them meant nothing. They had now. They had the future. They had their daughter.

That was all that mattered to her. She sensed Sethios's agreement through the bond. He lifted her into the air, carrying her back into the room and laying her on the bed.

Her legs spread for him, aware of his intentions.

He parted her robe and tossed his towel to the ground, then kissed a path down her body to the sweet spot between her thighs. His tongue continued that sensual assault, licking and tasting and sending her to the heavens with each skilled caress.

She'd left the knife in the bathroom with her clothes, but it didn't matter. They didn't need it. Because not all sex between them required pain. All they truly needed was each other.

He nibbled her clit, causing her to bow off the bed, her fingers threading through his thick, dark hair. *More*, she moaned into his mind.

Sethios didn't hold back or deny her, instead giving her exactly what she wanted, and sucked her nub into his mouth while spearing her with two fingers. She fell apart in seconds, her body starved for him after so long without consistent touch.

"I love the way you taste, angel," he whispered against her slick flesh before crawling up and over her again. He entered her without warning, his thrust causing her to cry out into his mouth as he claimed her lips in a harsh kiss.

She writhed for him.

Screamed for him.

Gave him everything.

Misted *with* him.

It was so erotic and beautiful and was punctuated by him biting her to send her over the edge into oblivion once more. She returned his bite, her teeth sinking into his neck and forcing him to come apart deep inside her.

He growled.

She growled back.

And their coupling turned feral in an instant, their bodies overcharged and ready to make up for years of lost time.

He slammed into her. She fought him with her thighs, squeezing him, pressing her ankles into his ass to encourage him to go harder.

She gave in to the experience, allowing him to consume her every thought and breath.

His name left her mouth on a prayer, just as he echoed hers in kind.

They were utterly absorbed in one another, falling into the bliss of their temporary tranquility. Their lives had constantly been in flux, spent running and hiding and preparing. They knew how to use a down moment to their advantage, which was exactly what they did now.

She indulged him, just as he indulged her.

Until they were a panting mess of tangled limbs, their sweat enough to warrant another shower, but neither of them was fit to move.

Caro nearly laughed.

Except she couldn't. That required too much energy.

"I think you've killed me."

"It's a beautiful way to die," he said, just as breathless as her.

She giggled in reply, the sound oddly liberating.

He rolled onto his side to face her, the two of them sharing a pillow. They'd just ridden each other to oblivion for what felt like hours and yet was still nowhere near long enough.

His palm found her hip. "Are you laughing at me again? Because I had no idea I was so hilarious," he deadpanned.

She kissed him, and he responded by rolling her onto her back and going to his elbows on either side of her head. Energy danced off his skin, the full weight of seraphic abilities seeming to ripple over him.

"Do you feel that?" he asked her.

"Yes. I think our intensified bond is what has strengthened your Seraphim genetics. That's probably why you can mist now." Which she loved. He had the most-gorgeous blue-tipped black wings. "Show me your feathers."

He did, igniting his ethereal state with a stray thought. "This took our daughter a week to learn, but it feels natural to me."

"Likely because your wings were suppressed, but always there. You just didn't know how to access them until recently. While Astasiya's needed to grow."

"I assumed mine were growing like hers over the last twenty-five years."

"Maybe," she replied, thinking it through. "I'm not really sure how it works. You're an abomination, after all."

He snorted. "I'm your abomination."

"You are," she agreed, smiling. "Hmm, but I wonder if my reformation impacted your Seraphim ascension."

"Or my father did," he replied. "He claimed it wouldn't have been useful to keep me grounded and unable to fly, but he's not exactly a trustworthy source."

"Yes." She considered it more, then added, "However, our bond feels fuller now. Like we completed something by reuniting."

"I sense that, too," he whispered, pressing his lips to hers. "I feel alive."

"Me, too." She kissed him back, reveling in all the sensations of his touch. "I love you, Sethios."

"I love you, too, angel." His tongue slid into her mouth, hypnotizing her all over again with his potent touch. She sighed beneath him, content to remain there forever. But she knew they had a future to face. A dark fate. One underlined in war and violence and blood.

Her daughter was the key to it all.

She just didn't fully understand what that meant yet.

They would figure it out together as a family. As a powerful unit. As Seraphim reborn beneath a renewed purpose.

"I think that was what the Fates had in mind," Caro

whispered, voicing her thoughts. "They wanted Astasiya to grasp humanity because they knew it would impact her decision-making. And rather than kill indiscriminately, she'll think through each and every resolve with compassion—something the council lacks. They're all about practical decisions, but she follows her heart."

It was so obvious to Caro now. Her daughter had loyalty to family and friends, not a blind purpose tied to a council of ancients. Astasiya would always do what was right for those she cared about, something the council would never understand.

"She's going to destroy them by shredding apart the system," Caro continued. "By introducing them to emotional reasoning. They won't know how to battle it."

He palmed her cheek, his green eyes sparkling with understanding. "I think you might be right, angel."

"But you think there's more."

"I think she's only begun to understand her power, which is why my father wants to train her. He knows something about her abilities—or the potential of her abilities—that he's not telling us."

"Because he wants to use her," Caro said.

"Yes."

"And you think we should let him," she added, seeing the strategy unfold in his features.

"I think we should consider it and ask Astasiya what she wants to do. It would be a risk, but it also might just give us the upper hand we've been missing since this all began."

"An attempt to be one step ahead of him," she mused.

"We could use the advantage," he replied. "But she'll need to agree."

Caro nodded, concurring. However, she already knew what her little warrior would say. "She'll take the risk."

"I know."

Her lips curled. "She's a lot like me, isn't she?"

"Very much so," he murmured. "We made the right choice, Caro."

"I know."

His eyes took on a serious gleam. "I don't regret it."

"Neither do I." She palmed his cheek. "She makes our sacrifices worth it."

"She does," he whispered, his nose gliding against hers. "She makes everything worth it. And so do you, angel. I'd suffer it all again, just for this moment."

"Me, too," she replied, her voice equally quiet. "Kiss me, Sethios."

"Forever," he vowed, taking her mouth and sealing the promise with his tongue.

Caro's heart warmed, her soul reveling in their embrace.

She was finally home.

With her love.

Her Sethios.

For eternity.

EPILOGUE

VERA

VERA HID in the shadows just outside the coliseum, her wings folded against her back. This was her favorite place to spy because no one ever noticed her here, tucked between two pillars of decorative rock.

The security cameras were all angled away from her, thanks to Mateo's interference. She texted him now, letting him know her position.

Roger, he sent back.

She was here for the sole purpose of listening for the council's verdict on Elizabeth and her new daughter.

Osiris had gotten her out just in time, sequestering her to the manor he'd procured for this purpose. But that left Hydra exposed and vulnerable, which wasn't acceptable.

Mateo had stayed behind on the island, despite his cover being blown—a disappointing development he'd overheard via his penchant for technology. Regardless, he'd remained and put the lives of all those on Hydra ahead of his own, an admirable feat and one Vera very much understood.

She frequently put her life in jeopardy.

Such as now as she awaited the verdict.

If Vera reported a pending attack, Mateo would deliver

253

the message to Lucian and accept the penalty of confirming his allegiance to Osiris. It would alert the others to her recent activities as well, but they were going to learn about those soon anyway.

Attacking Osiris that day had resulted in a new understanding of him—one that had given her pause.

She'd witnessed his memories of what the council had really done to him.

A vile, horrid event that had knocked the wind from her lungs and forced her to return to him a day after ensuring everyone's safety at Gabriel's home.

"I have to know," she'd told him. "Let me see it again."

He'd studied her for a long moment, his green eyes flashing with fury. "If you alter my mind again, I will add you to my collection downstairs."

She knew what he spoke of—the immortals he kept locked away in conditions far worse than death.

But she'd taken a chance and agreed to his terms.

Then she'd relived his memory in each excruciating detail.

By the time she'd finished, she'd been on her knees in tears while he'd stood over her with a stoic expression. "Now you know."

There was no faking a memory like that. Even now, it sent a chill down her spine. Because it'd happened inside these ancient coliseum walls.

She might not agree with his methods or his penchant for cruelty, but she respected his goal of taking down the council.

They needed to go.

And he was one of the few beings with the power to do so.

His memories had also proved his intentions in regard to Sethios and Stas. He truly saw his actions as teaching methods, as ways to empower them and strengthen their abilities. Caro was slightly different, as he'd believed her to be a weapon sent by the council. Now he understood the truth and wanted her to prosper with Sethios in a twisted, dark, horrible manner.

Yet it was the right manner. Because he knew what they would face.

Vera shook her head.

It was troubling to be inside Osiris's mind for that long and actually understand his choices, to see the practicality behind each harsh decision, and realize his true intent wasn't to torture or harm but to grow.

She nearly blew out a breath, her mind exhausted from the myriad of tasks she'd performed over the last few days. But this one was too important for her to fail, which was why she stayed utterly still, waiting for the council to disperse.

They were quiet inside, just the bare minimum of rumbling, which meant they hadn't argued much.

That could mean anything.

The council wanted the Hydraians destroyed and could easily agree to take that path right now, under the guise of wishing to find and annihilate Elizabeth.

Or they'd unanimously decided it wasn't time yet—which had been their ongoing decision for millennia. Until the Hydraians posed a significant threat, they'd leave them alone and hope Osiris would come to his senses.

That was the party line, anyway.

Vera understood the truth now. Just as she knew that Osiris would never "come to his senses." Not after what they'd done to him.

Shuffling started, the sound echoing around her. She pressed herself more firmly into the stone siding, waiting in her ethereal form. If someone happened to see her—

which they wouldn't—she'd be able to mist to a safe location in seconds.

But no one ever looked back at the coliseum. It served no practical purpose. Just as they didn't anticipate eavesdroppers lurking about, because all the Seraphim believed in serving the council, not questioning them.

It was a perfect society of silent compliance.

Except for the few—like her—who saw through the inhumane treatment.

Murmurs touched the air, words flowing between councilmen and councilwomen as they walked and misted out of the infamous theater-like structure.

A few voiced irrelevant comments.

She ignored them, waiting for the signs of an edict being issued.

When Adriel appeared, her spine stiffened. A pair of warrior Seraphim immediately flew down to meet him.

Leek and Kital.

The former was Adriel's oldest son—a Seraphim Gabriel had bested in a fight three decades ago. The other, Kital, was within his line, but a much younger generation and not as highly ranked as Leek.

"An abomination and her offspring have been taken to a warded complex in The Bahamas. We need you to retrieve them."

Vera's eyes widened. *How do they know?*

"The coordinates aren't clear, but three of the Fates were able to pinpoint it to a general location. I recommend you take Patreel and Arvane with you. They're two of our best trackers."

"Of course, Councilman. Are we to bring the abominations back alive or dead?"

"Alive is preferred, as we would like to run a few tests, but if they prove difficult, then corpses are accepted."

"Consider it done," Leek replied.

Adriel nodded, then looked up to the sky. "You're dismissed."

The two warriors misted without a word.

No other comments or edicts were delivered, confirming Hydria was safe for now. However, Elizabeth and her child were in serious danger.

Vera texted a summary to Mateo, then she headed to the Caribbean to deliver the bad news.

Fortunately, several of them had experience in hiding those they cared about.

This situation would be no different.

An incoming message buzzed her phone as she landed in the sand outside the manor, the number belonging to Osiris. *I'll take care of the warrior Seraphim to buy you some time.*

She blinked at his words just as a second message vibrated through from the same number.

I suggest you move them to Iceland. Skye and Ezekiel will help protect them.

She agreed with a nod, then started her journey inside, all the while preparing herself for a complex conversation about truths and lies.

Some promises were meant to be broken.

Others were made to bend.

But she was about to shatter them all.

And would likely pay the ultimate price.

The Immortal Curse Series Continues with
Wicked Bonds

❧

Curious about what happened when Gabriel confronted

Clara about his "emotional enhancements"? Find out in *Blood Burden*, a free bonus scene available to newsletter subscribers. If you would like to see additional bonus scenes, let me know and I'll release more (there are several in my head!).

Have you joined the Immortal Curse Discussion Group yet? If not, click here for fun, behind-the-scenes details and conversations on this series.

Looking for more vampires? Check out my Blood Alliance series for a darker world where lycans and vampires make the rules… But be warned, these alphas bite.

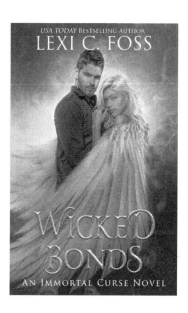

Continue the Immortal Curse journey with Balthazar and Leela in Wicked Bonds...

Welcome to the Immortal Curse world where angels and vampires exist in secret... for now.

A passionate affair of sizzling heat.
Forgotten and buried.
Because what happens in Brazil stays in Brazil.

That was the plan, anyway. Until Balthazar started to remember everything. Now he's forcing Leela to pay the ultimate price—by making her *beg*.

Every hot touch ignites her soul. Every smoldering glance makes her thighs clench. And worse, there's no escaping him.

They're on the run from a horde of warrior angels, protecting an innocent from a fate worse than death.

The High Council of Seraph has issued an edict.
Comply or die.
Only the faithful will survive.

WICKED BONDS

MUSIC PLAYLIST
BLOOD SEEKER

Addicted, Saving Abel
Carry Me, Eurielle
Hard for Me, Michele Morrone
Hate Me, Eurielle
Here We Stand, Hidden Citizens
Hold Your Breath, Ruelle
Is This The End (feat. Young Summer & Sam Tinnesz), Hidden Citizens
Out of the Fire, Digital Daggers
Sacrifice, Mars Lasar
State of Seduction, Digital Daggers
Strange Young World, Ranya & Hiden Citizens
The Razor's Edge (Piano Version), Digital Daggers
Too Far Gone (feat. Svrcina), Hidden Citizens
Until It Hurts, Fransisca Hall
We Hit a Wall, Chelsea Wolfe
Whispers, Eurielle
You Said, Eurielle

ABOUT THE AUTHOR

USA Today Bestselling Author Lexi C. Foss is a writer lost in the IT world. She lives in Atlanta, Georgia, with her husband and their furry children. When not writing, she's busy crossing items off her travel bucket list. Many of the places she's visited can be seen in her writing, including the mythical world of Hydria, which is based on Hydra in the Greek islands. She's quirky, consumes way too much coffee, and loves to swim.

Want access to the most up-to-date information for all of Lexi's books? Sign-up for her newsletter.

Lexi also likes to hang out with readers on Facebook in her exclusive readers group - Foss's Night Owls.

Oh, and don't forget to check out B's Blog for exclusive Hydria updates (if you're into that kind of thing).

Where To Find Lexi:
www.LexiCFoss.com

Book Six: Blood Seeker

Book Seven: Wicked Bonds

Immortal Curse World - Short Stories & Bonus Fun

Elder Bonds

Blood Burden

Mershano Empire Series - Contemporary Romance

Book One: The Prince's Game

Book Two: The Charmer's Gambit

Book Three: The Rebel's Redemption

Midnight Fae Academy - Reverse Harem

Ella's Masquerade

Book One

Book Two

Book Three

Noir Reformatory - Ménage Paranormal Romance

The Beginning

First Offense

Royal Fae Wars - Omegaverse Paranormal

Wicked Games

Underworld Royals Series - Dark Paranormal Romance

Happily Ever Crowned

Happily Ever Bitten

X-Clan Series - Dystopian Paranormal

Andorra Sector

X-Clan: The Experiment

Winter's Arrow

Bariloche Sector

Other Books

Scarlet Mark - Standalone Romantic Suspense

Printed in Great Britain
by Amazon